An Indie Next Pick
An Amazon Best Book of the Month

"Jonathan Evison takes a battering ram to stereotypes about race and class in his fifth novel, *Lawn Boy* . . . Full of humor and lots of hope . . . An effervescent novel of hope that can enlighten everyone."
—*The Washington Post*

"Evison excels at finding the humanity in his characters . . . This tender bildungsroman follows Mike from one setback to another, each interaction involving slyly observant and brilliantly witty dialogue that also poignantly conveys vulnerability. Evison skillfully weaves the American Dream into a subtle social novel to illustrate how race and class can thwart aspiration. In his bighearted portrayal of Mike Muñoz, Evison has created an indelible human spirit content to live authentically, which just might prove to be the true American Dream."
—*Booklist*, starred review

"Mike Muñoz is a Holden Caulfield for a new millennium—a tenth-generation peasant with a Mexican last name, raised by a single mom on an Indian reservation . . . Evison, as in his previous four novels, has a light touch and humorously guides the reader, this time through the minefield that is working-class America . . . [His] subject matter and wit are a welcome departure from self-conscious MFA trust-funded prose—one of his many comic targets, along with Walmart, puppy mills and inbred, rich white folks. As he chases the American Dream, Mike loses two teeth in a kitchen extraction scene (no insurance), but gains so much more—a social conscience, romance and his niche in life. Not to mention a laughing, sometimes teary, audience who stay with him until the very last page." —*The New York Times Book Review*

"A roller-coaster ride of a novel . . . Moving, evocative and beautifully written . . . Evison meticulously evokes a richly detailed marginalized world."   —*The Providence Journal*

"Moving . . . Evison convincingly evokes the small disasters and humiliations that beset America's working poor. Mike's gradual growth into self-awareness is punctuated by moments of human kindness and grace that transpire in and among broken-down trucks, trailer parks, and strip malls. Focusing on the workers who will only ever be welcome in gated communities as hired help, Evison's quiet novel beautifully considers the deterioration of the American Dream."
                                              —*Publishers Weekly*, starred review

"Few authors handle their characters with the compassion that seems to come naturally to Jonathan Evison. [His] latest work, *Lawn Boy*, explores the struggles of the modern American Dream through Mike Muñoz, a young Chicano landscaper in Washington State."
                                              —*Seattle Weekly*

"*Lawn Boy* is an important, entertaining, and completely winning novel about social class distinctions, about overcoming cultural discrimination, and about standing up for oneself."   —*BookBrowse*

"Jonathan Evison can write about anything and make it sing with hard-bitten empathy. I love it that he writes about working men without condescension. I had jobs like this. And you can tell that he did, too. Tough and strangely sweet at the same time."
                                              —Luis Alberto Urrea, author of *The House of Broken Angels*

"Evison's enthusiasm for his protagonist and his book's message is evident on every page. It's the kind of book that elbows its way into your head and forces you to think about your world in a new way."

—*The Seattle Review of Books*

"Jonathan Evison's voice is pure magic. He is a consummate world builder; in his unique universe, there is heartbreak and love and tragedy, and—always—laughter. In *Lawn Boy*, at once a vibrant coming-of-age novel and a sharp social commentary on class, Evison offers a painfully honest portrait of one young man's struggle to overcome the hand he's been dealt in life and reach for his dreams. It's a journey you won't want to miss, with an ending you won't forget."

—Kristin Hannah, author of *The Great Alone*

"Joyful, funny, and life-affirming." —*Signature Reads*

"Evison's characters are fully realized, and his protagonist is lovable despite his flaws—a believable young man whose future we want to see go well, but for whom life and present-day culture may have other plans. Hilarious and sad all at once, Evison's newest book is fantastic."

—*Read It Forward*

"*Finally* a book that zooms in on social strata without flinching or copping out. *Lawn Boy* takes us into the heart, mind and body of Mike Muñoz as he makes a coming-of-age trek from landscaping crew to navigating the dead American dream—all the way to reimagining a future on his own terms. I loved reading this book so hard I wanted to SHOUT 'fuck yeah,' because the underdog doesn't just transcend the forces holding him down (yawn), he rearranges the terms of human identity in the face of the false fiction called capitalism. A triumph from the ground up that reminds us how full of shit the topside is."

—Lidia Yuknavitch, author of *The Book of Joan*

"It's a difficult thing to write uproariously humorous fiction that has heart, passion, and inspiration rolled into it as well. The life of Mike Muñoz is a comedy of self-inflicted errors and familial obstruction, but his positive outlook toward achieving the American Dream is infectious and inspiring and will make you laugh and cry, often on the same page, sometimes for the same reason."

—*The San Diego Union-Tribune*

"The book explores the lives of people like Mike with humor and compassion, wrestling with how you get ahead when you can barely stop falling behind." —*Salt Lake City Weekly*

"Moving, hilarious, and uplifting . . . The genius of the novel, and of its author, lies in the complexity of emotions Mike's journey evokes, both from its hopeful beginning to its unexpected fulfillment. But it's also in the nature of that fulfillment—in the subtle sleight of hand Evison works to show that the grass can be greener on either side of the fence."

—*Four Corners Free Press*

"This book has one of the best first chapters that one could ever read. It is compelling, tragic, and funny at the same time. It is worth buying the book just for that wonderful chapter with its masterful writing . . . A very timely novel that rings very true to life."

—*Manhattan Book Review*

"*Lawn Boy* is empathetic and angry in its portrayal of class, poverty, discrimination—destroyers of dreams. But Mike perseveres—'I had poetry in my heart, goddammit'—and learns to blaze his own trail. He 'gets his mow on'; he even finds unexpected true love. As he learns that no man is an island, he's able to see increasing moments of grace with his 'ragged tribe.' In Evison's tough and wry novel, Mike Muñoz is every person who wants a living wage and a little dignity, 'the opportunity to think beyond sustenance long enough to dream.' Jonathan Evison has written a fierce and funny novel about a young man's attempts to transcend class and poverty."

—Marilyn Dahl for *Shelf Awareness*

"In *Lawn Boy*, we encounter Evison's empathetic genius once again . . . A uniquely uplifting read . . . Sharply written and laugh-out-loud entertaining, this novel explores the class system in America, and how the ladder to the American Dream is fraught with broken rungs and splinters."   —*Coast Weekend* (OR)

"A swift, engaging read, with an alternately wry and wistful sense of humor. But it also addresses painful territory head-on, especially when it comes to American economic and cultural inequality."

—*Cascadia Magazine*

"Laugh-out-loud funny . . . A book about triumphing over obstacles."

—*Kirkus Reviews*

LAWN BOY

Also by Jonathan Evison

All About Lulu
West of Here
The Revised Fundamentals of Caregiving
This Is Your Life, Harriet Chance!

LAWN
BOY

A NOVEL

Jonathan Evison

ALGONQUIN BOOKS
OF CHAPEL HILL
2019

Published by
Algonquin Books of Chapel Hill
Post Office Box 2225
Chapel Hill, North Carolina 27515-2225

a division of
Workman Publishing
225 Varick Street
New York, New York 10014

First paperback edition, Algonquin Books of Chapel Hill, March 2019.
Originally published in hardcover by Algonquin Books of Chapel Hill in April 2018.
Printed in the United States of America.
Design by Steve Godwin.

LIBRARY OF CONGRESS CATALOGING-IN-PUBLICATION DATA
Names: Evison, Jonathan, author.
Title: Lawn boy / a novel by Jonathan Evison.
Description: First edition. | Chapel Hill, North Carolina :
Algonquin Books of Chapel Hill, 2018.
Identifiers: LCCN 2017032613 | ISBN 9781616202620 (hardcover : alk. paper)
Subjects: LCSH: Mexican Americans—Social conditions—Fiction. |
Working class—Social aspects—Fiction. | American Dream—
Fiction. | LCGFT: Bildungsromans.
Classification: LCC PS3605.V57 L39 2018 | DDC 813/.6—dc23
LC record available at https://lccn.loc.gov/2017032613

ISBN 978-1-61620-923-0 (PB)

10 9 8 7 6 5 4 3

For Matty, Tup, and Thomsen, salt of the earth

LAWN BOY

The Happiest Place on Earth

When I was five years old, back when my old man was still sort of around, I watched a promotional video for Disneyland that my mom got in the free box of VHS tapes at the library. Basically, the video was a virtual tour of the Disneyland grounds. I guess you could say it was a harbinger of things to come, because what really sparked my burgeoning imagination, more than all the fanfare and rides, was the fastidious landscaping: the big, perfectly formed Donald Duck– and Pluto-shaped bushes, the vibrant floral beds depicting Mickey and Minnie, and the impeccably manicured lawns. It looked like paradise to me. I would have given anything to experience Disneyland. For months, all I talked about was the Happiest Place on Earth. Mom said if we scrimped and saved hard enough, and we stayed with my dad's family in El Sereno, maybe we could pull off such a visit.

"What do you think, Victor?" she said to my old man, sprawled on the sofa.

"We'll see about it," he said, turning up the Mariners game and repositioning his ass.

I knew he was just blowing us off. But I wouldn't let it go. I kept pushing for weeks, to where my old man would get really irritable every time I brought it up. Finally, one day he dragged me out to the driveway.

"Get in," he said.

"Where are we going?"

"Disneyland."

Even at five, I was a little circumspect. But what choice did I have except to jump into the Impala?

"What about Nate and Mom?"

"Don't worry about them."

We drove through Poulsbo in the rain and took the junction south to Silverdale, my old man unshaven, in a dirty T-shirt, stonily silent, gripping the wheel at ten and two. After twenty minutes, I started getting impatient.

"How much longer?"

"Hold your horses."

Then I recognized East Bremerton, and I thought maybe we were going to pick up our food stamps on the way or that this was all a big trick to take me to the walk-in clinic again to get a flu shot. My old man stopped at a minimart and left me in the car. He came back out with a big can of beer in a brown paper bag, and a Sprite, which he tossed across the seat at me, so when I opened it up, it fizzed all over the place. But he didn't yell at me—not this time. He just drank his beer calmly out of the brown bag and kept on driving in silence.

"Are you sure this is the way?"

"It's the way."

We kept driving until we got downtown near the old naval ship-yard, where he parked the car on a deserted side street, and we just sat there looking at the brick facade of an old warehouse while he sipped the last of his beer, his eyes darting back and forth between the street and the rearview mirror.

"Are we here?" I asked.

"C'mon," he said, stashing the empty beer can under the seat.

It's not that I was stupid, okay? I was five years old. Yes, I imagined Disneyland would be a lot farther away. I had no idea that Bremerton was in Southern California—who knew? It took a leap of faith to believe such a thing could actually happen to me, but I chose to believe, with all my heart. As I trudged along the Bremerton waterfront in the trail of my father's cigarette smoke, I was practically weightless with joy and wonderment—I still remember that sensation. And that's the thing of it, I never want to forget it. That brief blossoming of expectation, those few delicious moments before the fall, those moments in which I let myself believe something extraordinary was about to happen, that I, little Mike Muñoz, with the dad who called him Polla Pequeña and the chain-smoking mother and the mentally retarded big brother, was actually going to enter the Happiest Place on Earth—they are still among the most poignant moments of my entire life.

When I peered through the chain-link fence, across the expanse of half-barren concrete, at the rusting hulls of the great gray navy vessels, I was perplexed. The place looked big enough, sure. But where was the castle? Where were Mickey and Goofy and Pluto? Where were the big animal-shaped shrubs and the frothing sea of colorful flowers and the lush expanse of green grass that had so thoroughly sparked my imagination? Also, shouldn't we be hearing the laughter of children? Shouldn't it smell like cotton candy or roasted peanuts?

Instead, there were only the frenzied cries of a dozen feeding seagulls and a waterfront redolent with the stench of dead clams and urine. The only bush in site was a blighted thing about three feet high, an Almond Joy wrapper clinging to one of its bare limbs.

My old man clenched the chain-link fence and looked out over the shipyard in the rain, drawing irritably from his cigarette.

"Well," he said, exhaling. "Looks like they moved. C'mon, let's get out of here."

That was Victor Muñoz for you, world's greatest dad.

Needless to say, I cried. The entire walk back to the car, I followed in my father's shadow, chin quivering, vision blurred. But I didn't let my old man see me crying. I wasn't gonna give him the pleasure. The whole drive home, I gritted my teeth and tried to make myself believe that it could still happen someday, if only to spite my father, that one day in the not-so-distant future, if I hoped hard enough, I might still gain entrance to the Happiest Place on Earth.

A kid can dream, can't he? And that's what I did, for a while, anyway, until the relentless indignities of privation wore my innocence to a nub, awakening me to the reality that dreams were for dreamers. The point is, I'm not a child anymore. I'm almost twenty-three fucking years old.

This Was Not the Plan

F riday night, while Mom was pulling a double down at the Tide's Inn, I was at home, babysitting Nate for the third night in a row. Not that I'm complaining, but I could use a break. I watch my brother pretty much every night except Tuesday and Saturday, which consists mostly of placating him so he doesn't go ape shit. Surrender to Nate's will and it's pretty smooth sailing, most of the time. Overexert your own will, however, and you're asking for trouble.

Because unlike me, Nate knows exactly what he wants.

Mom and I make an effort to limit his TV time, because it seems like the right thing to do. So after a dinner of mac and cheese with turkey-dog slices and banana-flavored instant pudding, we screwed around with Mr. Potato Heads in the bedroom for a while. Nate likes to jam the arms and legs into the eye sockets, then hurl them across the room. He thinks it's hilarious. I can't really say that I share his amusement, but then I'm pretty much done with Mr. Potato Head at this stage of my life.

Nate smelled pretty ripe, so I finessed all three hundred pounds of him into the bathtub, using a couple of Oreos as incentive. After a hot bath, he's usually pretty sedate, which is when I cave in and set him in front of the TV in the kitchen, where he slouches at the table drowsily watching *Despicable Me 2*. As long as Nate's hypnotized by the television, I can generally count on him to stay in one place, which means I can almost have a life of my own, which mostly means reading.

I read at least two books a week, sometimes as many as four. Call it self-improvement. You see, old Mike Muñoz would like to figure out who the hell he actually is, what he'd actually like to do with his life. He aches to be a winner. I'd like nothing more than to spread my proverbial wings and fly the fuck away from my current life, or maybe just get above it for a while. At this point, I feel like I'm nothing more than what everybody needs me to be or whatever the situation demands of me.

Nebulous, that's the word I'm looking for.

"Nate, you good in there?" I shouted from the living room.

No reply.

"Nate?"

Nothing.

Had I been paying closer attention, my first clue that all was not right in our household would've been the fact that the relentless burbling of those idiotic Minions had ceased at some point. But the truth is, once you've sat through *Despicable Me 2* enough times, you stop hearing the little fuckers. Besides, I was too wrapped up in my book to notice. It's called *The Octopus*, by a dead guy named

Norris, and it was recommended to me by the new librarian. The novel is about corporate tyranny in the 1800s, about how powerful outside forces impose their wills on us and disenfranchise us and beat us to jelly, until we're seemingly powerless to fight them because they own the game. They are the landlords of the world. Sound familiar? Take away the sheep-herding poet, and *The Octopus* could've been written yesterday.

You'd think I would've smelled the smoke before the fire alarm started squalling, but oh no. It wasn't until Nate shouted that I raced to the kitchen to find smoke so thick that I could hardly see him through the haze, fists clenched, tears streaming down his face.

I grabbed the hot mitts and threw open the oven door, exposing a molten pizza. Molten, because Nate had neglected to take off the plastic wrapper and remove the cardboard Frisbee from underneath. It didn't help that he was broiling it. I rushed the pizza to the sink, where I deposited it in a smoldering heap, opening both taps full throttle.

"You okay?" I said. "Did you burn yourself?"

That's when he gritted his teeth and raised his balled fists to chest level, and I knew that unless I could calm him within the next three seconds, he would go Incredible Hulk on me.

"Here, buddy, have an Oreo," I said. "Have as many as you want."

Tears still streaming down his face, he grabbed a fistful of cookies. As soon as he stuffed them in his mouth, his breathing began to quiet.

You've got to hand it to my brother—the man knows how to leverage his position. You don't want to negotiate with Nate. If things had gone a little differently with his birth, he might have ended up being one of those people who invented themselves and did whatever the fuck they wanted with their life. Become the first Muñoz to wriggle out of the primordial mud and grow some balls. Why not? He's got the single-mindedness. He doesn't take no for an answer. He might've cured cancer for all we know. But things didn't work out that way. As is often the case in the 360, complications arose. Shit happened. And instead of being an astronaut, my older brother is a three-hundred-pound toddler.

The tears, it turned out, were mostly for the pizza, our last. I shepherded Nate to the living room and, with expert finesse, convinced him to eat a microwaved burrito instead of a pizza. Turning on the big TV, I plugged in the first *Despicable Me*, whereupon, with the aid of the Minions, I soon managed to restore order.

Mom came home almost two hours late, noticeably tipsy. Apparently, she was unable to smell the aftermath of our near disaster over the blue tendril of smoke curling off her Vantage.

"Sorry I'm late, honey," she said.

She set her purse down on the dining-room table and proceeded straight to the kitchen for a tumbler of chardonnay with ice. That's pretty much her go-to. But don't judge her. Let's see you take it on the chin from three husbands, your boss, the state, the insurance companies, and anyone else who stands in your way. Let's see you bring home the bacon, get slapped on the ass all night, do zero self-care, take three vacations in twenty-five years, and not make a mess of raising kids all by yourself. Yes, it's true, she's been unlucky and unwise in love. It happens. And anyone who has ever been a waitress at the Tide's Inn, with its "colorful characters," its gazillion cast-off scratch tickets, and its signature bouquet of mop water and burnt hamburger meat, will tell you that the place just takes the *umph* right out of you. Between the job and Nate, she hasn't got much left for herself by day's end.

So, you see, my life is not totally without purpose. After five caregivers in three years (two of whom Nate physically assaulted), we've burned so many bridges with the Aging and Disability Services Administration that we don't even bother asking for help anymore. But we manage to maintain a household, just barely. There's a lot of broken shit around here and not a lot of resources. So if you're wondering why our showerhead is an empty plastic liter bottle riddled with fork holes, why don't you run down to Home Depot and price a new showerhead?

When Mom emerged from the kitchen, tumbler in hand, she sat in the old brown La-Z-Boy that used to be Ronnie's. She picked up the remote and turned on the TV to nothing in particular, firing up a fresh heater and drawing deeply from it. Maybe it was just the sickly light of the TV, but behind her veil of smoke she looked a thousand years old. You could see the new crown on her front tooth and how it was whiter than everything else—and it ought to be for six hundred bucks.

"You okay, Ma?"

"Fine," she said, exhaling. "You?"

"I'm good."

She flipped around the channels a bit, puffing her cigarette, until she landed on something called *American Pickers*, wherein two guys who seem a little gay drive around the country in a van, rummaging through people's old crap and offering them money for it. Initially, there was something hopeful about the premise, but it turns out it's not as simple as just being a hoarder. You need the right crap.

Finally, Mom stubbed out her cigarette and pushed herself to her feet. "When you get a few minutes, honey, could you look under the kitchen sink? It's still leaking."

"Sure, Ma, I'll take a look."

When she was halfway to her bedroom, she turned back, as though she'd forgotten something.

"Oh, and I hope it's okay, but I picked up a shift tomorrow night. It's gonna be tight this month with the—"

"But I was—"

"Oh, never mind, honey. If you've got plans, I'll just call Jerry and—"

"Nah," I said. "Don't worry about it. It's okay."

"You're sure?"

"Yeah, I got it."

After Mom went to her room, I took a cursory look under the sink and quickly determined that the drainpipe (cheap-ass PVC) was cracked, and the elbow seal was also a lost cause. Probably the whole works would have to be replaced. A small pain in the ass, and twenty bucks if you did it right.

I'd be lying if I said I wasn't disappointed. Not about the sink but about tomorrow night. I'd planned on heading down to Mitzel's to sit in Remy's section, and eat another crappy entrée and drink a lot of water, so she'd have to come by and refill my glass. And no, I'm not stalking her. Some slow night, when there's a break in our conversation that feels natural, I'm gonna ask Remy out. Nick says I need to "hurry up and hit that shit." But then, Nick's kind of a dipshit.

Nothing Auspicious

I have this old picture, bent and tattered around the edges, that sits atop my dresser next to my pickle jar full of coins. The photo was taken a few weeks after my old man moved out for good. Not that there's anything particularly auspicious about the occasion of the photograph, but it's one of maybe a half dozen I have from my childhood.

In the picture, I'm standing with Nate and my best friend, Nick Colavito, out in front of the Bainbridge fire station, where my mom brought us for the annual BIFF pancake breakfast. Maybe it's because I look at the picture so often that I remember the details of that day so vividly. Or maybe I'm embellishing. But I remember my mom paying our admission with her previous night's tips, a tired but scrupulous stack of small bills. I remember that Mom didn't buy a plate for herself and that it was only after Nate went back for thirds and couldn't clean his plate that she devoured a half a strip of bacon and part of a soggy pancake.

Afterward, we waited in line for a free ride on a fire truck. I distinctly remember not having the heart to tell my mom that I was a little too old to get any kind of kick out of a fire truck, and so was Nick. But looking back, the engine ride was probably for Nate's benefit. He was always talking way too loud about fire trucks—often in church or in line at the grocery store. Anyway, that's when Mom lined up the three of us and snapped the photo.

Nate is on the left, a half foot taller than Nick or me. At eleven, he's already pretty thick around the middle, his T-shirt clinging to his bloated torso like a sausage skin and barely reaching the waistband of his cotton sweatpants, which are also too small. His hair is cropped short, so he won't pull it out or catch it on fire. Other than that, he looks somewhat content, if not a little cross-eyed.

On the far right is Nick, same age as me but older looking, his good-natured grin unable to belie the considerable defiance in his eyes. The effect is sort of a glower, like he's daring the world to do something or say something. Sometimes I wish I could go back and tell Nick to just hold his horses, that the world has plenty of shit in store for him. But I think he already knew that from experience.

That's me, little Mike Muñoz, standing in the middle. A sad-eyed ferret of a kid, skinny and bewildered, slight olive complexion, dark rings under my eyes. Greasy bangs plastered to my forehead, faded Toughskins jeans riding halfway up my shins. On my back, a dirty brown coat with a fake-fur collar. Not exactly the kid from the Sears catalog but a kid all the same. Eight years old and looking for a little security, a little self-confidence—any confidence, really. Just a third grader, bottom lip chafed from obsessive licking, little fingernails bitten to the quick, aching for a good time.

I don't know why I keep this old photo around, but it serves as a constant reminder of where I came from. Not that I really need one. I could just as easily look out the window. But sometimes, as with Nick, I wish I could go back and tell little Mike Muñoz a few things, tell him to relax and leave the worrying to the adults. Tell him he'll find love and security one day, if he can ever figure out where to look for it. And maybe I'd tell little Mike to start by looking outside himself instead of within the murky, undefined recesses of his heart. In my experience, a kid doesn't gain much through introspection. A kid gets more by throwing a ball or wrestling with a dog or burning anthills with a magnifying glass. Sometimes I wish I could just go back and tell little Mike Muñoz to quit biting his fingernails and have some laughs.

That's what kids should do, they should laugh. If there's a better, righter sound in the whole world than the laughter of children, I don't know what it is.

The Flying Saltshaker

What I like most about Remy is that she seems comfortable in her own skin, like she's not trying superhard to impress anyone. She's not apologetic about being a waitress at Mitzel's, and why should she be? I hate that everybody is so self-conscious about how much money they make, and how much freedom their big important job allows them, and all the cool places they go, and how good looking their kids are, and all the sexy pictures of jumbo shrimp and giant margaritas they post on their Instagrams. Remy's not like that. When she tells you to have a good day, you feel like she really means it.

Of course, Nick doesn't find Remy attractive, but what does Nick know? He's got something negative to say about almost every girl I've ever tried to get with, even though he's the one always pushing me. According to Nick, Shannon (the ticket taker from the AMC 7 in Poulsbo) looked like a pteranodon. And yeah, she kind of did, but that didn't bother me. I've got nothing against a slight cranial crest. It's not like she had wings. I was more bothered by the fact that I had nothing in common with her. According to Nick, Amy (the checker from Rite Aid) looked like Matt Damon. Personally, I thought she looked more like Hilary Swank, but that's beside the point. The real disconnect with Amy, once again, was that I had nothing in common with her. Nick called Monica from the bookstore "Skillet," because she looked like someone hit her in the face with a skillet, which was not entirely true. But the thing with Monica was, she didn't really read books, even though she worked at a damn bookstore. She may as well have been selling bathroom tile. I guess I don't see the point of dating somebody just because. Sex doesn't seem like enough.

The lone exception that Nick was ever willing to grant me was Shelly, the barista at the Coyote Coffee drive-thru on 305, to whom Nick assigned "semihot" status, from the neck down, anyway. He said I should "hit that shit," even if her face was "butter." And maybe I could have, if my heart had been in it. But the truth is, things always felt forced with Shelly, what with me ordering three coffees a day at the drive-thru window and trying to start conversations based solely on customer familiarity. With Remy, I don't feel quite as much pressure. The familiarity was there the first time I sat in her section, and it seems to grow with every visit.

Since Mom was working, I had no choice but to bring Nate with me when I went to Mitzel's the following night. This was bad news, of course, on a number of levels, not the least of which was a financial one. In case you didn't know, mowing lawns doesn't exactly make a guy rich. You'd think Nate would be grateful for a free, fancy meal. But let me tell you, coaxing him inside was no easy task, though the drive to the restaurant went relatively well. It wasn't until we parked my truck that things started to go south in a hurry.

"This isn't fucking McDonald's!" he shouted.

"Shhh," I said. "You can have anything you want."

"You said McDonald's!"

"Shhh. Look, they've got all kinds of cheeseburgers here. They're huge—way bigger than Mickey D's."

"You said Big Macs!"

"Shhh."

Clutching two menus, the hostess arrived just in time to run interference.

"Two of you tonight?"

"Yeah."

"Remy's section?"

"Uh, yeah, sure, I guess that'll work."

I swear, the hostess rolled her eyes as she shuttled us briskly to a booth in the middle of the dining room.

"How's this?" she said.

"Not McDonald's," grumbled Nate.

"Great," I said.

Begrudgingly, Nate turned his attention to the sticky picture menu.

"Anything you want under twelve bucks," I told him.

"This one," he said, pointing to the prime rib dip.

"That's fourteen. Try the bacon cheeseburger. It's only eleven."

"This one!"

"Shhh. Calm down."

"You said anything!"

"Fine," I said, heaving a sigh. "But no dessert and no soda."

He stiffened in an instant, thunderheads gathering behind his eyes.

"Okay, soda. But no dessert."

On this occasion, it was Remy's arrival that saved me.

"Oh, hey," she said, fishing her pen from behind an ear.

It's not her fault if her uniform is a little frumpy, with its padded shoulders and baggy sleeves and shapeless black slacks, any more than it's her fault that she always smells like pancake batter. That stuff is all superficial, anyway.

"Uh, this is my brother, Nate."

"Hi, Nate," she said.

"This one!" he demanded, pointing to the prime rib dip.

"Ah, okay," she said, scribbling down the order as she shot me a sly little wink. So sympathetic, so understanding. She could tell right away that Nate had special needs. What was stopping me from asking this woman out?

"How about you?" she said.

"I'll just have a side salad."

"You're sure?"

"And, uh, fries, I guess."

"Anything to drink?"

"Soda!" said Nate.

"Just water for me."

Nothing to set the world on fire, sure, but a successful exchange— or at least not a disastrous one. We were still getting to know each other. What was the big hurry?

When Remy delivered the food, I redoubled my efforts to develop intimacy.

"Wow. That's a big salad," I said.

"Yeah," she said. "It's pretty big."

"Really big," I ventured.

"Yeah, I guess so. Can I bring you guys anything else?"

"I think we're good. Thanks."

I thought I saw a little spring in her step as she waltzed back down the aisle to the wait station.

About two minutes later, Nick came down the aisle, with his trimmed little goatee, which made him look like a NASCAR driver, and his twelfth-man jersey. Muscling into the booth, he immediately started plucking fries off my plate.

"Man Hands working?"

"Quit calling her that," I said.

"Did you get her digits yet? Get it, digits? Like because of her big fingers."

"Just shut up about it."

Nick speared another fry off my plate and was eyeing Nate's.

"Make a move already, Michael. It's getting a little creepy, you eating here twice a week. No wonder you're broke all the time."

"Just get off my back for once, would you?"

"Jesus, why are you so sensitive? Speaking of fags: look at that homo by the window."

"And lay off the fag stuff," I said. "You don't even know the guy."

"Oh, are you a fag, too?"

"No, as a matter of fact, I'm not. It's just that what difference does it make about somebody's lifestyle or whatever. Fags are just people."

"Yeah, people who stick shit up their butts."

"You like The Rock, don't you?" I said.

"What the fuck does that have to do with anything?"

"Everybody knows he's gay."

"Fuck off! That's the stupidest shit I've ever heard. The fucking Rock, gay. Pfff."

Somewhere under all the bravado and the habitual bigotry and the general stupidity, Nick's got a good heart, I swear. And he's had my back many times, and Nate's, too. I guess I'm a loyalist at the end of the day. Just about everybody lets you down sooner or later, so if you know anybody who hasn't totally betrayed you, I figure you're pretty smart to stick by them, warts and all.

But there's one thing I'd never tell Nick in a million years, not that it really matters: in fourth grade, at a church youth-group meeting, out in the bushes behind the parsonage, I touched Doug Goble's dick, and he touched mine. In fact, there were even some mouths involved. It's not something I'd even think about all these years later, except that Goble is the hottest real-estate agent in Kitsap County. His face is all over town—signs, billboards, Christ, even on shopping carts. Do you know what I think three times a day when I see his picture? I wonder, all these years later, why he just kicked our friendship to the curb like that. Was it shame?

"How about you, Nathan?" Nick said. "How you holding up?"

Nate grunted through a mouthful of prime rib dip.

"Always the conversationalist," said Nick, before turning his attention back to me.

"Dude, it's just Man Hands. She's not even hot. She's like a five and a half. How much money are you gonna waste in this place? Ask her out right now."

"Not with you here."

"What, I'm gonna cramp your style? What about him?" he said, indicating Nate, his face slick with grease, his shirt front damp with au jus.

"Just leave me alone, okay?"

"Fine, whatever," Nick said, snatching one last fry. "Anyway, I saw your truck in the lot and just dropped in to say hi. You wanna go down to Tequila's later? I think the chick with the octopus tattoo is working."

"It's a giant squid, Nick, not an octopus. It's called a kraken, it's a legendary sea monster."

"So who the fuck cares?"

"I care."

"That figures."

"Just go," I said. "Please."

Nick stood up. "Fine. Michael, I don't know what's gotten into you lately, but you've got a real stick up your ass."

Thank God, he finally relented, leaving Nate and me in relative peace, a peace that lasted for a while, anyway, until Nate set his sights on dessert.

"I said no. We can't afford it."

"You said anything!"

I should have given in. It would've lengthened our stay, if nothing else. But as it was, I knew I'd be hitting up the Money Tree by the twenty-third and taking a 30 percent hit on my paycheck.

"Forget it. No dessert."

That's when Nate snatched up the saltshaker.

"Relax," I said. "You can have some Oreos when we get home."

Before I could persuade him further, he hurled the saltshaker across the dining room, and I mean winged it like King Felix. It whistled past some old geezer's head so fast that he didn't even look up from his soup before it crashed against the far wall, not three feet from Remy at the wait station, shattering a glass picture frame.

Nate went pale when he saw what he'd done. The dining room set to buzzing. Remy and the hostess immediately started tending to the broken glass while some guy with cropped hair and an earring, who carried himself like the manager, started striding purposefully toward our table. I was standing before he got halfway there.

"What seems to be the problem here, gentlemen?"

The guy's voice threw me. Turns out he was a she, at least I think, just kind of butch.

"My brother's developmentally disabled," I explained, for about the nine-thousandth time in my life. "He's got impulse-control issues. One time he hugged the neighbor's cat too hard."

"Is he okay?"

"He broke its spine."

"I mean your brother."

"Yeah, I think so."

"Are you okay, sir?" she asked Nate, slyly confiscating the pepper mill.

Without even thinking, I fled, leaving Nate with the manager, and the next thing I knew, I was kneeling on all fours, grazing elbows with Remy, close enough to smell her pancake-batter scent, as she plucked glass off the carpet.

"Ugh, this is so embarrassing," I said. "Here, let me get it."

"I've got it," she said.

"He does that sometimes. It's hard to see it coming, you know? It's not like a daily occurrence or anything. Look," I said, and I could see in her eyes she knew what was coming. "I know this is weird timing, but sometime—"

She stopped me short. "Maybe you should go check on your brother."

I felt like an asshole. Why the hell was I flirting at a time like this?

"Oh yeah, right, my brother."

Remy stood up and walked away with her tray of broken glass.

As it turned out, order had already been restored to the dining room by the time I was halfway to the table. In fact, Nate was apparently getting chummy with the manager, who was still poised at the end of the booth.

I could feel myself blushing from anger and embarrassment.

"Your brother and I were just chatting," the manager said.

"Is that right?"

I was giving Nate the stink eye big-time. I know it wasn't fair to blame him for my falling flat on my face with Remy, but I couldn't help it. If he hadn't thrown the saltshaker, it never would have happened. If I wasn't stuck looking after him my whole life, who knows how many girlfriends I might have had.

Remy avoided us after that. We finished our meal in silence, and the manager cleared our plates. It was the manager who brought us our check, and the manager who cashed us out.

I Am Not a Virgin

Don't get the idea I'm batting zero. I've just been in a bit of a slump since I lost my virginity six years ago. Not that I was lighting the world on fire back then. Gina Costerello just happened to fall into my lap junior year. Actually, Nick sort of pushed her there.

Gina Costerello was a senior, and not unattractive in a horsey way. She was at least three inches taller than me, which was enough to put her out of my league. At least in my memory, Gina always wore dark sweaters with big boobs inside. Not to say that big boobs were important to me. They seemed like an awkwardly designed utility more than anything. Gina's were hard to ignore, though.

It was Nick who was standing beside me that cool spring night in the woods at Rob Vosper's birthday kegger—Rob Vosper of the underaged tattoos and the older brother named William who was in a band that gigged semiregularly in Seattle, the same older brother who dated Gina Costerello for three weeks the previous year.

"Dude," said Nick. "They look like baby seals."

"No they don't. They don't look anything like baby seals."

"I'll bet she's got those smooth silver-dollar nipples."

"Stop," I said. "She's gonna hear you."

"No way. She's shit-housed, dude. Hey, Gina," he called. "Gina Costerello!" And then he promptly darted off toward the keg.

Gina turned in my direction sluggishly, her big brown eyes swimming for focus in the whites.

"Do I know you?" she said.

"I'm Mike. I sit next to you in home economics. We were partners for the pizza thing yesterday. You actually burned me," I said, volunteering my wrist.

"Oh," she said. "Sorry."

"That's cool. It was an accident."

She scanned me up and down with her unsteady gaze, from my fake Adidas Superstars (one too many stripes), up past my off-brand, faded jeans, to my ragged gray sweatshirt, and finally to my face: slightly greasy, with the faintest beginning of a molester mustache. I think she must have seen something pitiable in my brown eyes.

"You're actually kind of cute," she said.

"Uh, thanks."

"C'mon," she said, without taking my hand.

And that was pretty much the extent of our courtship. It was more like a transaction. Gina led me businesslike up the gravel road past a half-dozen parked cars. I did my best to be charming as we crunched along.

"Wow, it's dark," I said.

"Yep," she said.

"Really dark."

"Uh-huh," she said.

My thoughts were racing. My frustrated sexuality was on the cusp of relief. I could feel something big about to happen, though Gina seemed pretty matter of fact about it.

"Watch the ditch," she said when we finally arrived at her white Malibu, and I circled around to the passenger's side, nearly falling in the ditch.

Once we were in the cramped environs of the car, Gina was mostly business.

"Relax," she said. Reaching over me, she groped around for the lever, reclining the passenger's seat. "How's that?"

"Uh, good," I said, looking up at her in the dark.

Placing her knee between my legs, she wrestled off her sweater and unbuttoned her blouse and pulled off her panties, and she climbed on top of me before I even had a chance to savor the moment. I'm not saying I wasn't grateful. To this day, I remain grateful to Gina Costerello and whatever whim, or combination of alcohol and restlessness, prompted her to unbutton my jeans and straddle me in the passenger's seat of that Malibu. And don't get the idea that it didn't feel good, either. It was a revelation, a delirious paroxysm like I'd never known, a welling of rapture from my heels to my temples. The experience literally emptied me.

For ninety seconds after Gina climbed off me, roughly the time it took to get her clothes back on, I felt shucked like an oyster as I gathered my breath.

"Don't tell Rob about this," Gina said, buttoning her blouse.

"I won't. He doesn't talk to me."

"And crack that window, so it doesn't smell like mushrooms in here."

Cracking the window, I pulled up my pants, still wondering what had just happened to me. I spilled out of the car into the ditch, righting myself as gracefully as possible. I followed Gina dazedly back down the gravel road to the party.

"You're cute," she said. "Don't sulk so much."

Then she squeezed my hand once and headed directly for the keg before I could interpret whether or not I was supposed to follow her. I got the feeling she didn't exactly want me to, but then maybe I was sulking again. Anyway, that's where my romance with Gina Costerello ended as abruptly as it had begun twenty-five minutes earlier.

Gina Costerello was always nice to me after that, up until the time she graduated two months later. There was the time Joe Club stuffed me into my locker, and Gina managed to verbally persuade him not to lock me in there. And there was the time she actually signed my yearbook and told me to "take it easy."

But it was always painfully obvious to me that there would never be a repeat performance with Gina.

That never really seemed fair. Or maybe I'm just sulking again.

A Place to Land

Not to belabor the point, but I had good reason to be a nervous kid. A few weeks after that picture was taken in front of the fire station, we lost our house on the res when the landlord jacked our rent without warning. We kept what we could carry and left behind the rest of our worldly possessions, which didn't really amount to much beyond some tired furniture.

For nearly a month, Nate, Mom, and I lived in our 1987 monkey-shit-brown Astro van, eating cold SpaghettiOs out of the can, reading by flashlight through the fog of our own breath, and showering weekly at the state park. I wish I could tell you it was an adventure, at least for the first few days, but it wasn't. The experience was terrifying from the start.

We parked on the streets most nights, under the sodium glare of a streetlamp if we were lucky, where the shadows played tricks on my uneasy imagination as I lay awake. Other nights, we parked at the end of a dirt road, where I was equally terrorized by the crunch of footsteps over gravel and the clashing of limbs in the wind somewhere in the darkness. Invariably, we awoke damp and chilled to the bone, still wearing our clothes.

Weekends were the worst, because there was no school. School was warm and dry, and a green ticket meant a free hot lunch. Thank God the library was open on Saturday and there was church on Sundays, so we got some relief. Let's just say I've never been much of a camper. Been there, done that.

Eventually, we moved in with my diabetic aunt Genie in South Kingston, a situation that was less than ideal since Aunt Genie lived in a single-wide trailer in a motor court with strict guest regulations. Not to mention that she and my mom never got along.

The first thing Aunt Genie said when we showed up on her doorstep with our damp blankets and dirty laundry was, "This is what you get for marrying a Mexican."

At the time, I thought she was talking about Nate and me.

The three of us slept in the living room, Mom on the floor, and Nate and I on a fold-out couch. The fact that we were all trying to sleep never kept Aunt Genie from watching television, sometimes all night long. Many nights, I slept dreamlessly to the babble of infomercials and televangelists, only to awake at dawn and find Aunt Genie still sitting there on her bile-colored La-Z-Boy.

After nearly two months of this, my mom picked up a second job, at the elementary school. By that time, Aunt Genie was so anxious to get rid of us that she lent my mom half the money for a new rental on the res. And no, in case you're wondering, you don't have to be an Indian to live on the res. Apparently, all you need is a bunch of broken shit in your yard.

We managed to stay afloat for a year at that place until the landlord jacked the price, and my mom was forced to rent a one-bedroom apartment, or we might have been back at Aunt Genie's again. That didn't last, either. It was simply too hard for my mom to support us, even with two jobs. That's probably where stepdads 1 and 2 came in, at least in theory.

Stepdad 1 was Chuck, who was about five two and carried a comb in his pocket, right where his wallet should have been.

Stepdad 2 was Ronnie, a guy who liked to pump a little iron and go crabbing, until he married my mom, that is, after which point he simply enjoyed being a fat fuck and sitting in a chair.

Both Chuck and Ronnie suffered very audibly from chronic back pain, migraine headaches, and a general, debilitating condition called "the fucking system." Both stepdads, in the Victor Muñoz mold, were work averse, and both played a little guitar. In the case of both Chuck and Ronnie, the honeymoon ended abruptly, with neither marriage lasting two years.

I'm not making excuses here, but I've come to believe that to a large degree we are products of our environment. So I suppose it's no small wonder that expectations for Mike Muñoz have always been low. But mark my words: somehow, some way, I'm gonna change all that. Old Mike Muñoz fully intends on going out and getting his one of these days.

Getting My Mow On

Just in case I seem like another disgruntled wage slave, don't get the idea that I don't actually like landscaping. Maybe it doesn't pay a fortune, but I'm outside in the fresh air eight hours a day, seeing the immediate results of my labor. There's a lot of satisfaction in that. Think about it: why else would all those old fogeys who retire do nothing but work in their gardens all day long? I'd way rather mow your lawn or deadhead your rhodies or even mulch your flower beds than do your taxes or make your sandwich. At least with grass, you get the last word. Not like a sandwich, where somebody eats it. And what's more beautiful than a great green field of new-mown grass? What's more pleasing than a tidy edge or the clean lines of scrupulously pruned box-wood? I'm not gonna get all nuanced about the art of landscaping or start in with any of that navel-gazing philosophical crap like they do in books—it's not a metaphor for the human condition, it's a fucking yard. Just know that I'm a guy who really enjoys maintaining them, generally speaking. And yeah, maybe someday I'll write the Great American Landscaping Novel, but in the meantime, Tuesdays are a bitch.

All our Tuesday accounts are located across the Agate Passage on Bainbridge. We call the bridge the service entrance because virtually nobody on the island, as far as I can tell, mows their own lawn or maintains their own pool or cleans their own gutters. Nobody drives a broke-dick truck, either, unless it's from 1957. Even the high-school kids —with names like Asher and Towner—drive new cars. They seem happy and healthy, if not a little bored. They all appear harmless enough on the surface, except that most of them don't seem to realize how good they've got it or how people less fortunate than themselves have helped account for their good fortune, have even suffered, so that they can enjoy their wealth and security.

But like I said, one day I'm gonna get mine. It probably won't be a Tuesday, though. Tuesdays start with a half day at Truman's, a huge residence over on the east side of the island, with two hundred feet of high-bank waterfront on the sound, facing Ballard, all of it hemmed in by neat boxwood borders. There's an acre of manicured lawn, which Truman makes us mow with an old rotary mower that he must've inherited from Fred Flintstone. No leaf blowers allowed at Truman's, either. No radios, and especially no salsa music, which is fine by me. I guess when you're a big rich, important person, sitting around on your ass, meditating on your big important, rich-guy thoughts, moving your money around in the "free market," the one built on the backs of slaves and children, you can't be bothered with noisy lawn mowers.

Truman is an uptight little bearded guy about five foot three, who's always home on Tuesdays. I have no idea what he did to become so rich, but my guess is next to nothing. Whatever the case, he sure doesn't know how to enjoy it. Every time you look up, the guy is watching you out a window, and he wants you to know it. You had best be raking or pruning when he looks out the window, or you might end up like Eduardo and Che, both of whom got fired due to Truman's watchdogging. That's why I usually hide behind the boxwood for a few hours, pruning.

With boxwood, it's all about crisp edges and clearly defined boundaries, which are two things my life could use more of. So the work is pretty gratifying that way. It would be a hell of a lot more gratifying if I could make of that boxwood anything I chose. Not to brag, but I'm kind of a savant when it comes to topiary. Though I'm never called upon to do so professionally, I can coax zoo animals, naked chicks, or just your basic geometric shapes out of your garden-variety shrubs. Sometimes when I'm walking around, I'll see a shapeless clutch of holly and imagine an obelisk or a spiral. Or I'll see a line of yews and picture a Greek colonnade.

I do most of my creative work in our backyard, where nobody will complain about it. A cluster of mushrooms in the myrtle. A pair of pom-poms in the privet. In the barberry, a gnome eating a hot dog. But my masterpiece, liberated from the shapeless clusterfuck of Japanese holly behind the shed, was originally supposed to be a mermaid, in homage to the Little Mermaid. But ultimately, the shrub refused to submit to my artistic vision. One pesky limb in particular thwarted my efforts—one very proud and protruding limb. It was a teachable moment, really. I learned that sometimes it's better to give in to the thing itself than to fight it. Which is to say, my masterpiece ended up being a merman with an erection. I guess you could say that the erection was already there, and I just freed it.

Working beside Tino is one of the bright spots on Tuesdays. I've learned a lot from Tino, but don't tell him as much. I'm not saying I like the guy. He calls me *puto* five times a day, and his laughter grates on me. But he's efficient and detail oriented, and he takes pride in his work. He's got a good eye for the big picture: the lay of the yard, the importance of definition and balance, the subtle transitions in terrain that create flow. And he's holy hell with a pole pruner.

But this Tuesday, Tino was out of sorts. One of his uncles had a birthday party the previous night. A *gran fiesta*, as he put it. Multiple barbecues, four cases of Tecate, three fifths of tequila, and 2:00 a.m. soccer in a parking lot. Bottom line, Tino didn't look so good Tuesday morning: bleary eyed and kind of pale for a Mexican. You could smell the tequila coming out of his pores. Within a half hour of arriving at Truman's, he chipped in the hostas, then blew chunks again on the flagstone walkway, not three feet from where I was working.

Well, guess who must have been peering out the window and soon came marching down the walkway?

"What exactly am I looking at?" Truman said, indicating the pile of chum.

Sheepishly, Tino began to ramble some kind of explanation in Spanish.

"*No hablo español*," said Truman. "Did you do this? Is this yours?"

Tino looked at his feet.

"That was me," I said. "I was just about to clean it up."

Truman subjected me to a doubtful once-over.

"I ate some funky Indian last night," I said. "Pretty sure it was the masala. But it sure looks like the *paneer*, doesn't it?"

I'm not sure whether Truman bought it or not, but I'm pretty sure about this: the guy is a prick. If I were running this show, Truman wouldn't even be a client. I'd have standards: no creeps, no ingrates, no busybodies, no racists. No clueless rich fucks. I'd also pay my crew more than twelve bucks an hour, but don't get me started.

"Well, kindly take care of it," Truman said.

Kindly, my ass.

And things only got worse from there. An hour later, my fat boss, Lacy, showed up on the work site. Not that I ever really liked him, but he's changed in the past year. For starters, he never works alongside us anymore. He just delegates, usually by yelling on the phone. Back in the day, he used to always have good medicinal weed for his bad back. Black Rhino, Blueberry Kush, you name it. These days, safety meetings are strictly forbidden. In fact, if Lacy smells weed on you, he'll send you home. But the worst part about Lacy is that he's a social climber, and not a very good one. Basically, he's just a brownnoser.

"What the fuck, Muñoz? I just got a call from Truman. Are you drunk?"

"No, I'm sick. Should I go home?"

"It's too late now. You already puked."

"Sorry," I said.

"Fuck you. Look, I got a call from McClure," he said. "You need to start picking up the dog shit on the back deck. Like now."

"But you said—"

"It doesn't matter what I said. We can't afford to lose an account over some dog shit."

"Why don't they hire a—"

"A dog-shit picker-upper? I looked in the yellow pages, and guess what? I couldn't find one. So that leaves you, Mike. Is this gonna be a problem? Because I know Tino's cousin is looking for work."

"But, Lacy, you said—"

"Look, every crew needs one, and it turns out you're my dog-shit guy. Get the hell over there and clean the deck."

I hate working at the McClures' to begin with, but for different reasons than I hate working at Truman's. If I were in charge, we'd dump the McClure account, too. They don't want any pruning or bed maintenance, and the lawn is only about fifty square feet, hemmed in by shaggy cedars on all sides and riddled with roots everywhere. It's awkward as hell to maintain. You can't push the mower more than three lengths in any given direction before you've got to swing it around again, careful to keep the front wheels off the ground, or the mower will clip a root and stall. It's perpetually shady as fuck, so the grass is wet in July—and it grows two inches every time you turn your back.

That's not the real problem, though. The real problem is Duke, the McClures' two-hundred-pound St. Bernard, who takes elephant-sized dumps everywhere. And I mean everywhere: on the gravel footpath and in the beds lining the walkway. And yes, on the deck. And guess who the McClures expect to pick up all those turds? I'll give you a hint: not Hillary Clinton.

It was dumping rain by the time I got there. As usual, there were lawn cigars everywhere. The fucking dog had managed to shit in a pot of nasturtiums three feet off the ground. I couldn't even get my brain around it. As always, the McClures were thoughtful enough to set out a little fireplace shovel on the deck for me, and let me tell you, the instrument is sorely deficient for the task.

First, I tried the spatula method, but no matter how firm they looked, the turds were too soft in the middle, like one of those lava cakes. To make matters worse, the only bag I had was paper. And meanwhile, the rain was running a rivulet down the crack of my ass, and the stink of Duke's ass goblins was damn near unbearable. After about six waterlogged turds, the paper bag ruptured, in spite of my desperate attempt to stop the breach with my bare hands. The whole mess hit my boots like a rotten pumpkin. Seething, I glared up at the pitiless gray sky for a second before I lost it completely.

"Goddamn-fucking-cunt-fuck-shit-ass-fucker!" I yelled.

I flailed and stomped my boot in disgust as a dollop of shit hit the sliding glass door like refried beans. In a blind rage, I kicked the ruptured bag of shit across the deck, then marched down the steps to the lawn, where I began dragging my boot and wiping my hands in the wet grass.

"Shit-fucking-mother-of-fuck!"

I must have gotten old Duke's attention, because he'd lumbered to his feet and was standing there behind the glass, gazing out impassively, both eyes milky with cataracts.

"Fuck you," I said.

But Duke didn't bat an eye. He just lay back down with his big square head on his paws, let out a sigh, and closed his eyes.

This was the final indignity. The McClures' fucking dog had a better life than me. Sure, he was bored. But he was warm, dry, well fed, and he could shit anywhere he pleased, and some poor schlep like me would clean up after him. And here I was, disconsolate in the rain, with shit on my hands. Again, I'm not blaming Duke. But what the fuck is wrong with this picture?

I won't bore you with the details. Suffice it to say, I spent a half hour trying to clean up the mess, and you can damn well bet I wasn't happy about it. But without another bag, there was only so much I could do.

So I left.

Boldly, into the Future

Look, I'm not stupid. There was really no use in going to work the next day. I knew damn well I was a goner. But I wanted to see Lacy one more time and let him have it, let him know he could clean up his own dog shit if it was so important to him. I guess I needed to prove to myself that I did the right thing.

So the following day, Tino, Ramiro, Tomás, and I were lunching up at the top of Magnuson's driveway on Hall's Hill, when suddenly the three of them fell silent and went to skulking behind their tamales as Lacy pulled up in his white Econoline.

"Muñoz," he said, climbing out. "I specifically told you to pick up the shit on McClures' deck, did I not?"

"We talked about this from the beginning, Lacy. The dog shit was their responsibility. I was hired to mow the lawn and beat back the blackberries. I'm sick of people changing the rules on me. Promising me one thing, then giving me another. Maybe they think they're too good to pick up their dog shit, but that's their problem, not mine. You can hire a new dog-shit picker-upper, I'm out of here."

"Nice try, but you're fired," said Lacy. "Pack up your gear and get out of here. I can't believe you even showed up today."

Tino and the guys were all averting their eyes as I slammed my tailgate shut. Tino gave me a little nod, and when Lacy wasn't looking, he gave me a clap on the back as I climbed into the cab.

"Shit, ese, what you thinking, man?" he whispered.

"I'm a landscaper, not a shit picker-upper, that's what I'm thinking."

He shook his head, looking genuinely disappointed.

"You got to watch your temper, *vato*. Is only dog shit, right?"

"That's plenty."

"I keep my ears open for you, amigo. Maybe my cousin Sergio knows somebody. You cook?"

"Not really."

"Construction?"

"Not so much."

"Too bad. You gotta learn some other skills, homie. Don't get me wrong, you good with a lawn mower, best I know. And you prune really good, too, Miguel, but—"

"Don't call me Miguel."

"What about cars? You fix cars?"

"No."

"What about bikes?"

"Not really. I mean, maybe. Fuck, I don't know."

He shook his head solemnly. "I keep my eyes open, Miguel."

As I pulled away, I flew Lacy a bird out the window.

Maybe I'm my own worst enemy. Maybe I made my own miserable bed.

But I can't tell you how goddamn sick of the indignities I was, how fucking tired of Lacy's petty, patronizing ways. The way he kept me in my place, the way he seemed to relish my humiliation. Nothing would have pleased Lacy more than to watch old Mike Muñoz pick up dog shit in the rain. And don't get me started on some of the clients. Like the old lady in the wheelchair who treats me like her personal servant: always tasking me with fetching her an umbrella or moving boxes around in her three-car garage or dragging her garbage cans a half mile up the driveway. I don't mind helping somebody with special needs—hell, I've been doing it my whole life. It's the way the old lady expected it of me that made me want to wheel her off a cliff. The way she spoke to me, like I was beneath her. The way she never asked me how I was or even greeted me with a hello. Fuck the old lady and anybody like her. If I had my own outfit, I'd find clients that respected my work, people who appreciated my professionalism and my mad topiary skills and my immaculate edges. So, who knows, maybe getting fired was me turning a corner. Maybe this was Mike Muñoz finally sticking up for himself and asking for more.

At once dazed and energized, I watched my old life recede in the rearview mirror. Something had to happen now, right? Something had to give, my life had to begin. Didn't it?

Drinking the Kool-Aid

I was in third grade when my mom took the job as the milk lady at our elementary school. Nate, who should've been in the sixth, repeated fifth grade, where he spent his days in the moldering portable out by the soccer field. I envied him, actually. He got to watch videos and screw around with finger paints and construction paper and eat paste all day long. Meanwhile, little Mike Muñoz, still wearing the same dirty coat with the fake-fur collar, stuck to the far end of the cafeteria at lunch, not drinking milk, clutching his free meal ticket tight as he inched his way through the line, pretending not to notice his mom waving at him from across the room.

Yeah, I know, it was a dick move, ignoring my mom. What can I say? I wasn't exactly flush with social currency in third grade. Beyond Nick, I didn't really have anyone I could call a friend. I was a scrubby, undersized half Mexican, whose brother was a freak of nature. My high water pants and my green lunch ticket were indignity enough. I couldn't have my mom waving at me in the cafeteria.

After school, three nights a week, Mom went to her second job, waitressing at Campana's in Poulsbo, which left me to take care of Nate. Since the library was about the easiest place to keep him occupied, we'd spend two or three hours a day there, Nate flipping through piles and piles of board books, sucking and twisting his shirt collar until it was heavy with spittle and hopelessly stretched out. He'd spend hours rapping his knuckles on the side of the aquarium so that the startled clown fish darted about crazily. Always nearby, I read *White Fang* or *Treasure Island* or *Gulliver's Travels*, books with vivid settings far from my world and far from Nate.

Mom started taking us to a little Methodist church. The church was good to us. I'm not sure how much Mom believed in the gospel, or whether she prayed for our sins or knew the words to the hymns, but she believed in the church—as a resource, anyway. So on most Sundays she dressed us in our cleanest clothes, combed our hair, and we went to church, smelling of stale cigarette smoke. Mom stayed after the service and served coffee in the banquet room, and the married men chatted her up as Nate and I ate lemon bars and stale cookies and filled our pockets with sugar packets and creamers.

Thursday evenings, Nate and I went to the youth-group meeting at the church and played wholesome games designed to engender trust and communication and unwavering faith in God. We sang songs about building our houses on rocks and about how Jesus loved the little children. There were always snacks, of which we partook greedily: graham crackers and little paper cups full of grapes. I drank the Kool-Aid, but I didn't drink the Kool-Aid, if you know what I mean. It's not that I had anything against Jesus or God, I was just underwhelmed by the evidence.

I think those nights when we were at youth group were about the only break my mom ever got from us, an hour and a half a week on Thursday evenings. And you know where she spent it? At the Laundromat. These days, it may look like my mom's not trying very hard, but then I consider how far she's come and all the bullshit she's had to endure, and I figure she's doing all right.

As dull as the Bible study and singing were, I looked forward to Thursday nights. For one, I didn't have to manage Nate. There was a teacher for that. It gave me a break for a while. All told, there were eight or nine other kids, including my hero, Doug Goble, long before he became the hottest real-estate agent in Kitsap County. It's not that Doug Goble was particularly winsome or athletic or anything like that. He had a fetal cast to him, actually, like he wasn't fully cooked when he came out of the oven. I'm not saying he was all curled up or anything, but his head had a lightbulb aspect to it, and his nose was flat and undersized. I think the appeal for me was that Doug Goble had confidence, charisma even, though he was poor like me and, like me, lived on the res in a manufactured home with dirty siding and a cluttered carport. Doug Goble could talk to girls and adults. He was decisive and self-assured, which made him persuasive. He possessed that quality I most associated with winners: certainty.

"You see this church?" he'd say. "Someday, I'm gonna live in a house twice as big as this dump. And the roof won't leak. And it'll be right in town, where everybody can see it. I'm gonna have a huge laundry room with a maid. And she'll have big jugs, too."

And I believed it, every word of it. I guess I needed to believe it. I would have done just about anything to impress Doug Goble. I laughed at his jokes, listened raptly to his plans of world domination, hoping that at the very least he'd let me ride on his coattails.

"It's all just a big game of Monopoly. Dummies and nice guys always lose."

God, how I wanted to be a winner. How I longed for that certainty, when everything in my life was so uncertain. Goble tolerated me for the most part, as long as I kept laughing and listening. Until one day, he just abandoned me with no explanation. I always reasoned it was because I was a loser or maybe just a sucker. Anyway, our lives took different trajectories after that. Goble grew into himself and became one of the popular kids who sat at the same table in the cafeteria with the other popular kids who, in retrospect, weren't actually popular, just feared and admired, and mostly wealthy. Goble was forced to bluff on the wealthy part or to compensate with confidence and guile.

As early as sixth grade, Goble started distinguishing himself as an entrepreneur, trading in lunch tickets and selling his mom's cigarettes to high-school freshmen, who lined up behind the bleachers before school. Sophomore year of high school, he somehow finagled the school into paying him five cents per tray for collecting lunch trays from the cafeteria and commons, then outsourced the job to Vic Burzycki for a penny per tray.

Goble always had a plan, always knew what he wanted, never lacked ambition or nerve. He was a worthy hero for little Mike Muñoz, while he lasted.

The Usual Bullshit

Okay, I blew it. What do you want me to say? I probably shouldn't have kicked the bag of shit. I probably should have driven down to Jiffy Mart and asked for a plastic bag, even if I had to buy something. Then I probably should've gone back and cleaned up the mess and called it a day.

But I didn't.

Dazed and numb with apprehension, I had neither the inclination nor the courage to go home with the bad news. So I took comfort where I usually took comfort: the library.

As kids, Nate and I spent untold hours in the library while my mom was at work. We ate bruised apples and crumbling saltines, napping on the quilted sofas. The library was the most stable thing in our lives, the only thing in the whole damn society that said to little Mike Muñoz: "Here you go, kid, it's all yours for the asking." No matter that your ears were dirty and your hair was greasy. No matter that your mentally challenged big brother didn't have much of an indoor voice or that he tended to throw books and pee on the bathroom floor and scare the clown fish shitless. At the library, a little ferret of a kid like me had a chance. The only currency he needed was a library card.

For two hours, waiting for Nick to get off work at Les Schwab, I scanned the fiction section for distraction. What I wanted was a book written by a guy who worked as a landscaper or a cannery grunt or a guy who installed heating vents. Something about modern class struggle in the trenches. Something plainspoken, without all the *shiver-thin coverlets of snow* and all the rest of that luminous prose. Something that didn't have a pretentious quote at the beginning from some old geezer poet that gave away the whole point of the book. Something that didn't employ the "fishbowl lens" or a "prismatic narrative structure" or any of that crap they teach rich kids out in the cornfields.

I wanted a book that grabbed me by the collar and implored me to conquer my fears and embrace the unknown. I wanted a novel that acted as a clarion call for the disenfranchised of the world. Not 250 pages of navel-gazing about the nuances of saddle making, topped off with some hokey epiphany. I wanted realism. Grit. I wanted my transcendence with grease under the fingernails and unpaid bills piling up on the countertop. Where were the books about me?

Maybe I should write the goddamn Great American Landscaping Novel. Why shouldn't I have a voice? Just because I never went to college? Because I haven't traveled the world or lived in New York City or fought in Iraq or done anything else of distinction? I suppose you could make a strong argument for any one of those. But I believe the world could use the Great American Landscaping Novel.

After all, most of us are mowing someone else's lawn, one way or another, and most of us can't afford to travel the world or live in New York City. Most of us feel like the world is giving us a big fat middle finger when it's not kicking us in the face with a steel-toed boot. And most of us feel powerless. Motivated but powerless. Entertained but powerless. Informed but powerless. Fleetingly content, most of the time broke, sometimes hopeful, but ultimately powerless.

And angry. Don't forget angry.

The problem, I soon came to realize, was that landscapers, especially unemployed ones, and cannery grunts and heating-duct installers didn't have time to while away their days writing novels. They had bills to pay. Cars to fix. Disabled siblings to care for.

I finally picked up a handful of titles off the new arrivals' rack, though none of them really appealed to me. One was a dystopian novel about a global pandemic with metaphorical implications. So was another. The last was by a woman named Hannah, who'd won a prize I'd never heard of and was billed as "a stunning meditation on race, gender inequity, and sexual identity."

"MFA fiction," said a voice.

I looked up to discover the same broad-shouldered librarian with the mop of dark, curly hair and the prominent Adam's apple, who had recommended *The Octopus* to me. He was pushing one of those tan wheelie-carts loaded with recently returned books. Not your usual librarian, this guy, nothing like those formidable librarians of my youth, with their translucent nylon stockings. He was wearing a puke-colored sweater and a T-shirt that said BE THE CHANGE YOU WANT.

"I mean, the writing's good," he said. "Lyrical and all that. If it's sentences you're after. But so much of it just feels like affectation and craft to me."

"Got any recs?"

"What are you looking for?"

"Something angry," I said. "I like the last one you gave me—*The Octopus*. It made me want to put a brick through a window."

"Ah, follow me, then," he said.

He led me back to the fiction section and began running his fingers gingerly over the book spines. He picked out something called *The Jungle* by a guy named Sinclair.

"Is this guy dead?"

"Yes. You might've read it in high school," he said.

"Not if it was assigned."

"Then you should definitely check it out. Classic muckraking."

"Cool. Thanks, man."

"I'm Andrew," he said, extending a hand.

"Mike," I said.

He smiled, exposing a big pileup of crooked teeth that looked like a miniature Stonehenge. It was sort of a heartbreaking smile, but it didn't seem to bother him.

"You should go ahead and check out the new fiction, too," he said. "By all means. Don't take my word for it. See what you think. Maybe you'll like the acoustics."

Once again, the library had my back. I left feeling a lot less desperate and scared than when I'd arrived. I clung to that security as I walked down the hill to town, clutching my five books.

Around five fifteen, I arrived in the murky environs of Tequila's, where Nick awaited me in back. Before I could even tell him about getting fired, he started in on his usual bullshit.

"You see where they're puttin' a Mexican market across the street?"

"So?"

"Who do you think's gonna shop at it?"

"Uh . . . Mexicans? People who like Mexican food?"

"Bingo."

"So, why do you give a shit?"

"Because this place is starting to look like Tijuana."

"You ever been to Tijuana?"

"Fuck no. Why would I go to Tijuana? Hey, look at that fag over by the jukebox," he said.

"That's Ron Strobeck's little brother. He's a youth pastor."

"He's a total homo."

"Nick, do you have any idea what a dumbshit you sound like? I mean like ninety percent of the time?"

"Hey, you're the one mowing lawns, chowder hound. I stopped mowing lawns for money when I was twelve. I made thirty-one grand last year at Les Schwab. So who's the dumbshit?"

"But c'mon, don't you want more?"

"Yeah, more pussy."

"I'm being serious, Nick."

"So am I. I'd like to be getting considerably more pussy than I'm currently getting."

"What about a steady girlfriend, then?"

"Fuck that noise. Then I'd never get laid."

"See? You sound like a total misogynist when you say stuff like that."

"Fuck you, I don't see you getting laid."

"This isn't about getting laid, Nick. This is about your life."

"What are you, my guidance counselor now?"

"Where do you see yourself in ten years? Seriously, Les Schwab?"

"What is it with you tonight?"

"Just answer the question."

"I don't see myself in ten years. Why would I want to do that? I'll probably be fat. And my hair will be gone. You're really starting to piss me off with this superiority complex of yours, Michael. You work with a crew of illegals mowing old ladies' lawns. I just don't see where you get off judging anybody, I really don't."

Maybe Nick was right, maybe it wasn't my place to judge. But his ignorance seemed willful. Or maybe it was just lazy, which was also willful. Whatever the case, I was running out of patience for it, growing weary of the exercise—mostly fruitless—that comprised coaxing out Nick's good side. Such was my fatigue that over the course of the next two beers, I didn't even bother telling him I'd quit my job or how I'd struck out with Remy. Already besieged by doubt and insecurity, I couldn't see how telling Nick anything would make me feel better.

The Pavement

The next morning, I slumped at the kitchen table with a splitting headache, combing through the *Kitsap Herald* classifieds—all two columns of it. Nate was at the table with me, plowing mechanically through his third bowl of Rice Chex.

"Do you have to chew so loud? I'm trying to concentrate here."

Actually, it took very little concentration once I conceded that I had no sales experience and couldn't swing a hammer or program computers or even do an oil change. My broke-dick truck disqualified me from the delivery-driver position or even a job with those fascists over at Uber. And of course, there was nothing in the *Herald* for landscapers.

My mom emerged from the bedroom, her hair in a sleepy jumble, squinting as she reached for her cigarettes.

"Rained out today, sweetie?"

"Not exactly."

"Are you sick?"

"Nah, Ma. Actually, I sort of quit."

She lowered herself into a chair. "Honey?"

"Lacy is such an asshole, Mom. I was only making twelve bucks an hour. I want to do more with my life than clean up dog shit."

I could see the annoyance in her face as I rationalized the decision. As it was, our EBT card was nearly maxed by the fifteenth of every month.

"I'm gonna find something better, Mom. It'll work out, I promise."

I could see that she was anxious, but she didn't let on. Instead, she patted my hand.

"I know it will, sweetie."

Don't get the idea Mike Muñoz wasted any time on his job search, either. Not five hours after breaking the news to Mom, I'd already filled out an application and secured an interview by 3:00 p.m.

The manager at Subway was a three-hundred-pound guy named Jay, who had the perpetual throat rattle of a blown woofer.

"I don't see any food service here," he said, perusing my application.

"I've made a ton of sandwiches. Just not professionally."

"You got a handler's permit?"

"I'm working on that."

"What about evenings? What's your availability?"

"Evenings are tough. I watch my big brother."

He glanced at my application again and scratched his neck.

"*My Big Brother*, huh? Is that HBO?" he said. "I like *Game of Thrones*. Even though the end of the last season kinda blew. The thing is, Mike," he said, releasing a Darth Vader sigh, "I'm really looking for evenings. Let me hold on to this, and if something opens up, I'll give you a holler."

Four days passed, and I received no holler from Jay. Undaunted, I continued to pound the pavement, submitting a half-dozen more applications and working up a résumé that included . . . well, land-scaping, while emphasizing my enthusiastic personality and ster-ling work ethic. I was teachable, hardworking, eager, flexible. I had a strong back, a quick mind, a willingness to endure repetition. I was punctual, honest, and conscientious; I sometimes played well with others. So what happened to all the fucking jobs? There had to be jobs out there for a guy like me. Wasn't the American dream built on the idea of equal opportunity? So where was my opportunity? I wasn't asking for handouts. All I wanted was a job that provided a living wage and a little dignity. That seemed like a reasonable launching pad for any further ambitions I might have. All I needed was the opportunity to think beyond sustenance long enough to dream.

I was so desperate I even asked Nick to put in a word for me at Les Schwab.

"Not gonna happen," he said. "There's a waiting list."

"Can't you do something?"

"I wish I could."

Meanwhile, my mom immediately started picking up more doubles to make up for my unemployment, which left me in charge of Nate 24/7. That didn't stop me from combing the classifieds and sending out résumés. I began casting a wider and wider net, fudging my credentials with increasing abandon until finally I was applying for jobs that were way over my head. Once, I even applied for a job at the *Kitsap Herald* itself, though I had zero experience in the field of journalism, no college degree, and nothing more than six measly pages of notes on the Great American Landscaping Novel. Chalk it up to a rare moment of conceit. Why not bluff? Isn't that how the wealthy and successful folks of the world did it, by demanding more, by not accepting less?

I was shocked when I actually got an interview.

I wore the only tie I owned, the one Mom bought for me to wear to Aunt Genie's funeral, ten years ago. It was a little short, I think, not that I'm any expert on ties. My ass was sweating like two canned hams as I sat across from the managing editor, who looked exactly like my idea of newspaperman, which is to say gray and unhealthy, with some paunch around the middle. He was wearing a dress shirt, but it looked slept in. A little mustard stain sullied the collar. Here was a guy who knew the taste of cold chow mein and the scratchy texture of a sofa pillow against his cheek. A guy who left little coffee rings in his wake wherever he went.

"Can you type?" he said.

"Yessir."

"How fast?"

"Pretty fast, I guess."

He looked at me blankly. "Can you give me an estimate?"

"Sir?"

"How many words per minute?"

"Depends on the words, sir."

"Look, I'm not looking to make a cub reporter out of you—this isn't the *Washington Post*, and it's sure as hell not 1943. Do you have any idea what a newspaper looks like in 2016? I *am* the reporter. *And* the managing editor. I write the obits, too—that's our moneymaker. How are you on the phone? Can you sell?"

"Uh, I think so, I guess."

"Wrong answer."

He sighed, rubbing his face like he just drove from Flagstaff to Fort Collins with a belly full of truck-stop coffee.

"Tell me, kid, what possessed you to apply for this job?"

"Did you see my writing sample?"

"I didn't ask for a writing sample."

"Did you read it?"

"No."

"It's a fictitious news story about a—"

Without further ceremony, he stood up behind his desk and extended a limp handshake.

"Thanks for coming in, kid. Try Subway. I hear they're hiring."

The Guest Cottage

It would've been great after my most recent humiliation to come home and find Nate zoned out in front of the TV with Mom sitting beside him, flipping through a magazine. Instead, I arrived home to discover Freddy, the doorman-slash-bouncer from the Tide's Inn, sitting in my living room, smoking a joint, and eating an egg salad sandwich.

Freddy is this black dude about my mom's age with a gut like a medicine ball. I'd known him casually for a few years, though to my knowledge he'd never been to our house. Once, when Mom was home with Nate, I ran into Freddy at the Masi Shop, where I was buying a tallboy, and he invited me up to his studio apartment behind the fire station to smoke pot. We sat on an enormous blotchy, cream-colored sectional that took up practically the entire apartment while Freddy showed me vintage pornos on VHS with the volume turned down, providing his own accompaniment on electric bass. Besides casual exchanges at the door of the Tide's Inn, that was the extent of my experience with Freddy.

"Uh, hey, Freddy," I said, stepping into the living room. "What's up?"

Before Freddy could reply, my mom emerged from the kitchen with a glass of weak orange juice for him.

"We found a renter," she said. "Freddy's gonna be renting the guest cottage."

"You mean the shed?"

"I mean the guest cottage."

"Where's he gonna keep all his pornos?" I said.

"Hey now," Freddy said.

"Mom, what am I supposed to do with the lawn mower and all my tools?"

"We need to prioritize, Michael."

"But somebody will steal my shit."

"No one wants a dirty old lawn mower, sweetie."

"She's right, little man," says Freddy. "Nobody wants to mow their own lawn nowadays."

"Shut up, Freddy," I said.

By the next morning, I was so depressed I couldn't get out of bed. I could hear Freddy out in the kitchen talking to my mom. I didn't feel like reading anything angry, so I picked up one of the dystopian novels, which didn't do much for me. So I picked up a twentieth-century short-story anthology instead and started reading a story by this old British gasser, W. Somerset Maugham. It was exactly the kind of long-winded thing you'd expect from someone named Somerset. I was actually sort of relieved when I was interrupted by a call from an unidentified number.

"Miguel, is Tino. *¿Qué onda, vato?* I got a job lead for you, man. You know who is Vandermeer?"

"No."

"Rocindo's brother work on his crew. They doing big jobs—business parks. One of their guys got his foot ran over by a backhoe yesterday."

"Damn."

"Yeah, is not good. He gonna be out of work for six weeks. But now Vandermeer need a guy with a lawn mower and truck. They need a guy like yesterday, so you gotta call right away, ese. Oh, and don't tell my cousin I called you. He trying to get the job for his nephew."

"Thanks, man—I mean *gracias*. I owe you one, *ese*."

"Is no problem, amigo."

I called Vandermeer, and he seemed okay. He said if I showed up with my mower at 1:00 p.m. at the Seaboard Building in Winslow, he'd give me a shot, at least for the day. And all Mike Muñoz ever asked for was a shot.

So I cleaned up my mower before I packed it in the truck. I even hosed the truck down and gave her a coat of wax. I wore my clean green pants and my green sweatshirt, and brought along my ear and eye protection, just to look legit. I loaded up my edger and my rake and my weed whacker. I didn't even ask the guy how much he was paying, because it didn't matter. The truth is, after twenty fruitless job applications, I would have mowed a lawn for free, just to win back a shred of my dignity.

Well, you can probably guess what happened as soon as old Mike Muñoz got a little wind behind his sails. Yep, the old crash and burn. My truck gave out about a half mile past the bridge. It wasn't the usual lurch and stall. This time it was electrical. Everything quit at once. Coasting at two miles per hour, power steering locking up, I found enough shoulder space to pull over across from the Methodist church, right in front of one of Doug Goble's realty signs.

I actually prayed. Or maybe *begged* is the proper term. I beseeched God: Please throw me a crumb here. Let this be a loose battery cable. I've still got twelve minutes to get there. I turned the ignition over again. Nothing. I popped the hood and checked the cables. I jiggled some wires and tried to work a little voodoo with the distributor cap. I tapped the alternator a few times like it might be sleeping. Then, purely as an act of faith, I patted the hood after I closed it. Climbing back in the cab, I buckled my belt and, with another prayer on my lips, turned her over again.

Nothing. I must have turned the ignition over thirty times. And the whole time Doug Goble leered at me from his realty sign like the smuggest jack-o'-lantern you ever saw. Yes, opportunity finally came knocking and left a burning bag of shit on my front step. The irony is not lost on me.

Well, I didn't even bother calling Vandermeer, though I probably should have. I couldn't call my mom, because she had enough problems. And there was no way in hell I was leaving the mower. Freddy, though he was ostensibly a grown man, did not own an automobile, nor could he operate one to my knowledge. Otherwise, he'd probably be living in it—instead of our shed. As for the truck, I didn't have AAA, and I couldn't afford an eighty-dollar tow. So I emptied the glove box, unscrewed the plates, and using the stubby blade of my Leatherman, pried off the VIN by the rivets.

Sometimes you gotta walk away, even if you've got nowhere

to go.

A few fun facts: It's about three and a half miles from the Seabold Methodist Church to Suquamish, and there are no fewer than six Doug Goble realty signs along that stretch. If you position a weed whacker and an edger just right, you can get them to rest on the bar of a push mower reasonably well, and you can balance the gas can on the motor as you trundle the whole mess along the shoulder of the highway in your green sweatshirt in eighty-degree weather. If looking at the expressions of passing drivers is your thing, you can expect anything, from the bemused grin, to frowning contempt, to the smart-assed grin of some guy throwing a Pepsi can at you. I got one sympathetic look from a Mexican guy in a shitty truck with a lawn mower in back, who was probably headed toward Vandermeer.

I arrived home in the middle of the afternoon as Mom was ironing her slacks for work and smoking a cigarette. Nate was watching *Megamind* with the volume up too loud, oblivious to the world as he shoveled Cheetos into his mouth. Freddy plucked his bass on the sofa, smoking a joint. You could see one of his nuts poking out the leg of his jeans shorts, along with the inside pocket liner.

There are times when a man needs a garage. A shed. A god-damn tree fort. A little piece of real estate. The place can be riddled with oil cans and rat turds, it doesn't matter. There can be a lawn mower and a gang of broken flashlights and a busted jar of drywall screws. Half a croquet set, a rusting putter, and a ruptured air mattress. The point is, a man needs somewhere he can go to decompress, shake off all the shit life throws at him, dust off his bong, and feel like the king of his moldering little domain for an hour or two. A place to listen to Mozart or Rush, drink a couple tallboys, regather his wayward optimism, and convince himself the whole endeavor is worth the effort—and by endeavor, I mean breathing. But sometimes there's a guy living in his shed. Sometimes there's no optimism left to be gathered. Sometimes there's just enough room under the canopy to stow his lawn mower.

This was one of those times.

"You all sweaty," observed Freddy, from his place on the sofa.

"How'd the job go, honey?" said Mom. "I didn't hear you pull in."

"It didn't," I said. "My truck bit the dust on 305."

"Oh, Mike."

"Bound to happen with an old truck like that," said Freddy, Cheetos dusting his gray stubble. "Boy, you twenty-two years old. Time to jump-start your life."

"Is that right, Freddy? And how do you propose I do that?"

"You gotta start by finding gainful employment."

"Uh-huh."

"Then you gotta find yourself a woman."

"Mm-hm. Go on," I said, wresting the Cheetos from him.

"And, boy, you got to get your own place. Look around you. Ain't no woman gonna come around here."

"You don't think?"

"Hell, no! Ain't no woman gonna sleep in no bunk bed. And you got to get yourself into a new truck while you're at it."

"And how do you propose I do that?"

"By findin' some gainful employment. Ain't you been listenin' to me?"

"Thanks, Freddy. Good talk."

"Anytime, man. Old Freddy seen a few things. When you're black in America, you anywhere from invisible to a bright red. Gives a man a number of different perspectives on the world. You pay attention, Mike Muñoz, and maybe you can learn somethin'."

Coinstar Blues

The days of unemployment ran into weeks. I didn't even know what day of the week it was when I bused over to Safeway on the island for my monthly visit to the Coinstar. Allowing for my fare and the 10 percent Coinstar charge, I still figured to clear about thirty bucks by my estimate. And thirty bucks buys a lot of frozen burritos. On the ride to Safeway, I resumed reading the book that crooked-toothed Andrew recommended, *The Jungle*, by the dead guy, Sinclair. The writing was a little clunky at times but serviceable. It's about a dude named Jurgis, from somewhere in eastern Europe, who comes to America, like everybody else, looking for a better life. The whole thing starts out with a wedding feast, and by page 50 you just know this Jurgis fella is wishing he would've rationed all that food instead of springing for the feast, because things start getting thin really fast. It didn't help that his wife and his whole family were counting on old Jurgis to bring home the bacon. Poor Jurgis couldn't get a break. It was one indignity after another, and they were all more or less familiar. Poverty. Injustice. The Man. Hell, take away all the funny names and it could've been my life. And yeah, that pisses me off. I can't tell you how the book ends yet, but I can tell you this much already: I won't be eating a hot dog anytime soon.

There's this Indian kid from the res who is a fixture at the Bainbridge Safeway. He's usually staged out front by the shopping carts with his guitar, bungling through a stilted version of "Seven Nation Army," utilizing only his E string. He never takes his eyes off the fret board. His finger work is pretty jerky. But I admire him all the same for his nerve. He's pretty haggard, this kid. Nineteen going on fifty-one. He has a broken front tooth, and he always wears a leather vest, hand stitched with a cross-eyed eagle. You can actually see the dirt caked around his extremities, like a human bath ring.

Yeah, he sucks at guitar, I get that. But you see how it is? Some rich kid with a college education can go fuck around and pretend to be whatever he feels like. He can go save the world doing missionary work in Ethiopia, or pretend to be a poet in Brooklyn, or join a band, or be a political activist on weekends, or get an internship on Wall Street. I see them on the island in the summer, back from their East Coast colleges and prep schools, sitting around to no practical purpose, talking about XR and Vampire Weekend. But the minute some broken-toothed Indian kid exercises a little initiative in front of a grocery store, he's automatically a bum.

For this reason, I usually stand around and watch him suck for a couple of minutes before dropping a couple singles into his battered guitar case. But this particular day, he wasn't out front by the carts. Instead, I found him standing in front of the Coinstar machine, looking even shaggier than usual with a couple of sad weeks' growth for a beard. From the looks of it, somebody had recently used his vest to beat out a campfire because it was sooty and singed around the edges.

The kid just stood there, holding his guitar carelessly, apparently befuddled, but visibly unconcerned, smelling like armpit and car exhaust. I caught him admiring my pickle jar.

"You ever used this thing?" he said.

"Yeah, tons of times."

I walked him through the process and got him his voucher. The kid only cleared four and a half bucks. How long he had to stare holes in his fret board, how many ham-fisted versions of "Aqualung" he had to struggle through to make four bucks and change, I couldn't tell you, but I felt for him.

"Peace, bro," he said, clutching his voucher.

By the time I emptied all my change onto the tray, scooped up the remainder, and cashed in my twenty-eight-dollar voucher, the kid was already back out front by the carts, butchering Steppenwolf. I watched him for a little longer than usual, until he finished "Magic Carpet Ride," then started into something unrecognizable. When it felt like I had finally fulfilled my obligation to listen, I dropped three singles along with what was left of my change in the case.

"Right on," he said. "Peace."

The thing about the kid, the thing that made me a little melancholy as I hoofed it back to the bus stop with my twenty-five bucks, is that even though I don't know him from Adam, I know his story without having to ask. All I have to do is smell that leather vest and see that broken tooth and those sad brown eyes and the desperate determination in his knit brow as he tries to make music, and I can guess roughly what the household he grew up in looked like. Probably a lot like mine. If he was lucky, he had a diabetic Aunt Genie somewhere. Or a mom and a brother. Or maybe not. Maybe he was on his own, trying to make music.

When I arrived home from the Coinstar, I was only halfway up the driveway before I noticed that something was amiss: my lawn mower was gone! Somebody had stolen it in broad daylight.

"Fuuuuuck!" I hollered, pounding the trunk of the dead Festiva. "Shit-fucking-suck-fuck-piss!"

Chest heaving, fist still clenched, I marched into the house.

"Well, I hope you're happy," I said to Mom. "My fucking mower is gone."

"What happened to it?"

"Exactly what I told you would happen when we moved it out of the shed. Somebody stole it. Fuck, Mom. What if I get a fucking landscaping gig?"

"Honey, just cut out all the swearing. Every other word out of your mouth is 'fuck.' You're smarter than that."

"She's right, you know," said Freddy from the sofa, where he was smoking a joint. "Profanity is a class indicator."

"Fuck you, Freddy. You live in a shed. You lay down bass riffs to old pornos. What does that indicate?"

"Those are original compositions."

"Leave Freddy alone!" yelled Nate from the bathroom.

You see? This is what I'm up against. The whole world is conspiring to sink me. If it's not some asshole stealing my lawn mower, it's my own mother renting out my shed to a man who dispenses wisdom with one nut hanging out.

Three-Dollar Minimum

Sunday afternoon, when Freddy and Mom were both home with Nate, I took the opportunity to escape the house, hoofing it all the way out to the Masi with $2.39 to buy a tallboy of Schmidt Ice. I called in advance for a price check and had to hit up Freddy for sixteen cents.

As usual, the line was six deep when I finally got there, and the place smelled, as always, of corn dogs and gasoline. I realized that spending money on alcohol when I was totally broke was patently irresponsible. But like Freddy once said, "A man ain't no good to the world until he finds some relief."

Just when you thought old Freddy had dipped into his well of tired axioms one too many times, he dispensed a little pearl of wisdom like this one. The fact is, I was no good to the world, and I needed twenty-two ounces of relief.

Well, I never got it, not really. Because guess who got in line directly behind me at the Masi? I'll give you a hint: she recently came within three feet from being brained by a saltshaker. At once mortified and ecstatic to see her, my scalp tightened.

"Uh, hey, Remy."

"Oh, hey! What's up? How's your brother?"

"He's doing great. He's sort of got a new caregiver, which, you know, frees me up a bit. Dang, we haven't been to Mitzel's since, well, you know."

She laughed. "Oh my God, that was hilarious," she said. "I actually heard that thing whistle past my ears."

"I thought you hated us after that," I said.

"Not at all. I just didn't think I could serve you guys without cracking up. Oh my God, that old man—he had no idea!"

"Next," interjected the checker.

I set my tallboy on the counter.

"ID?" he said.

I pulled out my wallet and flashed my license. He checked the date and scanned my tallboy.

Stuffing the wallet back in my pocket, I started digging out my change. It was accounted for, every penny of it—all $2.39.

"Two seventy-one," said the clerk.

"It's two thirty-nine."

"Tax."

"I thought there was no tax on food."

"Beer isn't food."

I started patting my pockets. "Ah man, I forgot my wallet."

"I just carded you, remember? It's in your back pocket."

"Oh, right, duh." I pulled out my wallet and handed him my debit card. "Just put the difference on the card."

"The difference? You mean thirty-two cents?"

"Yeah."

"Sorry. There's a three-dollar minimum."

Here's the thing. There was exactly $2.03 in that account, and I didn't have overdraft protection. If that guy used my card, it would get declined for sure, and Remy would witness the indignity.

"Um, shoot, let me run out to my truck."

You know, the truck sitting in impound.

"Or you could just buy a pack of gum," said the clerk.

"Yeah, I don't really like gum. . . ."

"Or a Slim Jim," said the clerk.

"Not a big Slim Jim fan."

The checker heaved a sigh. "Look, anything that costs thirty-two cents will put you over the three-dollar minimum."

"I've got change," said Remy, sparing me further embarrassment, sort of. She fished through her purse at length, looking for the difference.

Clearly, I was the biggest loser ever. There was the clerk, wearily holding all my nickels and dimes as the line stacked up behind us.

"Don't worry about it, I'll just run to my truck," I said.

"No, no, I've got it," she said, setting her ChapStick on the counter. "Just put it all together."

We walked out of the store side by side, my heart beating in my throat.

"Where's your truck?"

"Oh yeah, I totally spaced. I walked down here."

"So you live close?"

"Just down the road two and a half miles."

"C'mon, I'll give you a ride."

My knees almost gave out. Remy was inviting me into her car—Remy! I must have spent a thousand bucks eating rubbery steaks and powdered mashed potatoes just to get this woman's attention. Now she was not only forgiving me for being a complete loser, she was actually willing to contribute to the cause. This should have been some kind of turning point for me, right?

"Nah, that's cool," I said. "I need the exercise."

"Are you're sure? You look sweaty. Let me give you a ride."

"Nah, I'm good."

"It's like ninety degrees. I'm giving you a ride."

In the car, she asked me what I did. I knew she meant what did I do for work, but I wasn't about to tell her I was an unemployed landscaper.

"I'm a writer," I said, regretting the lie immediately.

She looked impressed, or maybe just really surprised.

"That's so cool. What do you write?"

It pains me to remember our conversation. All I know is, I didn't want to blow it. I was desperate to redeem myself.

"Oh, you know, Great American Novels. I'm currently working on something big."

"What's it about?"

"Well, it's difficult to give you a synopsis. It's pretty sprawling. A lot of the book is about class issues. Wealth inequity. Race. And a bunch of other things."

"Like what?"

"Well, there's some stuff about poultry."

"Sounds amazing."

"Well, I'm no Frank Norris, but it's getting there."

Remy seemed genuinely engaged by my psychobabble. She was

actually buying it. Things were going inexplicably well, until the bottom fell out.

Suddenly, as we neared my neighborhood, I got panicky. I didn't want her to see where I lived. If she saw where I lived, everything would fall apart. I'd get caught in all my idiotic lies. She'd see my truck not sitting in the driveway. She'd see our crappy double-wide. If she dared to venture inside, she'd soon see that I shared a room with Nate, that our beds were in fact two estranged halves of a single bunk bed. Mom would still be home, puffing away. Freddy would be scratching his taco on the sofa. The place would stink of Blueberry Kush and cigarette smoke. There would be no type-writer, no stack of pages. Who was I fooling thinking I could ever be with this girl? She'd see through me in two minutes flat. By the time we got to the abandoned grocery store, I had no choice.

"You can just drop me here."

"I can take you all the way."

"Nah, this is great. I wanna walk at least a few blocks."

Without further ceremony, I opened the door and hopped out of the car.

"Great seeing you," she said.

"Yeah, you, too."

"Don't forget your beer."

I leaned back into the car and grabbed my tallboy off the dash.

"Come in and see me," she said.

"I will."

She winked. "You better. And bring your brother."

"Well, I'm not sure about that," I said.

When I walked away from Remy's car, I didn't even look back as I heard her circle halfway around the lot and give me a little honk.

What was I supposed to do, ask her out? Out where? With what? Christ, I didn't even have wheels. She'd have to pick me up, and soon she'd realize that I'm just some unemployed, unenlightened wannabe trying to figure out who the hell he was. So, yeah, now you're starting to get the picture. Maybe she liked me, maybe she saw something in me, but that's because she didn't know me. I'd rather she never see me again and maybe remember me as something I'm not. Like a writer or at least a guy with a job.

When I got home, things were as expected. Freddy and Nate on the couch. Mom in the kitchen, smoking cigarettes.

"Boy, shut that door, you lettin' the heat in," said Freddy.

I shut the door all right. I shut it good. I proceeded straight to the bathroom and locked the door, where I nearly put my fist through the wall.

"What the hell, boy?" Freddy shouted.

"Let me handle this, Freddy," my mom said.

I heard the back steps creak as Freddy walked out to the shed. Mom was soon at the door, jiggling the knob.

"Honey, is everything okay?"

"I'm just taking a shower, I'm fine."

"Why is the door locked?"

"Privacy, please! Jesus Christ, I'm twenty-two years old, can't I lock the door?"

I heard the ice cubes in her tumbler slosh as she went away. I turned on the shower, and like an idiot, I broke down and sobbed as quietly as I could. And it wasn't all about Remy, either, but a cumulative depression. The depression of experience. The futility of knowing I was stuck on a hamster wheel, and it would always be the same. Whatever I did, things were not going to get better.

I'd always be living on this lousy street or some other lousy street. My mailbox would always be crooked and full of bills I couldn't afford to pay. I'd always be broke.

Even if I could get Remy and somehow keep her, I'd only be dooming her. Maybe I could convince her to squirt out a few kids in a moment of weakness, and doom them, too. The futility of accepting that I couldn't physically afford to plan ahead, I couldn't even afford to look that direction.

Look, I'm not gonna lie. I was feeling sorry for myself. But beneath the self-pity seethed an anger, raw and abiding, hot and blind, an anger getting harder to suppress by the day. It just needed placing, needed focus, needed a voice.

"Mike," Mom said, again outside the bathroom door. "Are you sure you're okay?"

"Go away," I said.

You're Just You

After he moved out, I saw my old man once, maybe twice a year, until he disappeared completely when I was eleven. My mom must have known he was about to go AWOL, because she called Victor on the phone one Sunday morning after church, and though I wasn't meant to, I heard her side of the conversation from my place in the living room, where I was reading an illustrated Bible aloud to Nate.

"Yes, I heard, Victor," came my mom's voice from the kitchen. "Of course you are, Victor, that's what you've been doing all along, which is why you're going to come over here, and . . . no, it *is* your responsibility . . . this has nothing to do with—Victor, Victor, you listen to me . . . no, no, you listen to me . . . he's eleven years old . . . he hardly even knows you. He's confused, you owe him some kind of an explanation for why you just—I don't care what you think is best for you, you're gonna do this, or—oh, no, no, no . . . why,

Victor? Why? Because he's just a boy. Because you haven't been there to—wait, me? Me? Are you kidding? I'm the one who—oh, no you don't . . . well then, how about I call my old friend Bud Ellingson, you know, *your* boss, and tell him how you and your girlfriend borrowed his—oh, no? How about I tell him about all the times—oh, you don't think so? You don't think I could get your butt fi—oh, really? Just watch me . . . you're damn right, I'm serious . . . that's right, Victor . . . now you're getting the picture . . . yes, that's right."

What can I tell you about myself at eleven? I was awkward, insecure, mired in doubt about myself and the world around me. I was quiet, thoughtful, mostly afraid to ask questions, though very curious by nature. I was privy to more adult information than I cared to have access to. Given the choice, eleven-year-old Mike Muñoz would have just as soon been invisible than to have to confront uncertainty on a daily basis. He didn't like conflict. He didn't like excitement. As much as he loved books, he lived in mortal fear of real-life drama.

The day after my mom called to berate my dad, he picked me up in his dented green pickup truck and drove me unceremoniously out to McDonald's by the junction, where instead of going inside, we ordered drive-thru, then parked in the lot facing the street, across from the auto-parts store.

I couldn't wait to get that hot cheeseburger in my mouth. The whole cab smelled like french fries. But my stomach was in knots, because I knew something was coming.

"Look, Nate," my dad said before we'd even unwrapped our food.

"I'm Mike."

"Right. Look, I don't want you to feel like anything was your fault—me leaving and the rest of it. It's not your fault I couldn't deal with you or your brother or your mom, that's on me. You guys were probably fine, hell, I don't know, you were kids. I just didn't want you, okay? You're not what I signed on for. And that's not your fault."

"Okay," I said.

"Good," said my dad. "See, no shame in not being wanted. It's not like being unwanted."

"It isn't?"

"Of course not. There's an old saying, but I don't remember it. It has to do with being what you want to be, not what . . . anyway, I can't remember. You didn't do anything wrong, that's the point here, and your mom wants you to remember that. You couldn't help it. You're just you."

"Okay."

"Good," he said.

"Dad?"

"Don't call me that."

"Okay, but what about Nate?" I said. "Shouldn't he know?"

"He probably wouldn't understand. But you tell him if you want."

"Okay."

Then my dad tossed the bag of food onto my lap and turned the ignition.

"C'mon," he said. "Let's go. You can eat that on the way home."

Do the Math

Just when things were coming to an impasse on the home front, I got a callback.

"You Mike?" a voice said.

"Yeah."

"This is Chaz Linford. You applied for a production job with me."

"Yeah."

"You're hired."

"I am?"

"It's a competitive position. I'm looking for a motivated candidate. It's yours if you want it."

"You're sure?"

"What about you? You sure you want it?"

"Yeah, of course," I said, though I wanted to ask him how he arrived at the conclusion that I was a motivated candidate. Surely, it wasn't my four and a half years of landscaping experience. Could this be the opportunity I'd been pining for? A job whose only requirements were that I was strong, bright, willing, and motivated to learn? The sort of job the politicians were always yammering about creating? The job that paid seventeen bucks an hour?

The place is called Chaz Unlimited Limited, which sounds ambiguous, I get that. Anyway, we're in the business of "production and assembly"—as in, we assemble promotional crap for other companies. By crap, I mean bobblehead dolls, novelty key chains, posters, and weird little Japanese dolls with puckered lips that sing "On Top of Old Smokey" when you squeeze their bellies. Think of me as a machine but human. I repeat the same tasks over and over, some days a thousand times. I didn't even know this sort of job existed anymore this side of China.

Chaz Unlimited Limited is located on Bainbridge in a chichi new business park called Copper Top, across the street from the middle school. Our production warehouse and home office is surrounded by a boutique coffee roaster, a boutique brewery, a charcuterie slash deli, a wine-tasting room, and a yoga studio. Not a single nail studio or minimart. I guess that's the difference between a business park and a strip mall.

My work station is the only one with a window. The other two employees, both long-term temps, are conscripted to the corner of the warehouse under the central heating unit. As far as I can tell, neither one of them speaks or goes to the bathroom. I'd put them both in their midthirties, a pale, weak-eyed tandem, slump shouldered and indistinct. I call them Thing One and Thing Two. They work always with their heads down, moving with a mechanized efficiency, the trebly blare of their earbuds a constant.

Every afternoon as I piece together bobbleheads, I watch the coffee roasters convene on the lawn and eat their lunches, which they invariably procure at the charcuterie slash deli, sandwiches wrapped in butcher paper. They're all guys around my age, all scrawny as hell. They wear big beards and skinny jeans and boots and T-shirts that are too small. The T-shirts are always something random: DICK'S TOWING SERVICE, PETE'S AUTO BODY, BUSY BEAVER SEPTIC CLEANING. Usually, they sit in a circle staring holes in their phones for a half hour, but sometimes they talk to each other in a lazy, impassive way. Eventually, I get bored watching them and start thinking of other stuff. Like what I'm going to do with all this money. Not only am I making five bucks an hour more than I was with Lacy, I get a solid forty-hour week with overtime possibilities—at time and a half! Let me do the math for you: that's $25.50 an hour—cha-ching! And no picking up dog shit!

Sometimes, though, as I'm looking out the window at the business park, my fingers employed thoughtlessly, I get a little wistful for landscaping. I miss the fresh air. I miss the satisfaction of pruning hedges and raking out flower beds. Hell, even deadheading rhodies. Don't even get me started on topiary. If Copper Top were my account, I'd tidy up those edges in front of the yoga studio and contain that unruly salal around the front entrance. I'd also get that laurel hedge in shape and cut back that ivy before it took over the southeast corner. Whoever installed the sprinkler system left a few blind spots, which are beginning to turn brown. That row of arborvitae along the back edge would make a nice Greek colonnade. Everywhere I look, I see room for improvement, and I wish I could do something about it.

But forget all that, I've got key chains to assemble, paychecks to cash.

On Friday, at the end of my first week, I decided to buy lunch at Provence, the charcuterie slash deli. Freddy and Nate had eaten all but one slice of the ham I'd left in the fridge, and it's the Buddig brand, so one slice is about as thick as a skin graft. I took one look at the Provence menu and was about to walk out. Thirteen bucks for a BLT, and it didn't even come with chips and a Sprite! They didn't even have Sprite! I would've bolted right then and made a run to Mickey D's, but the coffee roasters were in there with their pet beards, and I didn't want to look like a cheapskate.

"Cool shirt," one of them said flatly.

I had to look down to see what I was wearing: TIDE'S INN, SUQUAMISH, WASHINGTON, a T-shirt my mom gave me.

"My mom works there," I said.

"No way." He actually sounded mildly impressed.

"Dive bars are cool," observed one of his friends, with all the passion of a tollbooth operator.

"Yeah," I said. "I guess."

I lunched with them on the lawn, eating my thirteen-dollar sandwich deliberately and feeling a little self-conscious that I didn't have a beard. I had to admit, the sandwich was pretty damn good. The three of them kept asking me questions about Suquamish. Was I Indian? Was it crazy on the Fourth of July? I felt like an exchange student. Since they were so interested, I told them how my truck broke down and how I said the hell with it and how I just pried off the VIN and let it get impounded. Why didn't I just buy another truck, they wanted to know. I told them it was a long story. I told them about the stolen mower, too. Why didn't I just get a new mower, they wanted to know. Their solution to everything was to get another one, as though such a thing were a given. I guess maybe I didn't have much in common with those guys.

I feel pretty safe in saying my boss, Chaz, has a bit of a drinking problem. Because after work that day, he had me follow him out to his BMW and breathe into his blow-and-go so the engine would start.

"Get in, I'll give you a lift," he said.

"You sure?"

"No problemo, amigo."

Man, his car was quiet. No tapping or dinging or choking. And boy, could it accelerate. For a guy on DUI probation, a guy who clearly had liquor on his breath, Chaz wasn't what you'd call a cautious driver. He consistently drove ten over the speed limit, even in school zones.

"Muñoz, that Mexican?"

"Californian," I said.

"Ha. Good one. I like that."

He reached across to the passenger's side, popped the glove box, and fished out a plastic minibar vodka.

"Sorry, bud, no tequila. You want one of these?"

"Nah, I'm cool."

With one hand, he unscrewed the cap and tipped the bottle my way. "To free enterprise," he said.

Tossing back the vodka, he threw the empty bottle out the window and smacked his lips.

"I like your style, Muñoz. You keep your nose to the grindstone."

"I do?"

"Sure. But not too much, not like those other two. You don't want to work too hard in this world, or it'll make you cynical in no time flat."

"It will?"

"You've got a nose for opportunity."

"I do?"

"Sure you do. And that's what it takes to get on in this world."

Thus began his ten-minute soliloquy on entrepreneurship. Old Chaz had a lot more irons in the fire than just glow-in-the-dark key chains and the like. I could barely keep up. It seemed that Chaz Unlimited Limited was only the flagship. There was Chazy Chaz LLC, Chaz in Charge LLC, and All That Chaz LLC. He admitted to having no liquid assets at the moment but contracts up the yin-yang.

"Smoke and mirrors, smoke and mirrors," he explained.

The thing about never having any money your whole life is that you have no way of learning about money. It's like learning to play Yahtzee with no dice. If I understood Chaz right, everything I knew about finance was ass backward. Apparently, you don't want to pay your bills on time; in fact, you don't want to pay them until someone puts a gun to your head. If you can avoid paying them at all, that's the best scenario. And here I'd been worried about late notices all these years. Oh, and it turns out that debt is actually a good thing. You want to owe the bank money.

"If you've got the bank's money, you own the bank, see?"

That was a real eye-opener. I can't say for certain how scrupulous Chaz is, but he's paying me more money than I've ever made in my life, so I'm willing to listen and learn. Not only that, he hinted at better opportunities.

"I'm cooking up a new venture called Razmachaz. I might need a point man."

"What's it about?"

"Import and distribution. We'll get into the particulars once I get all my ducks in line. Think Mexico. That is, if you're interested."

"Sure," I said. "Sounds good. Go ahead and hang a left here."

He leaned over to the glove box as he took the turn, groping around for another mini. I'm not sure why, but I didn't care if Chaz saw where I lived. I guess he didn't seem like the judgmental type. Plus he was kind of sloppy, anyway, a few days' unshaven, slacks rumpled. Really not my idea of a successful guy, if you want to know the truth. Take away the BMW, and he could've been working at the Masi.

"It's the gray one up here on the right." I said.

"Got it."

"Thanks again for the lift."

"No problemo, amigo," he said, coasting up to where the curb should've been. "Nice place."

As he pulled away, he threw the minibottle out the window. It bounced a few times before it rolled into my neighbor Dale's unruly yard, where it would never be noticed.

The Social Thing

Desperate to acquire new friends, I soon started taking lunch regularly with the coffee roasters out on the lawn, even though I hated them. No more thirteen-dollar sandwiches, though. Even if I could afford them now, it was the principle of the thing. The roasters—Dallas, Austin, and Houston—not only ordered overpriced sandwiches, they ordered frilly sides, like saffron deviled eggs and pickled watermelon rind, and they washed it down with three-dollar bubbly water. They looked at my ham sandwich the same way the Mexicans used to look at it, with a sort of thinly veiled contempt.

"You know that's not even ham, right?"

"Says ham right on the package."

They'd snigger, which was the closest I'd ever seen them get to actual mirth. Austin almost seemed to have a personality. When I told him I was a topiary artist, he seemed impressed, albeit in a not-very-demonstrative way. I told him about my mushrooms and my pom-poms and my hot-dog-eating elf, and of course my merman, though I didn't mention the erection.

"You should come check it out," I said.

And to my surprise, he actually consented to have a look. So, after work, Austin hooked his fixed-gear bicycle onto the front of the metro bus, and we made for Suquamish. It felt strange riding the bus and not reading a book. I was accustomed to having some dead guy to keep me company or at least some MFA grad, who was in love with sentences. Instead, I had Austin, who mostly checked his Facebook page while I looked out the window, thinking I should have offered him the window seat.

"You read?" I said.

"What, like books?"

"Yeah."

"Not really. You?"

"Yeah, quite a bit."

"You must have a lot of time on your hands."

I guess I was a little nervous. Not that I was trying to impress the guy, but when had I ever invited somebody I hardly knew to my house? I wouldn't even let Remy see where I lived. But I figured since Austin liked dive bars, maybe his tastes extended to squalor in general, in which case he might like the res or our house.

He was visibly unimpressed by our humble abode, averting his eyes as we walked past the moss-encrusted Festiva, the tarpaulin-draped swamp cooler, and the bevy of broken shit strewn willy-nilly under the sagging canopy—everything from engine parts to empty bleach bottles. He seemed particularly uneasy about leaving his bike out front. And of course I couldn't blame him.

Freddy had his fat taco parked on the sofa next to Nate, watching *Wreck-It Ralph* with his Gibson knockoff bass propped in his lap. It had to be getting on my mom's nerves having him around, the way he was always in the house, eating Cheetos in his underwear. But now that I'm employed, the writing is on the wall for Freddy.

"Freddy, this is Austin."

Freddy played a couple farty notes on his bass before giving Austin a stony-eyed once-over.

"Boy, how come you wearin' your sister's pants?"

Austin glanced over his shoulder to make sure Freddy wasn't talking to someone behind him. "Uh, hey."

"Don't look like no lumberjack to me. Why you wearin' all that facial hair, boy—that to keep you warm?"

"Um . . ." Austin appealed to me with his eyes.

"Ever swung an ax?"

"Don't mind Freddy," I said. "And that's my brother, Nate."

"Hey," said Austin.

Nate belched under his breath, never taking his eyes off the screen.

"Don't mind him, either. C'mon, I'll show you my merman. You want some grape soda or anything?"

"I'm good."

"Stay out of my grape soda," Freddy called after us.

I took Austin out back and showed him my work. The pom-poms were a little rough around the edges, and my merman was a bit shaggy from neglect, but as far as I could tell, Austin was mildly impressed.

"I'm thinking of adding a little school of sucker fish near the bottom of the merman," I told him. "You know, like circling suggestively around him or something."

"So, like, this is ironic, right?"

"What, you mean because mermen don't really get erections?"

He sniggered at that, shaking his head bemusedly, while running his fingers lazily through his beard. I was hoping he'd have more questions about my merman, but he only fished out his phone and checked Facebook again.

"You sure you don't want some grape soda?"

"Nah."

"Let's walk down to the Tide's Inn," I said. "It's a dive—one of the diviest, actually."

He checked the clock on his phone and petted his beard some more. "Nah, I gotta hit the road here pretty quick."

"You want a bong toke?"

"Nah, I'm good."

"We could walk down to the pier. You like fireworks?"

"Not really."

Austin was a tough nut to crack. His curiosity didn't seem to run very deep. But I'd be lying if I said my heart didn't sink a little when he left ten minutes later, following a few more stilted exchanges.

I've never been much good at the social thing. And that's actually rare for siblings of special-needs children. We usually have to develop strong social skills in order to help our siblings navigate a world that is generally unprepared to accommodate them. I was pretty good in that respect. I made sure Nate didn't get arrested when he dropped trou in the middle of a traffic island. I made sure he didn't shoplift or smoke cigarettes or do any of the other stupid things I did. I acted as his liaison and translator and diplomat. I read to him, I made sure he ate, I made sure he dressed warm. You'd have to call me a good brother. But in every other respect, I was a dud socially. How else would I end up with a best friend like Nick?

TMI

On Saturday night, Nick swung by and picked me up in his beloved Honda, House of Pain rattling the windows as he pulled up to the trailer. His love for bad hip-hop, like his love of that stupid Accord, is every bit as irrational as his fear of Mexicans and gays. He's already sunk a ridiculous amount of money into that car. Nothing on the damn thing is stock. The muffler belongs on a drag racer. The spoiler belongs on a Formula 1. The LED hubcaps spin to no discernible purpose.

At Tequila's, we got in a round of darts, in which he beat me handily—as usual. I'd lost what little dart mojo I'd ever had, but I didn't care. Though it was the first time I'd been there in weeks, I was sick of Tequila's, weary of the jukebox, tired of smelling the bathroom, sick of the ubiquitous neon and the endless repetition of SportsCenter, and most of all, done with the nagging hope that somehow tonight would be different, that something or someone would magically walk into my life, because I was in the right place. As though Tequila's in Poulsbo could ever be the right place.

"So, what's new?" he wanted to know. "How's the new gig?"

"Repetitive," I said.

"Well, that's the idea of a job, Michael. The minute it stops repeating itself, you're out on your ass."

"I guess so."

"Hey man, I might be able to score us some tickets this season—fifty-yard line, yo. Some big-shot contractor with like four different trucks says if I hook him up on some all-season Toyos, he'll give me a pair of tickets to the game of my choice. What do you think, Cardinals? I love watching Arians lose his shit."

"Just not the Rams," I said.

"Hell no," he said, taking a healthy pull on his beer. "Oh, hey, I got a joke. What's the difference between a fag and a refrigerator?"

"I don't want to know."

"A refrigerator doesn't fart when you pull out the meat."

"Nick, I *said* I didn't want to know."

"What is it with you?"

"What about you? Why are you always bashing people? Mexicans, fags, lesbians, I don't get why they offend you so much. What did a Mexican or a fag ever do to you?"

Nick doesn't answer, just sips his beer irritably.

"Seriously, I just don't get it, Nick. You don't even have a reason."

"Duh, Michael. Look around. They're taking all our jobs. They don't pay taxes."

"Fags don't pay taxes?"

"No, dumbshit, illegals. And for your information, they're not normal."

"Mexicans?"

"No, fags."

"What's normal, then, Nick? Tell me that. Your porn habit? The way you talk about women?"

"Oh, like you don't watch porn?"

"Actually, no."

"You're a liar."

"What if I told you I touched another guy's dick?" I said.

"Pfff." Nick waved me off and turned his attention back to his beer.

"What if I told you I sucked it?"

"Will you please just shut up already?"

"I'm dead serious, Nick."

"Well, I'd say you were a fag."

"I was ten years old, but it's true. I put Doug Goble's dick in my mouth."

"The real-estate guy?"

"Yeah."

Nick looked around frantically. "What the fuck are you talking about, Michael?"

"I was in fourth grade. It was no big deal."

Cringing, Nick held his hands out in front of him in a yield gesture. "Stop."

"He sucked mine, too."

"Stop! Why are you telling me this?"

"And you know what?" I said. "It wasn't terrible."

All the air went out of Nick, and he looked at me dully, his face a prairie of blankness.

"This is a joke, right?"

"No, Nick, it's not a joke."

"So you're saying you're a fag?"

"I doubt that. It's been twelve years since I touched a dick. But that's not the point."

Nick looked genuinely troubled. Averting his eyes to his beer, he looked just about as thoughtful as I've ever seen him look.

"So, wait," he said. "You're not, like . . . in love with me, are you?"

I swear, I almost punched him. "Fuck no. How could I—or any other guy—possibly be in love with you?"

"What is that supposed to mean?"

"You're still missing the point, Nick."

"No, why wouldn't a guy love me?"

"Never mind," I said. "Just drop it."

"You're wrong, asswipe, I happen to know gay guys like me. I've caught them staring at me."

"How'd you know they were gay?"

"They were gay."

"How'd you know?"

"They were staring at me, dipshit. It was in the city. Of course, they were gay."

"Okay, so assuming they were gay—" I said.

"Shhh!" he said, glancing up and down the bar.

"How did it make you feel?"

"Like kicking their asses."

"C'mon, honestly. What did it feel like?"

He scratched his neck and looked vaguely in the other direction. "It didn't feel like anything, Michael."

"You were flattered, weren't you? Admit it."

"Fuck off."

"Just admit it. It didn't really make a difference, did it, if it was a dude or a woman? Either way, you felt good about yourself. You felt wanted."

"You're sick, you know that? There's no way in hell you're gonna make a fag out of me. Is that what you're trying to do?"

"Is that what you think this is about? Believe me, Nick, even if I were gay, I'd have zero interest in you."

"Good."

"You hate women, you hate Mexicans, you hate gays—"

"I don't hate women."

"You hate these people because you're scared, Nick."

"Bullshit."

"Because you're insecure about your own intelligence, your own sexuality, your own measly job. Because you—"

And just like that, Nick stood up without a word and walked out of Tequila's. The truth is, I was glad to see him go. But still, I couldn't believe it. I'd never seen him leave a full pitcher like that.

Family

I was pretty shit-housed by the time the bus dropped me off a little after midnight. When I got home, I could hear Freddy in the shed, thumping away on his bass while watching, one could only assume, vintage porn. Mom was at the kitchen table, smoking a cigarette. There was no sneaking past her, so I ducked my head into the kitchen.

"Hey, Ma."

"Hi, honey." She smiled, so I could see her conspicuously white crown. The shadows played hard on her face. Despite the weariness, I saw an old spark of genuine satisfaction, too.

"You want to sit down?" she said.

"Nah, I'm beat. How was work?"

"Not too busy," she said. "How's Nick?"

"He's good."

"Tell him to come around more often."

I could tell she wanted me to hang around and talk for a while. But then I'd have to tell her about Nick walking out on me, and I didn't want to disappoint her.

"Well, good night, Ma."

She tapped her cigarette and picked up her tumbler. "Good night, honey. Could you remember to take a look under that sink?"

"You bet, Ma."

I stumbled into the bedroom and plopped down on my half of the disembodied bunk bed without taking my clothes off. The room spun slowly counterclockwise, to the tune of Nate snoring.

I got to thinking of Nick, way back in seventh grade, when he practically lived with us. His mom and dad were fighting constantly. Two or three times, the cops showed up at their house, and once they even hauled his old man off to county. Nick never talked about it, but we all knew that his dad roughed him up regularly. Don Colavito was a mauler. I'm pretty sure it's the reason Nick always tensed up when you touched him unexpectedly. I'm also certain it's why Nick goes by his middle name, Nicholas, and not his first name, Donald.

My mom treated Nick like one of her own, even though she had more than she could handle already. He was one of us, eating bruised bananas and crackers in front the TV while Mom was at work. He'd still be there when she got home with pizza and breadsticks. Some nights he didn't go home, and it was a rare night when anybody came looking for him.

And then there's the fact that Nick's been like a brother to Nate, too. He's spent countless hours in front of the TV with him, eaten a gazillion Big Macs with him, read a million books to him, stuck up for him in high school, though Nick was younger and a hundred pounds lighter. And he's never once run out of patience with Nate.

I'm not defending Nick, exactly. It's just that no matter what a narrow-minded dickhead he is, he's family. All these years, I've had no choice but to accept him, in spite of his bigotry and shallowness and willful ignorance. No matter how deep the infection runs, family is family. The only other choice is to cut them off like rotten limbs.

Like Butter

Having affixed my final bobblehead for the day, I was filing out the door behind Thing One and Thing Two when Chaz stopped me out front by the dead ficus. I assumed he needed me to start his car again.

"We need to talk," he said.

My ears started burning.

"You got time for a beer?"

"Uh, maybe," I said. "Let me call Freddy."

"That your boyfriend?"

"No. Not at all. Kind of a roommate, I guess."

"See what you can do, Muñoz. Razmachaz is heating up. I need to start getting you up to speed."

Though Freddy let me know on no uncertain terms that he'd have to shuffle some things around (presumably his nuts), he was willing to cover me on one condition.

"Pick up some chips on your way home. The cheesy kind. None of this baked-rice shit."

"Got it," I said.

"And get some grape soda at the Masi."

"They don't carry it anymore."

"Orange, then. The name brand."

"There's only one brand."

"Shouldn't be too hard, then, dog. Just don't be late. I got shit on my plate."

"Yeah, yeah."

"And remember: cheesy."

I heard Nate going ape shit in the background.

"Gotta go," said Freddy, hanging up.

Just as I'd suspected, Chaz needed me to start his car, the driver's side of which was caked in dry mud.

"Yeah, I kinda got stuck the other night," he said. "You got a license, right?"

"Yeah."

"Good. You drive today."

"You're sure?"

"What the hell," he said, riffling through the glove box for a mini.

Man, the transmission on that Bimmer was like butter. It was one thing to sit shotgun in the BMW. Driving it was something else. I truly felt like another person driving that car. I would've gladly driven all the way to Spokane right then if I'd had the chance, but Chaz directed me about a mile south and instructed me to park on a side street, where we climbed out and started walking toward the center of town.

After about four blocks, we stopped at a Mexican restaurant called Isla Bonita on the main drag and went straight for the bar.

Move a few walls around, get rid of the sombrero behind the bar, and Isla Bonita could've been the Tide's Inn or Tequila's. The stale air, the queasy light, the hoarse laughter. Within ten minutes, I'd be hearing Lynyrd Skynyrd. The bar patrons were a pretty rowdy crowd for five fifteen on a Monday afternoon. I recognized these people. They were not your characteristic islanders. They were my people. They hung Sheetrock and mowed lawns. They drove delivery trucks and repaired hot tubs. They lived fiercely and kept their blinders on and didn't look much past their next paycheck. People with grease under their nails and name patches on their work shirts and deep worry lines at the corners of their eyes. People who lived for the promise of a little immediate satisfaction, when they could get it. And they could get it at Isla Bonita. It was a revelation that such a place existed on the island. Chaz must have been reading my mind.

"Don't let the McMansions and the Mercedes fool you, Muñoz. Who do you think put this place on the map? I'll tell you: loggers, berry pickers, and shipbuilders. And they weren't all Scandinavians, either. They were Japanese and Filipino and Indian. Look at the street names if you wanna know the real story. Forty years ago, it was nothing but mom-and-pops on this island. Yeakel's shoes, Vern's Winslow Drugs, the Country Mouse. This place was Mayberry R.F.D.—Christ, you probably don't even know what that is. But there was no Safeway, no Subway, no Starbucks, nothing the modern world would call culture. There were three cops, and we knew them all by name. Not only that, we knew their secrets."

"So, you're from here?"

"Born and raised. Class of '83. My dad sold insurance at Farmers, my mom sold baskets and decorative birdhouses. This place was a hippie haven, Muñoz. Artists, outliers, eccentrics. It was an island in the truest sense."

"No man is an island, but Bainbridge Is.," I said.

"How do you know about that?"

"My mom had the T-shirt. She's almost as old as you. I know about Mayberry, too."

"If you listen hard enough, you can still hear the heartbeat of that place—just barely. But don't get me started. Look, I like your style, the way you keep your shoulder to the wheel and your ear to the ground."

I'd be lying if I said I wasn't flattered by Chaz's confidence in me. He was evasive concerning the precise nature of Razmachaz but kept assuring me that I was the man for the job. He was grooming me. I should be on my toes and ready to learn. Was I reliable? Was I ambitious? Did I want to escape that dump I was living in? It hadn't yet occurred to me why on earth Chaz might have selected me to be his protégé, when Remy walked in and sat down in a booth. I felt the blood drain from my face.

"You okay, Muñoz? You're not diabetic, are you?"

"I'll be right back," I said.

As bad as I wanted to run, I'm proud of myself for summoning the courage to proceed. I stood up and walked directly to Remy's booth, convincing myself that I was capable of things I hadn't been capable of the first time I sat down in her section. I was making seventeen bucks an hour now. I was the point man for Razmachaz LLC—whatever the hell it was. I was driving a BMW, sort of. And

I had poetry in my heart, goddammit. But none of that mattered when the dude in the straight-brimmed Yankees cap and the big black gauges in his earlobes sat next to Remy, draping his arm around her. I immediately did an about-face, I hoped before she saw me.

I looked the other way for the next half hour, which is to say I looked at Chaz, which is to say Chaz had an audience. He told me about everything from floating payrolls, to tax credits, to money laundering. He told me how money didn't matter, how it was just another tool, how finance should be all about freedom. Personal freedom. Freedom of choice, freedom of mobility, freedom to sit in your office and get drunk. It wasn't that he was ambitious, more that he was lazy—and by his own admission. That's why being an entrepreneur was the only life for Chaz. He could make his own hours. He could sleep at his desk. He could make businesses happen out of thin air, which is where credit came in.

"Hustling is overrated. It makes you bitter when things don't work out. I've seen it. The key is to take risks and court luck. That way, when you fail, you haven't got too much invested."

Chaz then proceeded to tell me everything *but* the particulars of Razmachaz LLC, and *where* exactly the "point man" fit in, ordering numerous rounds while I watched in the mirror behind the bar as the guy in the Yankees cap kept his arm around Remy. Of course I was jealous. But more than that, I was embarrassed that it wasn't me with my arm around Remy. It should have been.

Finally, Remy walked to the bathroom, and I ducked my head as she passed, determined to get out of there before she saw me.

"Let's go," I said.

Chaz tossed off his drink in a single slurp and left two twenties on the bar. I ducked my head again on the way out. I didn't even glance at Remy as I whisked past.

"Mike!" I heard her say.

"Oh, hey," I said, turning.

"Meet you out front," said Chaz with a little wink.

Simultaneously disappointed and relieved not to have to introduce Chaz, I stood at the end of Remy's booth, not knowing what to do or say next.

"This is my brother, Travis," she said.

"Oh!" I said, a little too brightly. "Nice to meet you."

"Right on," he said. "Is this the guy?"

Remy socked him on the shoulder and blanched. I felt bad for her getting put on the spot like that, even though I couldn't believe for a second that I was "the guy."

"So, what's up?" I said.

"You stopped coming around. You promised you'd come back and see me."

"Well, after the whole saltshaker incident, I wasn't sure if they really wanted us in there."

"Anyway, I don't work there anymore," she said.

"Where do you work?"

"Nowhere right now. What about you?"

"I'm in production."

"Ooh, like film?"

"More like bobbleheads."

"That sounds cool. Better than waiting tables, anyway. How's your novel?"

"Oh, you know, comin' along," I said. "Getting ready to publish it, actually."

Goddammit, I was doing it again, digging myself a deeper hole, creating expectations I could never live up to. It's like I wanted to fail.

"How exciting!" said Remy. "When can I read it?"

"Soon. Just needs some, you know, tuning up. Some editorial."

"I can't wait," she said. "Hey, you wanna sit down?"

"Nah, my friend is waiting for me. I've gotta give him a lift. I better get going. It was great seeing you, though."

I was about to make my exit, scalp tingling, heart clenched in self-contempt.

"Wait," she said, fishing around in her purse. She located a pen and scribbled her number on a beer coaster.

"Call me," she said.

"Uh, yeah, will do."

I must have been smiling like an idiot when I walked out and found Chaz leaning against the wall.

He looked mildly impressed. "Funny, the whole time, I kinda figured you were gay," he said.

"Why would I be gay?"

"I don't know. Just a feeling I got."

"Do I seem gay or something?"

"Not exactly. More like you don't seem *not* gay."

"Why, because I don't have a girlfriend?"

"That could be it."

"Well, where's your girlfriend?"

"I don't have one."

"Are you gay?"

"Absolutely not."

"Well, there you go. And besides," I hastened to add, displaying my coaster with Remy's number, the smiley face already beginning to smear with the sweat of my palm, "I got digits."

"Not bad," said Chaz.

Yes, I was pretty damned satisfied with myself as we walked the four blocks back to the car, Chaz lagging behind with uneven strides, stopping once to piss in a shrub. I felt like I was actually, finally, on the verge of something.

The Player

I treasured that coaster. I wore its edges smooth, contemplating the possibilities. I was really beginning to think Remy might be the one. She was engaging, quite attractive, and familiar enough to feel comfortable around. If I could only get close enough to Remy, I knew she would stir me in some special way, and I could get over the girlfriend hump.

But making the next move was a lot tougher than it should've been. Sad as it sounds, I actually wished I could've called Nick for advice, though I'm sure I knew exactly how that conversation would run:

"Generally speaking," he'd say. "I'd give it a week before calling her. But in your case, I wouldn't wait longer than three days."

"Why in my case?"

"She might lose interest."

"Geez, thanks."

"Well, Michael. Maybe you're just not alpha material, that's all I'm sayin'. Maybe you're one of those sensitive guys who's just gotta be around all the time, drinking with her while she complains about other guys and confesses a bunch of stuff. Then, eventually, she drinks too much and gives into your sensitive-guy charms."

"Dude," I'd object weakly.

"So, assuming you're that guy, Michael, and you probably are, I wouldn't give it a whole week. You see my point?"

It was like having a conversation with my own ego.

In the end, I decided to wait until payday to call Remy. I did my best to dial her number breezily, as though there were absolutely nothing at stake. But the second she answered it, I went blank.

"Uh, hey, it's me, Mike. You know, from Mitzel's and . . ."

"Oh, hi."

"So, uh, I was thinking like maybe we could, I dunno, grab some kind of food or something? Maybe some pizza. Or like maybe a drink? Like a cocktail or whatever."

"Oh, I see. You wanna get me drunk, is that it?"

"I didn't mean—"

"Typical man. One thing on his mind."

"No, really, I didn't mean like—"

"And what happens once I'm tipsy? What's your plan then, Mike?"

"I was just talking about—"

"Is that when you take advantage of me? Like in the back of your truck or something?"

"Look, I swear, I wasn't trying to say—"

"Mike, I'm kidding," she said. "I'd love to have a drink."

"How about this weekend?"

"The thing is, I'm leaving for Wenatchee tomorrow to see my parents for a couple weeks."

"Ah."

"It's sort of embarrassing, actually. I need to work at my dad's hardware store and make a little money to hold me over. I'm totally broke."

I found the news that Remy was broke thrilling. It released me from my own shame and potentially made me attractive, too, as a person who was not only gainfully employed but also soon to be the point man for Razmachaz LLC—whatever the fuck it was.

"How about the nineteenth?" she said. "It's a Thursday."

"Perfect," I said. "Where?"

"You decide."

"Uhhh."

"You don't have to decide now. Text me."

When I hung up the phone, I felt slightly changed. Like I'd just made some kind of major step. Granted, I was a little late in taking it, but still it was a confidence builder.

All You Can Eat

Three days later, Remy texted me, marking the beginning of a brief exchange:

OMG. It's soooo hot here. Ugh.

LOL. Only 70 here.

Lucky!

I'm feeling lucky!

Don't do anything naughty . . .

I'll try not to!

Again, on Thursday she texted:

Looking forward to the 19th!

Me, too! It'll be fun!

It better be! LOL.

Is that a threat?

Maybe.

And again on Friday:

I'm over Wenatchee. My dad is driving me nuts.

Hang in there.

Thanks. At least $$$ is good.

That's good.

See you when I get back!

Not only were we flirting, not only was Remy initiating it, but we were actually developing intimacy. These exchanges with Remy, the two of us perfect strangers, really, separated by 140 miles, were about the closest I'd ever come to having a bona fide girlfriend, pathetic as that may seem. And I must say, it had me feeling bullish.

Saturday morning, Mom, Nate, Freddy, and I all squeezed into the Tercel and drove the two miles to the casino. They've got a huge breakfast buffet over there with an omelet bar and twelve toasters and the whole shebang. It's called the Clearwater Buffet. We call it the Clearwallet Buffet, though. It's the kind of thing where in order to bring Nate, you've got to have backup because there's a high ape-shit probability. Too many choices, too much food. If you haven't noticed, food is a big trigger for Nate.

For all of Freddy's faults, he's really good with my brother, which I'm certain is the only reason my mom hasn't kicked him out yet. Freddy is like Nate's sensei. At the buffet, when Nate started working himself up into a state, Freddy remained calm and made eye contact with him.

"Look here, boy: I feel your pain. They ain't never enough blueberries in them waffles. Damn near drive a man crazy. But you a grown man, dog, remember that. Fact is, you a well-grown man. And sometimes a man gotta bear up in the face of adversity. They's a truckload of waffles not fifty feet from here, and they're all you can eat. You'll get your fill of blueberries. You just relax now, boy."

Freddy's silky baritone had an immediate calming effect on Nate. My brother was a pussycat the rest of the morning while we heaped our plates with bacon and potatoes, and eggs any way we wanted them. Tall glasses of orange juice and bottomless cups of coffee. We gorged ourselves on bear claws and dunkers and bagels with smoked salmon. We laughed, we grunted, we farted, we sighed. I felt like a king sitting at that table, seeing everybody so cheerful. Here was the Muñoz clan (and Freddy) on a sunny Saturday morning, with actual promise on the horizon. All the restaurant food we could eat and no anxiety or guilt about the expense. My mom looked ten years younger, sitting there with no cigarette between her fingers, no tumbler of wine, her crow's-feet turning to laugh lines before my eyes. Freddy was in high spirits, too.

"Mm-mm, I'll tell you what, Mike Muñoz," he said, snapping off half a crispy bacon strip. "Old Freddy could get used to this. A man grow weary of Rice Chex and instant oats, ain't that right, Nate?"

Indeed, Nate was lost happily somewhere between abstraction and diabetic shock. Things couldn't have been nicer or more pleasant. And dammit, I was grateful, but a little guilty, too. I really should have invited Nick.

Not Just Any Lawn Mower

After the buffet, Mom had to pull an afternoon shift, so Freddy, Nate, and I walked out to 305 and caught a bus to Hansville for the flea market. I had fifty-nine bucks in my pocket, and as much as I'd been promising myself I'd show a little financial restraint, I was itching to get there.

Flea markets are a glorious thing if you're not a millionaire. There's nothing quite like the pleasure of discovering lost treasures among life's flotsam, unless it's the pleasure of getting rid of rusty old shit and making a buck. It's a win-win situation—kind of like recycling for poor people. It was a thirty-five-minute bus ride to Hansville, and the window wouldn't open and Nate was a little gassy after the buffet. He's not inhibited that way. On top of the drive, it was a half-mile walk to the flea market from the bus stop, a warm stretch of highway in August.

Freddy's corduroys kept riding up on him.

"Goddamn," he said, digging at his crotch. "It's like a goddamn reuben sandwich down there."

"Spare us the details, please."

"You don't understand, boy. I hail from warmer climes. A man's privates gotta breathe."

"I didn't realize Tacoma was so much warmer."

"I'm talking about Africa."

"Kind of a stretch, don't you think?"

"How's that?"

"That was like five generations ago."

"Uh-huh. And I suppose you ain't Mexican?"

"Technically, my dad was born in California."

"Uh-huh. You just keep tellin' yourself that, Mike Muñoz. But far as anyone else is concerned, you Mexican. If it looks Mexican, and it has a Mexican name, it's probably Mexican. Even if it don't speak Mexican."

There must have been forty stalls spread out in roughly even rows on the dead grass, a couple of blue Honey Bucket outhouses on the far edge of the gravel parking lot. Most people don't realize it, but a flea market is a whole social order. First, you've got your pros, the ones who might actually own a home of stick construction. Usually, they're retired. Their stalls consist of foldout tables, the kind you see in church basements. The pros have canopies for shade. They have power strips and cash boxes. Their wares are varied and many, everything from pewter figurines to frilly, old lamps. Stamp collections, books, ceramic bowls, vintage postcards, Victorian doilies. Meanwhile, your rustics and fierce libertarians, the ones whose homes probably don't have cement foundations, operate from their tailgates, amending them with saw horses and plywood to accommodate their inventory. Their wares are also many but less varied: carburetors, chain saws, winches, wedges, mauls, old license plates, ammunition, and knives. The next rung down is the broke-as-hell working-class stall. This is your classic fire-sale scenario—everything must go: blenders, 28k modems, Foreman grills. Crock-Pots, treadmills, and terrariums. Even toys, which sort of breaks your heart. Farther down the line, your hippies operate exclusively on blankets or tarps. Candles, dream catchers, and handmade drums. Maybe a wood carving of two bears fucking. Always a sad cardboard box of records—some America, some CCR, some scratched-to-hell Steppenwolf, and maybe an old Andy Williams or Mantovani album, which belonged to their parents. By the time you get all the way down to the tweakers, you're almost to the Honey Buckets, and there's no more shade. You have some heavily tattooed kid with an oversized baseball cap and his fourteen-year-old girlfriend. A towel, a pit bull, and some stolen DVDs. That's where I usually start shopping. On this occasion, I scored a bunch of DVDs for Nate, including *Cloudy with a Chance of Meatballs* and *Scooby-Doo Wrestlemania Mystery 2*.

Farther up the line, I found a fishing rod for eight bucks and a tackle box for three fifty. Not that I fish, but I've been meaning to start one of these days. I always see Indians sitting on the dock downtown, with a can of beer in a brown bag, their fishing poles dangling over the edge. They never catch anything but bullheads, but it looks relaxing. I also bought another Leatherman for four bucks and, for five bucks, a Billy Bass wall hanging that lip-synched "Take Me to the River" and wagged its tail fin in perfect time. If you've ever seen one, you know they're hilarious and quite lifelike.

Yes, I realize I was spending immoderately. But dammit, I needed it. The fact is, I only bought one big-ticket item: a lawn mower for thirty-five bucks. I haggled the guy down from forty-five. Not just any lawn mower, either. A Snapper 3.5 horsepower mulching mower with a thirty-six-inch deck. Green, like my old one, but in better shape.

It didn't occur to me when I bought the mower that I'd have to push it all the way home. So, while Freddy and Nate bused back to the res, I began the journey on foot and started thumbing. After about eight steps I realized I should have sent the tackle box and the DVDs home on the bus with Freddy. Eventually, an old blue pickup with three dozen angry bumper stickers stopped for me. The driver, who wore a long white beard, watched me suspiciously in the side mirror, like a detective on a stakeout, as I hefted the mower into the bed. I was about to jump in back with the mower, but he waved me into the cab, where I squeezed in with a pair of overweight labs.

"Del Jeffers," he said, without extending a hand.

"Mike," I said.

"That all? Just Mike?"

"Mike Muñoz."

"Mexican, eh? Figured as much when I saw you pushing a lawn mower."

I was hot and tired and happy to have a ride. I wasn't going to disappoint him by not being an actual Mexican, so I didn't object.

"If you don't mind my asking, how does a fella find himself pushing a mower along the side of the highway?"

"It's a long story."

"Truck break down?"

"Yeah, but not today."

Del considered the information to see if it fit anywhere. "You always take it fishin' with you like that, the mower?"

"I'm not fishing."

"Hmph. Well then, how is it that you got yourself a rod and a tackle box?"

"I came from the flea market."

"Ah," said Del. "So it's all yours, huh? The mower, the rod, the tackle, all those there DVD videos."

"It is now. Like I said, I was at the flea market."

"Flea market, you say?"

"Yeah."

"Hmph. Just a coincidence, then, I reckon."

"What?"

"Daughter's brother-in-law got his mower stolen couple weeks back. Green, like that one. Turns out he's quite the angler, too. Where'd you say you live?"

"I didn't."

"Mind my askin'?"

"The res."

Why is it people always ask you so many questions when they've already got their minds made up about you? Del kept interrogating me as we passed Little Boston and Crazy Corners, and a little ways past the Indianola signal, where he dropped me on the shoulder.

"This is as far as I go," he said.

I was still a few miles from home, but I'll be honest, I was relieved to get out of Del's truck. He watched me intently in the side mirror as I wrestled the mower out.

"You take care, Mike Muñoz of Suquamish," he said out the window. "Stay out of trouble."

Changing of the Guard

I knew Mom would not be happy with the arrangement, but I figured Freddy's days were numbered, anyway, and since he spent most of his time in the house, we agreed to swap rooms.

I'm not saying the shed's a palace, but I made a desk out of eight cinder blocks and a half sheet of splintered plywood, and lined my books in even rows along the workbench, until the place started looking homey, in a third-world way.

I hung up my Billy Bass and pushed it a few times. "Take Me to the River," he sang, his big lips moving so lifelike, his tail fin wagging in rhythm.

The biggest improvement was the solitude. Besides the thrumming of Freddy's bass, the relentless screech of my neighbor Dale's band saw deep into the night, and the occasional bottle rocket or M-80, it was pretty quiet out there. The first night, I settled into my air mattress and read this old French geezer, Céline, and boy, was he pissed off at the state of the world. I had to admire his spirit.

In the morning, I walked into the house to eat a couple Eggos and make my lunch before work, and guess who walked out of my mom's bedroom in his hopelessly stretched-out tighty-whities? I'll give you a hint: it wasn't Bernie Sanders.

I was more stunned than anything else. "Freddy? Uhhh?"

"Mornin', Mike. How was the guest cottage?"

"Where's my mom?"

"I'm right here, honey," she said, walking out after him in her bathrobe.

"Oh," I said.

And really, what else could I say?

After breakfast, while I was scraping my plate into the garbage under the sink, I happened guiltily upon Freddy's recent handiwork. And I have to admit, his fix was pretty ingenious. He'd replaced both the cracked drainpipe and the leaking elbow with the Festiva's radiator hose and clamps. Cost: zero. I'd be lying if I said I wasn't a little jealous that I'd never thought of it. That's when I realized that there had been an official changing of the guard. My status as head of household had been usurped by a man who recorded homemade soundtracks to 1980s porn.

Chief Seattle Days

I guess you get used to seeing things a certain way, so that even when they change you stop noticing. Maybe that's why I haven't exactly raved about the res. Sure, there's a beautiful new tribal center where the slab used to be, but I still think of it as the slab, a hoopless basketball court riddled with potholes. They've dolled up Chief Seattle's grave, but the place remains largely forgotten in spite of the new infrastructure the casino dollars have provided. They've rebuilt the dock, but it still leads to the same old place. I suppose it might help if I were Indian; maybe that would imbue the res with a sense of heritage, maybe then I'd feel some vital connection to the place. But as it is, it just feels like the place I've been stuck my whole life.

Except, that is, for a single weekend at the end of summer, when the whole res is transformed, and Suquamish feels like somewhere for once. For forty-eight hours, everyone puts their misery on hold. Old grudges are temporarily forgotten. The drumming and the dancing never cease. And the whole town is redolent with barbecue smoke. Some of my best childhood memories are of Chief Seattle Days. With the parade, the canoe races, the pageant, the salmon dinner, the softball tournament, and the vendors, it's quite a powwow.

Mom had to work doubles all weekend, but somehow Freddy managed to get the days off. Saturday, around noon, Nate, Freddy, and I trudged downtown into the thick of the festivities. It was eighty degrees, and people who shouldn't wear shorts were wearing shorts, including Freddy. I bought us all Indian tacos and lavender lemonades and bottle rockets, and we listened to the drums and watched the dancing and ate more Indian tacos. We poked around the booths and watched part of a softball game and ate sno-cones and shot off our rockets. Then we rounded it all off with a salmon dinner for nine bucks a plate—my treat.

In the evening, we bumped into Nick down by the tribal center. Considering we had not spoken since he walked out of Tequila's a few weeks ago, it wasn't that awkward. Familiarity trumps just about anything in the end. Why else would we keep making the same mistakes over and over?

Nick had a bottle of Old Crow in his pack, and I staked us to a box of Henry's Private Reserve, and we all walked down to the beach. At the bottom of the stairs by the boat ramp slumped the snaggle-toothed Indian kid, looking disconsolate with his beat-up guitar case and an old gray wire-haired dog sprawled at his feet.

"Boy, can you play that ax?" said Freddy.

The kid shrugged. "Some."

"Well, come on, then."

The kid stood up and fell in line with us, the old dog following along at a distance of ten or twenty feet, nose to the ground. We walked north under the bluff, away from what was left of the revelers, spreading out to collect firewood along the beach. Nick and I were side by side out of habit.

"Dude, look, I'm sorry," I said.

"For being a fag?"

"For being a jerk."

He took a slug of the whiskey and passed it to me.

"Fair enough," he said. "I'm a jerk, too, if you hadn't noticed. But, dude, did you seriously put a guy's dick in your mouth?"

I passed the bottle back. "I was in fourth grade."

Nick immediately wiped the rim of the bottle off with his shirtsleeve. "That's it? That was the last one?"

"Does it matter?"

Nick took a slug and handed the bottle back, considering me in the dusky light, like he was looking for a different Mike.

"Fuck it," he said. "I guess not. Just stop talking about it. So, you think our offensive line is going to be shit again?"

"Depends on how things shake out with the draft and everything."

"Yeah, that's what I'm afraid of. What the fuck makes anyone think Britt can play center? Couldn't play guard, couldn't play tackle, now he's supposed to be the answer at center? Arizona scares me, bro. Fuck, I hate Arians. He looks so fucking stupid in that Kangol hat with his fucking red face. He reminds me of my dad."

"I can see that."

"Fuck that guy. I hope he drops dead."

"Arians or your dad?"

"Both of them."

We all converged about a quarter mile down beach, away from the fireworks, our arms loaded with driftwood. Coaxing logs around to serve as benches, we started a fire under the bluff and commenced drinking beer and passing around the Old Crow. Now and then, somebody patted the dog's head as we bullshitted and ate pretzels, and sometimes fell to silently watching the fire, hypnotized by the hiss and crackle of it. At one point, the kid's dog started vigorously lapping at its own nuts, and we couldn't help but pay attention.

"Wish I could do that," said Nick.

"Better pet him first," I said.

We all laughed at that and stared back into the fire, sipping our beers as the water licked the shore.

"Boy, what's your name?" Freddy said to the kid.

"Marlin."

"Like Brando?"

"Like the fish."

"Marlin, let's hear you play that hammer."

The kid looked into the fire and kicked some embers around with his old combat boots.

"Do I gotta?"

"Hell, yes," said Freddy. "Beach fire got to have a guitar."

Marlin reluctantly lifted the guitar out of the case. He set it in his lap and looked at the fret board for about fifteen seconds, as though it might finally reveal the answer to some mystery. Then, apprehensively, eyes still trained on the neck, he started picking "Seven Nation Army" on his E string.

Dun-dun-dun-dun-dun-dun-dun. Dun-dun-dun-dun-dun-dun-dun.

I thought I heard a little improvement myself, a little more confidence, a little less clumsiness, but Freddy was wincing.

"Don't you know any chords, boy?"

"I can play something else, if you want," the kid said.

"Well, no wonder you ain't got but fifty cents in your case. Boy, get over here and let me teach you some chops. Freddy's known primarily for his bass licks, but he can find his way around a six-string."

Marlin stood up and lugged his guitar over to Freddy's side of the fire, where Freddy immediately started instructing him, first in the art of tuning, as Nate watched on absently in a food-induced stupor. I scooted a little nearer to Nick, to where our arms were grazing, and Nick shifted ever so slightly on the log, like it might have made him uncomfortable. Then, as Freddy strummed a few soft chords, I leaned in real close and whispered in Nick's ear.

"Do you want to see my dick?"

"The fuck!"

Nick hauled off and punched me in the shoulder so that I tipped backward off the log, spilling my beer. I landed on my back, looking up at the stars, laughing my ass off. After a second, Nick started laughing, too, then gave me a hand and pulled me up. I dusted myself off and grabbed the whiskey from Nick and took a pull, then he grabbed it back and did the same, without wiping the rim of the bottle.

Marlin was holding the guitar now, trying to strum a chord, with Freddy's encouragement.

"That's it, boy, easy now. You ain't angry at the strings."

"Remember back in fifth grade," Nick said to me, "when we used to break into the school cafeteria at night and steal ice cream?"

"And cold Canadian Jumbos."

"Remember when Nate got stuck in the window?"

"How could I forget?"

"Man, we were lucky. Weren't we?"

"What do you mean?"

"Just running free like that. Nobody stopping us from doing whatever we wanted. We had it made."

"That's one way to look at it, I guess."

I couldn't help but love Nick a little more right then, knowing what his childhood looked like. The thought of it made me a little sad.

Before we knew it, Marlin was jerkily strumming "Wild Thing" in bona fide chords. The kid was thrilled, bright eyed and smiling. Suddenly his sound was so much bigger.

Freddy was pretty happy with himself, too. Hell, we were all happy with ourselves just then. Even Nate, who kept silently crop-dusting us. I looked around at everybody's face in the glow of the firelight, and I wondered why we didn't do this every night. Here we lived in this beautiful place, and I'd never even thought of it as beautiful before. It'd always been ugly by association, I guess. Now I felt like I was seeing it for the first time. The lights twinkling across the bay, the stars winking above, the forest rearing up behind us on the bluff.

I was pretty drunk by that time and pretty goddamn grateful for the crumbs life had been dropping in my path lately, like maybe they were leading somewhere new, some destination I couldn't see yet. I couldn't help but count my blessings: my job with Chaz Unlimited Limited, my new digs in the guest cottage, the $217 still miraculously sitting in my checking account. And then there were

Remy and all the great books waiting to be read on my workbench. And the dim but compelling possibility that I might one day write a book myself or do something else of distinction.

For now, I had this beach fire, the lapping of the surf, these people, this beer, this laughter. These pretzels, this music, this momentary sensation that in spite of all the unrest and injustice, and hatred and greed, in spite of the cold, uncaring stars wheeling above us, we live in the most beautiful of all possible worlds. And yes, the moments are fleeting, like my mom's smile, and it's not often we have control over them, and that just makes them all the sweeter. Fuck it, if that sounds like a Jack Johnson song, it's true.

I started misting over in spite of myself, wiping my eyes as though the smoke were to blame, but my friends saw right through it.

"What's the matter, boy?" Freddy wanted to know.

Nick put a hand on my shoulder. "What up, bro?"

"Just happy," I said. "That's all."

How to Seize the Day

My high spirits lasted through Sunday, and Monday morning I awoke refreshed, ready to go out and seize the day. On the bus, I read Richard Brautigan, and anything seemed possible. After all the vitriol of Céline, I'd told my library friend, Andrew, I was looking for something gentler, and he steered me to *Trout Fishing in America*. Old Brautigan made heartbreak seem jaunty, and the world, for all its messed-up shit, seemed like a place with soft edges.

But when I showed up to work, there were three squad cars in front of the warehouse, and Austin and his roaster buddies were standing in front of the warehouse in their skinny jeans and ironic T-shirts, drinking *macchiato* and rubbernecking at the scene.

"What's up?" I said.

"Pretty sure your boy Jazz is getting pinched," said Austin.

"What the fuck?" I said.

No sooner did the words leave my mouth than two cops escorted Chaz out, hands cuffed behind his back. Always the optimist, Chaz was smiling like Bill Clinton in a sea of big red balloons.

"Chaz!" I called out.

He looked at me and shrugged like it was no big deal.

"A minor setback, Muñoz, trust me. Nothing to worry about. Stay the course, comrade. Stand by and think big, Muñoz."

The cop gave Chaz a little shove and dug an elbow into his kidney as he guided him into the backseat.

"Keys are under the floor mat—driver's side," he said as he disappeared into the depths of the cruiser.

"What a loser," said Austin.

"Fuck you," I said.

Why the fuck I ever thought I could be friends with that guy, I have no idea. You just know a little punk like that has a safety net. Two parents somewhere with money. All I know is, whatever Chaz did, whatever crime he perpetrated to get busted (provided it wasn't human trafficking or child pornography), he was nobler in my eyes than that little phony Austin. What did Austin ever do but eat expensive sandwiches, pet his beard, and act superior?

It was looking like I had the day off, along with the foreseeable future—as in, the cops put a chain on the door. Hopefully, they cleared out Thing One and Thing Two first, or they could still be in there, not talking and not going to the bathroom. After the roasters dispersed and the squad cars pulled away in a motorcade, I was stuck standing in the parking lot. All I could think about was my last paycheck that I'd never see. Fourteen hundred bucks.

Yes, old Mike Muñoz was screwed again. Suddenly, a tidal wave of buyer's remorse crashed down on me. The fishing rod, the breakfast buffets, the Indian tacos, the bottle rockets, and salmon dinners—frivolous, all of it. Who did I think I was spending so thoughtlessly these past months? God, what an idiot I'd been. And now what? Two hundred seventeen bucks from destitution all over again. If only there was something I could do to get all that money back.

It took me a half hour to decide what I should do about Chaz's BMW. Probably the smart thing would have been just to leave it parked where it was, but Chaz seemed to want me to do something with it, and Chaz had always been a stand-up guy with me, so I felt obliged. Also, I figured the car gave me my best chance of seeing that last paycheck.

I found the key under the mat, activated the blow-and-go, and drove the limit all the way home. I parked it in the driveway, behind the moldering Festiva, where the BMW didn't take long to attract the attention of the whole neighborhood.

Don't get the idea that I had any intention of driving that car around town like I owned it. Oh no. That car was staying right where I parked it until such time as Chaz came to claim it or provided me with further instructions.

Standing By, Thinking Big

I stood by, just as Chaz told me to do. I tried to think big, I really did. I worked at it. I even wrote every afternoon for three hours and piled up eleven pages. They were terrible, but they were pages. As long as I didn't go back and read them, I was making progress. I didn't buy a single tallboy for at least a week. I went to bed early and sprawled on my air mattress in the shed, lulled by the screeching caterwaul of Dale's band saw. I tried to imagine my current situation as the minor setback that Chaz assured me that it was. I tried to imagine bigger and better things for Mike Muñoz. A new job, a new truck, my own place, a real novel with my name on it. But the thing of it is, I don't really know how to think big. God knows, nobody ever taught me. In fact, I was taught precisely the opposite. I was taught to always expect and prepare for something less, because eight times out of ten, that's what was coming. To actually expect anything bigger or better was simply beyond my reach.

But just for the sake of argument, supposing I actually did manage to envision some ideal for myself—a Pulitzer Prize, a BMW, a drawer full of matching socks—how was I realistically going to make such a thing happen, given my current circumstances? Yes, there was hard work, to which I was no stranger, but what had my hard work ever achieved? Maybe Chaz was right. Maybe it's smarter to take the path of least resistance. There was commitment, to which I was also no stranger, but what had my commitments ever done but shackle me to my threadbare reality? And like Chaz said, the more you committed to, the more you had at stake. That left luck and big risks, the very things that Chaz encouraged me to court. But when had Mike Muñoz ever been lucky?

By ten o'clock, I was biting my nails, tossing fitfully atop the air mattress. I turned on my lamp, and reached for my fourteen-dollar paperback, a "luminous debut" I'd recently picked off the new arrivals table at Liberty Bay Books, written by an MFA grad named Joshua. But it was no use. I couldn't connect. The writing was overwrought, and the story was lagging. I just couldn't concentrate. I kept reading the same sentence over and over. The protagonist was eating an apple and walking across a parking lot toward her mother's car, "her thoughts gleaming with a smoky chiaroscuro of nostalgia."

All I could think about was the money I'd blown the past few weeks; it had to be four hundred bucks—next month's rent. Somehow I had to recoup that money.

I'd like to think that I am somewhat self-aware. I've got some blind spots, that's obvious, but all in all, I feel like I've got a pretty clear view of reality. More often than not, I know when, and why, I'm making a bad decision. Most of us do—and by us, I mean broke people. Take smoking, for example. If Mom didn't smoke away ten bucks a day, we never would've had to rent out the guest cottage to Freddy in the first place, right? Mom knows that, she's done the math a million times. But there's more to consider. For starters, she's perpetually tired. She's been working fifty-hour weeks for as long as I can remember. And there's a good chance she's clinically depressed. Smoking gets her through that second shift. It relaxes her when the pressure is mounting. It gives her something to look forward to during her break and after work, and before work, and when she wakes up in the morning. It makes her heart beat faster. At ten bucks a day, that's a bargain.

Then there's the casino. You won't find Warren Buffett slumped at a one-armed bandit. Don't expect to see the CEO of Verizon hooked to a rolling oxygen tank, cigarette dangling from his lip, pumping tokens into a slot machine like an act of faith. No, it's usually us poor fucks. And yes, the very act of poor people gambling defies reason. Isn't that the point? All the observable phenomena in our lives, all our personal experience, encourage us to keep our heads down and not expect any windfalls. Hell, not even a fair shake. Your boss won't give you a break. The bank won't give you a break. The landlord won't give you a break. The politicians and the corporations sure won't give you a break. Even the clerk at the Masi won't give you a break. Why not give Lady Luck a shot? She's no crueler or more fickle than any other master. At least you feel like you've got a ghost of a chance with her. You know what you're up against. The rules aren't always changing like everything else. Gambling fools us into thinking we're somehow impervious to the odds, that the universe might grant us an exception.

But then, don't dreams do the same thing?

So, yeah, on the surface, walking to the casino last night was probably not a wise decision, not for a guy with two hundred seventeen bucks to his name. It was a dry seventy degrees with a slight breeze, so the trees whispered all around me. There were hardly any cars on the road. The old Milky Way was spray-painted across the sky, and when I stopped on the gravel shoulder to look up at it, it didn't seem hostile, just vast. It was almost a relief to see the casino squatting on the bluff, a garish display of throbbing light.

At first, I only withdrew sixty bucks from the ATM, so it's not like I wasn't showing some restraint. And I was up eighteen bucks by midnight, which is two salmon dinners, if you're doing the math, so it's not like I was losing. In fact, I was feeling downright impervious to the odds, convinced I could recoup all the money I'd blown if I just played it smart. I guess you could say I was thinking big when I staked myself to another sixty bucks and took to the blackjack tables.

I recognized the dealer by the little scar running down her cheek. She used to work at the Masi, an Indian lady about my mom's age, and like my mom, she looked tired and worry-worn in her rumpled work uniform. She didn't seem to recognize me, or maybe she was trained not to be too familiar with patrons. Not that she wasn't friendly. Even when I was up thirty-eight bucks, there seemed to be pity in her eyes. Her name tag said GEORGIA. Sweet Georgia, with the little pink scar on her cheek and the pity in her eyes. She was my lucky charm for the next hour and a half.

Before long, I was up eighty bucks. Then a hundred four. Then one twenty-six. Then one seventy! No, not life-changing money, not even enough to impress anyone at the table, but with every chip I collected, something was redeemed—a fishing pole, a DVD, a singing bass. And sweet Georgia was my redeemer, my dealer of good fortune. It was like she wanted me to win. If I ever found a stray cat or managed to buy another truck, I vowed to name it Georgia.

I was up two twenty-five when Georgia's shift ended. That's when the guy next to me, who was down big, cut his losses and called it quits. I probably should've done the same, but I was thinking big. I asked myself WWCD, as in, What would Chaz do? And I knew without a shadow of a doubt, Chaz would keep laying down his chips.

The new dealer was fresh. Clean and pressed, like he just woke up and took a shower and shampooed his beard. His name tag said PHILLIP. He had a sharp nose and a wolfish grin, and unlike Georgia, there was no pity in his small eyes. The first hand he dealt me was an eight up and an eight down, then he hit me with a queen. The next three hands looked about the same. Before I knew it, I found myself back at the ATM for sixty more bucks and paying another three-dollar surcharge, determined to win my money back.

Well, you can guess how it all ended, kiddos. Old Mike Muñoz shit the money bed. Yep, I lost everything—and mostly on decent hands, too. I don't blame Phillip, but if I ever find out which car is his, I'll slash his goddamn tires anyway.

"The casino offers a free door-to-door shuttle," he offered, sweeping up the last of my chips.

"Blow me," I said.

I left the casino on foot. With fifty-eight cents in my pocket, and twenty-eight dollars left in my checking account, I began the long, dark walk home. The stars were still out, and once I got away from the highway, I found a little peace. Things were only slightly worse than when the night began. What was two hundred bucks in the big picture? Nothing like the breadth of the night sky to make your worldly troubles seem insignificant.

Miguel Is El Mejor

After leaving the casino, I was about a mile down Suquamish Way when headlights washed over me, and a beat-up pickup slowed to a crawl as it passed. The driver promptly hit the brakes and swerved to the shoulder, stopping altogether. The way my luck was running, it gave me the creeps.

The pickup sat idling hoarsely on the dirt shoulder for a few seconds as I froze in place, aglow in the red taillights, spooked by the prospect of getting brutalized and left in a ditch. I don't know why, but I felt a little better once the passenger's door opened, and salsa music spilled out of the cab.

"¿Queeeé ooooonda, eseeee?"

It was my old compatriot Tino, obviously drunk.

"Hop in, *vato!*"

Approaching the truck, I deduced in the glow of the brake lights that there were already three bodies in the cab.

"What, you mean in back?"

"Naw, man. *¡Muévate, puto!*" he said, shoving the guy next to him. All three of them squished over, even the driver. Still, there were only about six inches to fit my ass on, and I could barely close the door.

"Rocindo," Tino said. "This is Miguel, the one I told you about."

"Hey," I said.

"Where you going, man?" said Tino. "Where's your truck?"

"At home," I said.

"You mean at your mom's house?"

"It's both our house."

"*Sí,*" said Tino. "*Su casa es la casa de tu madre.*"

The others laughed.

"Fuck you, *puto,*" I said just as Rocindo pulled back onto the pavement and started heading toward town.

"You wanna go to a party in Kingston, *vato*?" Tino said.

"Nah, man. Just drop me off."

"C'mon, *ese*. We have a good time."

I could tell he was sincere, and I would've gone. God knows, I could've used a party. Anything to forget the financial blood-letting at the casino, my unemployment, my miserable prospects, and the rest of it. I truly had nothing to lose by going with Tino. But somehow I just couldn't let him see how bad things had gotten. I guess somewhere in me, I still needed to feel superior to him.

"Sorry, man, I'm wiped. Got a bunch of stuff on my plate tomorrow."

"No problem, Miguel. We drop you off."

The whole drive to my house, I tried to talk myself into going with them. How could my night possibly get worse?

"Hey, Holmes," said Tino. "The old lady misses you. Same with Truman. His boxwood look like shit, *ese*. It look like a fucking dog pruned it. Lacy was stupid to fire you."

"Yeah, well."

"He got to find a better lawn man, too."

Ramiro promptly punched Tino in the shoulder.

"Shit, is true, *mi primo*, your edges suck!"

The little guy socked him again, and Tino just laughed.

"Sorry, but you ain't Miguel, *mi primo*. Miguel is *el mejor*. It means, you the best, *vato*. You a pro."

I can't say I didn't appreciate Tino saying so, just not enough to change my mind about going with them. It wasn't until Rocindo pulled up in front of the house that I remembered Tino would likely be looking for my truck.

"Shit, *ese*, whose Bimmer?"

"Uh, yeah, that's my boss's car."

"Nice," he said. "Where you working, *vato*?"

"All over. This and that. Production, import, export, that kind of thing. Anyway, thanks for the lift."

Rocindo tipped his cowboy hat, and Ramiro smiled.

Tino still had questions, though, I could tell.

"Well, gotta go," I said, climbing out. "You guys have fun."

"Gimme a call, *ese*. You still got my number?"

"*Sí*," I said.

When You Make Other Plans

When the day arrived to finally take Remy out, I was down to twenty bucks, which equated to two movie tickets—no Milk Duds, no popcorn. I thought about hitting up Freddy for a loan, but desperate as I was, I just couldn't bring myself to do it. I considered calling Remy and telling her I was down with the flu. But I decided I was done lying to her. If I had any hope of ever being with Remy, she'd have to accept me for what I was—broke.

So I bought a seven-dollar bottle of wine from Albertsons, along with some lunch meat, some bread, some cheese, and a couple of nonorganic Honeycrisp apples. I made sandwiches and cut them up into dainty squares, and sliced up the apples, and brought two mugs and some napkins and a bottle opener from home. I packed it all in the closest thing I could find to a picnic basket: the green tackle box I'd bought at the flea market. I rolled up a blanket, some newspaper, and some kindling and stuffed it in my old backpack from high school.

Remy was already waiting in front of the tribal visitor center when I arrived at five thirty. Her hair was different, but I couldn't tell you how exactly. It might have been the light, but she seemed to be wearing more makeup than usual. She had a little wart under her eye, which I'd never noticed before, and a skin tag on her arm that looked like a toasted Rice Krispie.

"What a great idea, a picnic," she said, clutching my arm. "I had no idea you were such a romantic."

I was terrified almost to the point of nausea as we walked down the steps and crossed under the pier heading north, toward the same spot where, a few weeks earlier, I'd seen Suquamish as never before. I was hoping to recapture some of the romance of that night. The gentle lapping of the surf, the crackle of the fire, the crying of the gulls, riding on the briny air. This is what I imagined for Remy and me as we nibbled our sandwich squares and sipped our wine and made easy conversation.

But conditions were different this time around. To begin with, it was pretty windy, and the tide was way out, and something stank, like maybe a dead sea lion had washed up on the beach somewhere nearby. Also, it was threatening to rain. And not only were the sand fleas infuriating, but I also couldn't get a decent fire going to save my life.

We ate the sandwiches, anyway, and made quick work of the wine. Remy did most of the talking while I blew on the fledgling fire. She told me about her two weeks in Wenatchee, and seeing her old friends and being glad that she'd moved on instead of getting stuck in Wenatchee, which didn't sound so bad to me. There was a river and a brewery and mountains that were green in the spring and snow covered in winter.

Lousy fire and sand fleas aside, things were going pretty smoothly until it started to piss rain. We tried to pretend we didn't notice for a few minutes, but eventually the smoke from the smoldering fire became unbearable.

Now what? Totally broke and no more wine. I definitely didn't want to invite Remy to my house. What could be more unromantic than watching TV with Freddy and Nate? I scrambled for a solution as we made our way south toward the pier. The shed was beginning to look inevitable until Remy arrived at another prospect, equally as mortifying.

"Let's duck into that bar," she said, indicating the Tide's Inn.

"You don't want to go there," I said. "Trust me."

"It's a bar," she said. "It's dry."

"Yeah, but . . ."

"But what? Come on, I'm buying."

I'm not ashamed that my mom is a waitress. It's just not something I like to watch. For this very reason, I rarely go to the Tide's Inn, though it's only five blocks from the house and I could probably score an occasional free beer. Add to that the discomfort of bringing Remy to my mom's place of employment, where somebody was bound to tease me, and you've got a pretty good idea why I was so itchy under the collar.

There were numerous BMX bikes parked out front, which is a hallmark on the res, because DUIs are kind of a thing around here. There was also an old St. Bernard with a giant tumor on his neck, lounging in the doorway. Stepping over the dog, we pushed through the door and made our way across a floor littered with scratch tickets, ending up at a wobbly table in back, where we sat in the glow of the ancient cigarette machine.

"Uh, just so you know," I said, "my mom is gonna be our waitress."

"That's your mom? Wow, she's pretty."

Mom was pleasantly surprised to see me, and I imagine even more surprised to see me with a girl.

"Ma, this is Remy."

"Nice to meet you, sweetie. You have excellent taste in men."

My scalp tightened.

"Yeah, so far he's a keeper," said Remy.

Goddamn, it was hot in there. My mom hovered over our table, small-talking with Remy for what seemed like an eternity. Honestly, I just wanted to get past the pretense and kiss Remy and find out whether or not it would be life changing.

My mom comped us a pitcher, which I knew would later come out of her tips.

"So when's your novel going to be published?" Remy asked, topping off our glasses with the pitcher. "When can I read it?"

"Actually, uh, there is no novel," I said. "Not really. I was just trying to impress you."

"Ah, I see," she said, visibly unimpressed. "So you lied?"

"It wasn't a total lie," I said. "I'm trying to write a novel, but it's terrible. I wrote a scene where a guy is sitting on the toilet eating a turkey leg, trying to figure out what he's doing with his life."

"Is he pooping?" she asked.

"I haven't really figured that out. I guess I assumed he was pooping, since his underwear is around his ankles."

"He should be pooping," she said. "Or he should get off the pot."

It was like she was talking about me.

When our beers were empty, we reached that awkward point where it was time to make a decision. I can't speak for Remy, but I had a pretty good buzz by then, between the wine and the beer. My instinct was to drink more, because I felt like it would only get us closer to something definitive, but I didn't have any money.

"Well, I better call it quits while I can still drive," she said.

I should've said something like "You can always take a cab" or "You can crash on my couch" and then ordered another pitcher or a couple of Jägerbombs and had my mom comp it. But then, maybe Remy was trying to preserve something. Maybe she really did think I was a keeper. Maybe she didn't want to move too fast.

Outside, the rain had let up. We stood in the parking lot for a while, prolonging the opportunity to take some elusive next step. I was compelled to take that step but mostly by voices in my head.

Nick: "Hit that shit."

Freddy: "What you waitin' for, boy?"

Mom: "She was awfully nice, Michael."

What was the big hurry, anyway? If Remy and I were meant to be, it would happen, one way or another.

"We should do this again," Remy said.

"Totally. I'll text you."

"Well . . ." she said.

I leaned into her, then stopped, then she leaned forward and halted. Finally, we leaned in at the same time and managed a kiss. It was clearly more than polite but still a little ambiguous. I should've put my hand on the small of her back and pulled her close to me and really locked lips with her, like in an old movie. I should have staked some claim to her immediate future.

"Thanks for the picnic," she said, climbing into her car.

"You bet," I said.

And then she drove off.

The Revolution Is Postponed

That night, I dreamed of landscaping, of clean lines and neatly raked beds. Of calloused hands and green boot tops, of steaming mulch and hissing sprinklers and sun-dappled rhodies in full bloom. I dreamed of tidy edges and shady corners and weedless gravel paths meandering between rose beds. I dreamed of a world where I was still getting a paycheck, still coming home each day exhausted but satisfied, ninety-six dollars richer. In my dream, I had a brand-new F-250 named Georgia. And it was divine.

I awoke to the dulcet strains of Dale's band saw, the rain beating down on the roof of the shed like pea gravel. The entire right side of my jaw was throbbing. The pain hit like a rubber mallet and ran like a shiver up the back of my skull. I reached in and wiggled the tooth with a wince until it was loose, and the pain took my breath away.

Believe me, it would have been easy to eat four Advils and stay in bed all day. But I got dressed and left without eating breakfast or even going in the house. By afternoon, with my loose tooth still throbbing ceaselessly, I put in job applications at KFC, Payless ShoeSource, and Taco del Mar.

On the bus ride back, wincing through my toothache, I read a half chapter of Knut Hamsun's *Hunger*, and I'll be honest, ravenous as I was, I didn't really buy the conceit of the whole thing. First of all, the hungry people I knew weren't bandying on about philosophy all the time. They talked about cheeseburgers, if anything. Also, they tended to look for jobs instead of wandering around refusing help. The guy in the book was basically kind of a pretentious bum.

Anyway, the bus broke down at 305 and Hostmark, right where some kind of protest was going on with a dozen or so picketers. So I watched it out the rain-streaked window while waiting for a new bus to arrive. The picketers' homemade signs were running and bleeding so badly from the rain, you could hardly read them, and they were all wearing those cheap ponchos, the thin kind they give away at sporting events. Nobody, it seemed, was paying attention to the protesters or their cause, which was presumably why they were there in the first place.

After a moment, I recognized the ringleader as Andrew the librarian, he of the big Adam's apple and the messed-up grill. He was the least miserable looking of the crusaders. In fact, there was something heroic about the way he was waving his sign defiantly, like a challenge, as though the weather were just one more oppressive force thwarting his cause, a cause I was still unable to ascertain, since his picket sign looked like a fucking Rorschach test. But

I'd be a liar if I said the protest wasn't sort of inspiring, whatever it was about. And I'd be lying if I said I didn't wish, if only for a moment, that I could be like Andrew, waving that sign as though he believed he could deter the ruinous forces of greed and global warming, as if he believed he could actually save the world with it.

I confess, I'm one of those people who complains about the world and doesn't do shit about it, aside from a little recycling, and only when it's convenient. Sometimes it's pretty hard to see past your immediate struggles, you know? But for a minute there, watching those miserable protesters, I felt the stirrings of a social conscience. How the hell else was anything going to change if people weren't willing to take to the street and air their grievances?

But just look at me, what could I do, especially in this rain, with this debilitating toothache? And shouldn't I be saving myself first, anyway? Wasn't it kind of like the oxygen masks on airplanes? Wouldn't I be more help to everybody else if I could breathe myself? Still, it got me to thinking that I could probably be doing more to make the world a better place. But first, old Mike Muñoz had to save himself, and that meant making some money—someway, somehow.

Stop-Gap Measure

Selling all my shit amounted to what Chaz would call a "stop-gap measure." I was "creating a little cash flow," "liquidating a few assets."

Freddy and I paid our fifteen bucks, and the organizer pointed us down to the end of the line. I pulled the Tercel around and started setting up shop next to the kid with the pit bull and the tattoos. Leaning against the car, Freddy drank an orange soda and watched me unload my fishing rod, my tackle box, my lawn mower, the Billy Bass, everything I'd bought at the flea market last month. Not to mention my Felcos, my rake, and my post-hole digger.

"Grab my stuff while you're at it," said Freddy.

Freddy had two VCRs and three cardboard boxes of porno tapes.

"Freddy, I'm telling you, you can't sell that shit at the flea market."

"Says who?"

"There might be kids here."

"Ain't no kids at no flea market. 'Sides, your mama say I got to get rid of this shit if I'm gonna live under her roof. Kills me, man, kills me. This shit is classic, dog."

"You're gonna get us kicked out."

"Hell no, boy. Discretion is my middle name. Why you keep grimacing, boy? Shit ain't that heavy."

"My fucking tooth."

"You want me to pull that shit?"

"Yeah, right. Because you're a dentist."

"Shit. Dentist ain't like no doctor. More like a mechanic. All you need is the tools and the basic idea."

"Thanks, but no thanks, Freddy."

I displayed the mower, scrubbed to a shine, right out front, with a tag marked fifty bucks and a sign that said LIKE NEW! I stuck the post-hole digger straight into the ground, so that it looked useful—ten bucks. Nine for the old Felcos. Six for the rake. I priced the rod and tackle box, fifteen for the pair. The few records my mom contributed were two for three dollars—Chaz calls that "bundling." It's a good way to "dump inventory."

When I finally finished laying out my wares, Freddy set to work methodically unpacking.

"Nobody gonna buy those VHS tapes, yo," said the kid with the pit bull, watching Freddy lay them out discreetly behind the Tercel.

"Shit," said Freddy. "Boy, if you knew anything, you wouldn't be sittin' your ass on that ratty towel. And you sure as shit wouldn't have no homemade scorpion tattoo on your neck, either. I want your business advice, I'll ask next time."

Well, that shut the kid up. He went right back to organizing his stolen DVDs.

Freddy was a hell of a salesman, as it turns out.

"Sir, I noticed you admiring that post-hole digger. You like movies?" *Wink wink, elbow elbow, nudge nudge.* "You know, like classics?"

Freddy had it all figured out. Discretion really was his middle name. He'd been collecting brown paper bags for a week.

As for me, my sales got off to a slow start. A kid with skinny jeans bought one of the CCR albums, but he saw right through my bundling scheme. And since I didn't have proper change, I had to give it to him for a buck. A woman in a visor unlocked my Felcos and inspected the edges for nicks before offering me six bucks. Since I believe in momentum, I took it. That was it, though. Mostly, I sat there next to our Tupperware cash box with the wrong lid, increasingly discouraged.

Freddy, meanwhile, was irrepressible.

"This one here got Christy Canyon," he'd say. "This here got Little Oral Annie."

By two o'clock, I'd slashed the mower down to thirty-five dollars OBO. By three, I was down to OBO.

Freddy kept right on selling, his rapport with customers growing more familiar as the afternoon unfolded.

"You can have your shaved lady parts." *Elbow elbow, nudge nudge.* "Old Freddy wanna look like a catfish when he come up for air."

He was out of brown paper bags by three thirty, and up nearly sixty bucks, while I flatlined at eighteen dollars. At four, we packed up the remainder of our wares. I would've been a financial wash for the day if Freddy hadn't kicked me down a fiver for gas and another ten for my trouble.

If there's a silver lining to this cloud, it's that we didn't have to triple-park the Tercel in the driveway when we got home to unload. That's because as we were swinging a right off of Division, we passed a tow truck. And I'll bet you can guess what car it was towing.

Freddy, DDS

That night, the pain got so bad it woke me at 3:00 a.m. The nerve under that incisor was a live wire, crackling deep beneath the surface. Advil couldn't touch it. This was the kind of pain that made you want to put an elephant gun to your head. The kind of pain that wouldn't allow you to contemplate or even acknowledge anything but its very existence, that wouldn't allow you to hope or pray for anything but its termination. I literally could no longer bear it. I would have given both my thumbs to be reclining in a dentist's chair, with or without anesthesia. And I hate dentists.

Whimpering, I trudged into the darkened house, bumbling like a wounded grizzly down the hallway, where I woke Freddy, startling him.

"What the hell, boy?"

"You got to do it. You gotta pull it."

"Shhh. You gonna wake up your mama."

"You gotta get rid of it, Freddy. You gotta."

"Come back in the mornin'."

"Now, right now!"

That woke up Mom, who snapped on the lamp to find my wild-eyed, grimacing personage hovering half naked over her bed.

"What is it? What happened?"

"I can't stand it any longer."

The three of us convened in the kitchen, where I sat rigid and perspiring in a straight-backed chair, beneath the sickly glare of the overhead light.

"This is a terrible idea," said Mom.

"If you're not gonna pull the fucking thing, then please shoot me," I said, tears streaming down my face. "I'm not kidding. It's like nothing I've ever felt. It's not worth it."

"Boy, listen up," said Freddy. "You *cannot* move, you hear? You gotta be strong. You gotta be a rock, you hear? You gotta put your pain in a box, okay? A little red box with a lid."

Shining his Maglite into my mouth, he primed the nearly empty Chloraseptic bottle a few times and managed a meager squirt.

"There, now. You let that settle in, and I'll prep my instruments," he said clutching the needle-nose pliers.

I watched on desperately, tears clouding my vision, as he ran scalding water over the pliers, then took the added precaution of dousing the ends in peroxide.

"Now, if this don't do the trick, we'll move on to the heavy artillery," he said, indicating the vice grips, laid out on a dish towel atop the counter.

I actually might have lost consciousness for an instant as Freddy rooted around with the pliers, trying to get a firm purchase on the offender, while Mom steadied my head.

"Now, now," said Freddy. "Stay with me here, big guy. This is gonna be over real quick."

Every second felt like an eternity as he worked the pliers around deliberately, Mom shining the flashlight for him. When he finally had a satisfactory grip, he said, "Now, I'm gonna count to three, and then it's gonna be all over, okay, dog?"

I clenched my eyes shut and moaned by way of consent.

"Okay, now. Ready? One—"

That's when he pulled it, on one. Immediately, blood started gushing out of my mouth, my mom frantically staunching it with a dish towel.

"Well, lookie here," said Freddy, holding the pliers up to the light.

There was a tooth in the pliers, all right, cleanly excised, root and all. Freddy had managed a tidy extraction.

"What'd old Freddy tell you: easy as one-two-three."

Though the evidence was right there in front of me, in the form of a bloody molar, something was terribly wrong. The pain had not relented one iota. If anything it had increased, which seemed hitherto inconceivable. The realization was not long in arriving. The tears came faster and hotter.

"Ong oof!" I hollered through the blood-drenched towel. "Ong ucking oof!"

"Come again, boy?"

I pulled the towel away, and the blood began gushing anew. "You pulled the wrong fucking tooth! It's the incisor!"

And I bawled unabashedly, chest heaving, blood running down my bare stomach to the waistband of my underwear.

"Goddammit, Freddy!" I shouted, my mouth pooling with blood.

Mom immediately stuffed the dish towel back in my mouth to slow the bleeding. Freddy calmly dropped the tooth in an empty coffee cup and began rinsing the pliers.

"Relax yourself now," said Freddy. "This here's gonna make it easier to access the other one."

"Uck ou!" I yelled, seizing the pliers.

Bloodied and faint, every solitary cell of my body screaming in agony, I harnessed all the strength I had and began groping for the right tooth, fending off Mom.

"Michael, don't do this! We'll go to the dentist. We'll get on a payment plan. I'll pick up some doubles. We'll sell the Tercel. Please don't do this."

But I had no choice.

"Okay, dog," encouraged Freddy. "You got this. Keep a good grip now."

With a firm, steady grip, I pulled with everything I had, then promptly blacked out.

After that, I dimly remember Freddy and Mom putting me in the bathtub and sponging me off.

Burying the Lede

stayed in bed for two days after that, with a mouthful of gauze and a bottle of peroxide, taking my meals through a straw. Miraculously, I avoided infection. And though I was quite certain that all my bottom teeth were already beginning to shift, I was grateful as hell to be rid of the agony and ready to face the future.

With Chaz's car repoed, and not a word from the man himself, I had no choice but to admit that I was no longer in a holding pattern. So Tuesday morning, having spent the entirety of both Sunday and Monday in bed convalescing, I ironed my button-down shirt and my baggy slacks and resumed my job search with a still-swollen jaw and a new, considerably more spacious smile.

But first I had to drop by the Verizon store and prepay for minutes in case I got any callbacks or in the increasingly unlikely event that Chaz tried to contact me. My data was dangerously low, which was why I didn't always answer Remy's texts.

At the Verizon store, there was a guy with Sheetrock dust in his hair and another guy with paint on his jeans, both in line in front of me. And of course, there was also the obligatory old lady who needed instructions for unlocking her screen. I waited forty-five minutes. When I finally got to the counter, they tried to give me a new phone at "no charge." But I'm not as stupid as I look. I knew there'd be all kinds of strings and data packages attached, so I told the guy no thanks, I just want minutes. But I was eligible for an upgrade, he said. I don't want an upgrade, I told him.

"But you're entitled to one."

"I don't want one."

"But you earned it."

"I don't want it."

"It's free."

We volleyed back and forth like that until I finally wore him down, and he reluctantly submitted to selling me thirty minutes, which I paid for entirely in singles and loose change.

My first exercise in pavement pounding was a return to the Subway up on Finn Hill, the one that was formerly filling night shifts. When I asked for the manager, I was expecting the big guy, Jay with the shallow breathing, but it turned out they had a new manager, whom I recognized immediately. He was maybe fifty years old, paunchy, and extremely tired looking. I knew this guy from somewhere, but for the life of me I couldn't place him. Was it my woodshop teacher from high school? Somebody from the bus? A regular at Tequila's?

"Sorry, kid," he said. "We filled evenings last week."

"What about days?"

"No dice. You try the store on 305?"

"Are they hiring?"

"No."

"What do you think? Should I go down there, anyway?"

"I wouldn't," he said.

"So why'd you ask?"

"Just curious, I guess. I'll tell you what, try back next week."

"You think you might have an opening then?"

"No."

He shook my hand, then promptly circled back around the counter, slipped on a pair of plastic gloves, and started dressing some lady's sandwich. On my way out, he called out, and it wasn't until then that I finally placed him.

"Oh, and kid. About your writing sample."

"Did you read it?" I asked.

"I read it," he said.

"And?"

"Full of split infinitives. Dangling participles, not to mention vague pronoun references, passive forms, fragments, comma splices, you name it. Didn't you take freshman comp? Kid, you keep dangling participles like that, and somebody's going to hit their head."

"Very funny," I said.

"Worst of all," he said, "you buried the lede."

"Bury this," I said, giving him the finger.

Try Not to Be Black

Nate's been short of breath the past couple days, and a little lethargic. So Wednesday, I made a three o'clock doctor's appointment for him. Did I mention Nate doesn't like doctor appointments? He was like a goddamn silver-backed gorilla in the back of the Tercel, pounding the seatbacks, stomping his feet, pawing at the side window. Thank God, Freddy was along for the ride.

Things were proceeding pretty smoothly until the cop pulled in behind me at Whale Dancer, flashing his red-and-blues.

"Fucking great," I said, pulling to the shoulder.

I kept my hands at ten and two on the steering wheel, like I read somewhere you're supposed to, so that the cop can see them at all times. That way, maybe he wouldn't beat the shit out of me or shoot me in the face. One thing became quickly apparent as we waited on the shoulder: the situation did not agree with Nate.

Maybe it was the combination of the flashing lights and being stuck in the backseat, but as the cop began walking toward the Tercel, Nate began pounding furiously at the back of my seat.

"Easy now, big dog," said Freddy.

The officer was a hatchet-faced dude with no discernible forehead. Not that I'm big into *Star Wars*, but the guy looked a little like Jar Jar Binks. He tapped on the window, peering first and foremost at Freddy's black personage with apparent suspicion. Only then, with something akin to alarm, did he seem to register the spectacle of my seething three-hundred-pound brother in the rear seat, pounding his fists against the side window.

I indicated that the driver's window would not roll down, and when the officer didn't seem to comprehend, I shouted as much, but he couldn't hear me with Nate going berserk. When I opened the door to explain, he unholstered his pistol in a flash and yelled at me to stay the hell put and get my hands up where he could see them. He circled around the front of the car to Freddy's side, pistol trained alternately on me, Freddy, and Nate. Mostly on Freddy.

"Roll down your window!" he barked at Freddy.

"It don't roll down!"

"Step out of the vehicle!"

"Door don't open!"

"Put your hands on the dash, where I can see them!"

Freddy complied as the cop circled back around to my side of the car, pistol trained, left eye twitching.

"Step out of the vehicle," he said.

Slowly, I stepped out.

"The rest of you, out."

Freddy tried to crawl out behind me, but his knee hit the stick, and the Tercel began rolling slowly backward toward the squad car with Freddy and Nate still in it.

"Oh shit," I said.

Freddy was hanging halfway out of the car when the flustered cop, trying to get a handle on the escalating situation, inexplicably took aim at a rear tire of the Tercel, and pulled the trigger with a pop, missing the tire completely and kicking up some gravel just as Freddy managed to reach between his legs and apply the emergency brake.

The Tercel lurched to a stop on the shoulder, mere inches from the cruiser. The cop rushed forward, pistol aimed at Freddy. "Out of the vehicle, all of you!"

Freddy flopped out onto the shoulder. But Nate, kicking and screaming, was not to be reckoned with.

"He has special needs," I explained.

"Calm him down," said the cop, pistol still trained on Freddy.

Even though he was the guy holding the gun, Jar Jar Binks was clearly the most nervous party involved, with the possible exception of Nate, who was going off like an air-raid siren.

"Get up," the cop said to Freddy.

Freddy stood without dusting off his knees, hands held out in front of him.

"Gotta talk to him, boss," he said.

"Shut him up, and get him out of the car," said the cop, twitching. "And keep your hands in the air."

Deliberately, Freddy leaned slightly into the car, hands up.

"Okay, now, big dog, I know you're upset. Don't nobody like to have a gun pointed at them. But the policeman need you to step outside the car."

It took some coaxing, but Freddy finally managed to calm Nate and persuade him to get out of the car, where the cop lined us up with our hands on the hood.

"You have any idea why I pulled you over?"

"Because he's black?" I said.

"What did you just say?"

"He didn't say nothin'," said Freddy, shooting me a look.

"I pulled you over because your muffler is nearly dragging," he said with a twitching eye.

"Is a nearly dragging your muffler against the law?" I said.

"I recommend you get it fixed."

"Are you gonna arrest us?"

"Don't tempt me," said the cop.

"Boy, keep quiet," said Freddy.

The cop looked at Freddy as though he'd spoken out of turn, then looked back at me.

"Consider this a courtesy stop."

"You gotta be kidding me," I said.

"Shut up, boy," said Freddy.

The cop smiled and steadied his twitching eye.

"Disorderly conduct is no joke, I can tell you that," he said. "You like to get a better look at the station, see what your tax dollars are paying for? Or if you'd rather, I could just hit you with a fine."

Well, the fine should have shut me up—I certainly couldn't afford that. I'll be the first to admit, we were a motley-looking crew, packed into that shit-can Tercel. But last I checked, there was no law against that. The fact is, besides our dangling muffler, we did nothing worthy of suspicion. If we were driving a Lexus, and Freddy were white, I doubt we would've been pulled over at all.

My advice: If your window doesn't roll down, get it fixed, even if you can't afford to. Also, if you get pulled over, try not to be black.

"Good thing you're such a crappy shot," I said to the cop as he walked back to the cruiser.

"What was that?"

"He didn't say nothin'," said Freddy.

In the car, Freddy berated me, mostly with silence but with a little mumbling, too. "Pfff . . . plain stupid . . . damn lucky to drive away from that mess. . . ."

Big Mac Attack

We were twenty minutes late to Nate's doctor's appointment, but it didn't matter, they would never have been ready for us, anyway. As ever, the waiting room was packed. I don't know what medical care looks like for the wealthy, but let's talk about the waiting room at Nate's doctor. You never see a guy in a polo shirt or a kid with braces or a girl in ballet shoes in there. No, it's always the miserable hordes, the morbidly obese, trundling oxygen carts. Diabetics in sweatpants. Bent old ladies with cat hair on the butt of their pants. There's always at least one person in a surgical mask with a relentless, rattling cough. And usually a kid with Down's, talking even louder than Nate.

A Mexican girl, who couldn't have been older than sixteen, nursed her dark-haired baby while a toddler lolled around at her feet and a dirty-faced boy of about three perched in the chair next to her, sucking on his finger. He had the dull-eyed, complacent look of somebody who's undernourished. Sometimes when I see a kid like that, I try to imagine what his life is going to look like in thirty years. Will he shape himself? Will he become a doctor or a lawyer? Or will he be shaped, bent, and molded by the external pressures of poverty and injustice? I think you can probably guess the answer to that one.

After about an hour, a squat lady in purple scrubs called out Nate's name.

"You want I should take him?" said Freddy.

"I got it," I said.

Scrubs led us down the corridor. She needed to weigh Nate, so I coaxed him up on the scale, where she had to move the top counterweight as far to the right as it would go. She jimmied the bottom weight until the arm achieved balance. Nate weighed 305—just like the highway. After she marked it down on her clipboard, Scrubs led us to a room down the hall and instructed Nate to sit on the edge of the exam table. Fastening the blood pressure apparatus to his arm, she pumped it up and released the air, looking slightly unnerved as she eyed the gauge. Immediately, she repeated the procedure and marked the results down on her clipboard.

"Any dizziness?" she asked Nate.

"Not that I know of," I said on Nate's behalf.

"You said shortness of breath?"

"Yeah, like he's been exercising or something. Except he hasn't been exercising."

She made a note briskly on her pad. "Dr. McFarland will be with you shortly," she said, hurrying out of the room.

Normally we'd be sitting there for a half hour, with me wishing I'd brought that issue of *House Beautiful* I was vaguely thumbing through in the waiting room, but today the doctor arrived almost immediately, looking every bit as tired as her patients. You could tell she was once athletic, before she started eating out of a vending machine and keeping bad hours.

"Hello, Nate," she said, glancing at the chart. "I'm Dr. McFarland."

"He's kind of shy," I said.

"Shallowness of breath?"

"Yeah, a couple of times. And he's just seemed kind of listless the past week."

She put a stethoscope to Nate's chest and a thumb on the inside of his wrist, and staring at a fixed point on the wall, she listened to his pulse, silently counting.

"His blood pressure is a major cause for concern," she said, glancing at the chart. "If we don't manage it, we could be looking at some real complications. We need to make some lifestyle changes immediately. Like yesterday."

The way she looked at me, the implications were inescapable. This was my fault. What the hell kind of brother was I? Nate was a child, incapable of making sound decisions. I was an adult. I should have monitored his diet. I should have kept him on an exercise regimen. I should have been coercing him all along, fighting him for his own good, no matter the inconvenience, no matter the black eyes, the errant saltshakers. But I took the path of least resistance. I accepted the fact that things would get worse for my brother. That's old Mike Muñoz for you: Take the easy way out. Accept the worst like it's inevitable. It's easier than changing the game, isn't it? Why bother changing the game when you can just talk a big one: talk about writing novels and saving the world, but at the end of the day, you're just plying your special-needs brother with cheeseburgers and Oreos and phoning in the rest.

We left with two prescriptions, about twenty pages of literature on high blood pressure and one very guilty conscience. The minute we climbed back into the Tercel, Nate had a Big Mac attack.

Los de Abajo

The following day, I dropped off an application at the new Rite Aid on 305, then wandered down the hill to downtown Poulsbo to kill some time. When I got to Front and Jensen, I found Andrew the librarian standing there with a clipboard, collecting signatures. He was wearing a pea-green cardigan sweater with big brass buttons over a homemade T-shirt that said ACT!

I had to hand it to Andrew, the guy took initiative. He was socially engaged, highly motivated, and unwavering in his convictions. Pretty much everything I wasn't.

"Hey, Mike. What's up?"

"Not much," I said.

"Spare two minutes to talk about the environment?"

"Uh, yeah, sure."

"Did you know that Shell plans to resume drilling for oil in the Arctic?"

"Yeah, I think I heard something about that."

"Experts say there's a seventy-five percent chance of a major spill, and oil recovery is nearly impossible in Arctic conditions."

"Bummer," I said.

"Not to mention the fact that there's no spill-response capacity in the region in the first place and that the Arctic is one of the most fragile ecosystems on Earth."

He gave me about two seconds to let the information settle in before soldiering on.

"Did you know that the Arctic is currently warming at twice the rate as the rest of the world?"

"That's fucked."

"Yes, it is," he said. "It is most certainly, unequivocally fucked. Especially if you're a polar bear or a ringed seal or a migratory whale or a puffin. But also if you're a human being. And the oil companies know this. They've known it for five decades. But they don't care about anything but quarterly profits. That's why we're collecting signatures to stop the drilling before it begins."

"Hell, yeah," I said. "I'll sign it."

Andrew flashed a Stonehenge smile, handed me the clipboard and pen. I proudly filled out my name and address. Yeah, I know a signature's not much, but it buoyed my spirits a little knowing that I'd at least done something to make the world a better place, which was more than I usually did. Hell, for all my complaining, I wasn't even a registered voter. I determined then and there to change that.

"Thanks for caring," he said.

"You bet," I said. "Thanks for, you know, standing on a corner with a clipboard."

But I don't think Andrew heard me, because he'd already moved on, accosting the next passerby. Too bad, because I'd wanted to hang around and talk about books for a while. I was about to cross the street to avoid Tequila's, when I ran into Tino in front of the Christian bakery.

"*¿Qué onda, Miguel? ¿Cómo lo llevas?*"

He was still wearing his work clothes; boots scuffed, dirt on the knees, baseball cap pulled down low over his forehead.

"Hey, man," I said.

"Whatchu doin', *ese?*"

"Just walkin' around," I said. "Savin' the Arctic, that kind of thing. What about you?"

"Just picked up *mucho* dog shit at McClures'. *Pinche* dog shit on the lounge chairs. I need a *cerveza, ese.* C'mon, I buy you one," he said nodding at Tequila's.

"Do we have to go there?"

"Naw, man, wherever you want."

So we walked down by the marina to the Dockside Tavern, with its murky light and its sagging, lost-puck shuffleboard table, its filthy bathroom, and its bar top sticky to the touch. The bartender, not the chatty sort, had a jagged three-inch scar across his forehead and a naked-lady tattoo on his forearm.

I ordered a PBR to go easy on Tino's pocketbook.

"So, what's new?" I said.

"Ah, you know, *ese.* Same old shit. Lacy, he just getting meaner and fatter. New accounts, bigger projects. We working most Saturdays now. Overtime on weekdays. But he don't pay us extra. He still payin' the same shit wage, no matter how many hours."

"So quit."

"Shit, I'm thinking about it, but it's the same everywhere.

Nobody want to pay a Mexican. I need to make more money, *ese*. I need some space, you know? That trailer is getting too small. Ramiro, he only four foot six, but he snores like a *pinche oso*. And Rocindo, all the time he having sex with his wife late at night. Then his *hijos* eating Skittles and climbing the walls at six in the morning. It's Locotown. I gotta get out, *ese*, gotta get my own place. But how am I gonna do that working for Lacy, when I'm sending half of what I make to Durango?" He shook his head grimly. "Is not supposed to be this way, Miguel. Is supposed to get better."

"It does get better," I said.

"Yeah?" he said, doubtfully.

"In my experience, yeah. Right before it all goes to shit again."

Tino sipped his beer soberly. "Something gotta change, that's all I know, *ese*. I gotta do more than just survive, or what am I doing here? I may as well be back in Durango."

"I know a guy who'd be happy to give you a lift to the bus station."

"Don't I know it, *ese*. Back home things are even worse, though. But still I miss it, my *niños*, my *esposa*. Is lonely, Miguel, you don't know."

"So go back."

"I can't afford to go back. It took me everything to get here. More than everything. I got people depending on me back home. I gotta make something happen."

"Bring your family up here."

"Ha, is not so easy, Miguel. And my money, it don't go so far, not here. Rocindo, he got help—his wife, she work part-time. Her brother help them out, too. And still they need me and Ramiro to pay the rent. Where do I put my family?"

"Gotcha," I said.

Tino drained his beer and held up two fingers for the bartender, who delivered two more, promptly and without a word.

"*¿Mi hija más joven?*" he said, taking a long draw of his beer. "She two and a half years old. *Mi* Isabella. *Mi chiquitita* Izzy. Look just like her mama, with her big feet and her little nose. She talking all the time now. Mia say she never shut up. Last week she say she gonna go get Papá. Bring Papá home. This kills me, Miguel. Seems like half my money I'm spending on my phone. *Pinche* Verizon gets half my paycheck."

"Verizon is fucked," I said.

"*Tienes toda la razón,*" he said.

We ended up talking for two hours. We joked a little about the old lady and the abundance of dog turds at McClures', but mostly we talked in earnest, grinding axes and regretting our lots. He asked me what happened to my teeth, and I told him about Freddy's foray into dentistry. He winced throughout the story, like a guy who'd been there, which in fact he had, opening his mouth to prove it. I could see the gap once occupied by a molar.

"Did it myself, *vato*. Five shots of mezcal and *alicate viejo*."

In spite of all his difficulties, financially, personally, geographically—and let's face it, they were worse than mine—Tino ended up buying me four beers and a shot of Jäger. I shouldn't have let him, but he seemed to want the company, and if I weren't broke myself, I would have done the same for him.

"I don't know, Miguel," Tino said, calling for the tab. "Something gotta change."

"I know the feeling," I said, clapping him on the back.

And boy, did I ever know the feeling. But at least my family wasn't a million miles away. At least angry white men weren't calling for my deportation, blaming me for their problems; at least they weren't trying to wall my people out. I had it better than Tino, and I'll admit there was a little comfort in that, but things were getting dire on the home front. As the days of unemployment mounted, the old revenue stream had slowed well past a burble or a trickle, past so much as a lonely drop, to a parched and heat-fissured drainage ditch, strewn with bleached skulls and faded beer cans. No callbacks and nary a word from my old mentor Chaz, who, for all I knew, was collating Walmart circulars at the state penitentiary in Walla Walla.

"All I want, Miguel, is to get by, *a ser tratado con dignidad, a caminar con mi cabeza en alto, ¿comprendes?*"

"*Sí.* I think so."

Is That You?

Snaggle-toothed Marlin was manning his post outside Safeway, staged in front of three dozen shopping carts, each emblazoned with Doug Goble's shit-eating grin, along with his slogan TEAM GOBLE. GOBLE OR GO HOME. I'm pleased to report that Marlin's ax work was much improved since Freddy's campfire tutorial. He was banging out "Enter Sandman" by Metallica, and he wasn't even watching the fret board the entire time. He looked like a guy who actually played the guitar. Clean him up, and he could probably play at somebody's wedding.

When Marlin finished the number, I reached for my pickle jar and started unscrewing the lid with the intent of scooping out a small offering. But I bungled it, and the jar slipped from my grasp and shattered all to hell. Small change and broken glass scattered everywhere. Marlin set down his guitar immediately and scrambled to my aid as people started walking around us like a couple of undesirables.

Within moments, the special-needs bag boy came out with a broom and a dustpan as Marlin and I scrupulously picked through the glass for silver, and yes, even copper, under the bike rack, behind the propane tanks, below the watermelon display, filling the fronts of our T-shirts. As I was scanning the pavement for coins, I heard a voice.

"Muñoz? Is that you?"

Confronted by a pair of pointy leather loafers, I reluctantly peered up to behold the living, breathing personage of Doug Goble towering over me, perma-grinning like a mayor on a parade float. Instinctively, my eyes darted to the queue of shopping carts, then back up at Goble.

"Great idea, right?" he said. "As long as some kid isn't sitting his ass on your face. God, I hate kids. What are you doing down there, Mike?"

"I dropped something."

"Your piggy bank?"

"Blow me," I said, blanching.

He grinned even harder, stooping down to help Marlin and me.

"You've got a small fortune here," he observed, dropping coins into my shirt. "Invest it wisely."

"I'm gonna punch you if you don't knock it off," I said.

"Relax, I'm just joshin'. C'mon, I'll buy you a cup of coffee."

So there I was at the Starbucks in Safeway with Doug Goble. For all my discomfort, Goble was downright chatty. He acted like we ran into each other all the time, and it had nothing to do with dicks. He talked about old times at the church but never mentioned our penises or the fact that he never said ten words to me after our little foray in the bushes. He talked about a few of his new listings and his plans to expand his real-estate empire into Jefferson County but made not a single reference to holding or tugging or sucking dicks. And yet I was convinced he was flirting with me. He talked about the five acres they were developing over on Weaver and the new parking lot at the casino.

"So, what about you?" he said, like someone who's not actually interested.

"I'm a landscaper."

"Ah," he said. "Landscaper."

"I'm also a writer," I said, a divulgence I regretted immediately.

"A writer, huh?" he said, doubtfully. "You make any money in the writing racket?"

"Not yet."

"Hmph. Who the hell has time to read, anyway? So what else you been up to? Inquiring minds want to know."

I was becoming increasingly certain that "buy you a cup of coffee" was some sort of euphemism. All I could think about while he was chatting me up over the rim of his cappuccino was his little salamander between my fourth-grade fingers, rapidly engorging with blood. Was he expecting me to do it again? Just like that? Not that I would. Not for a cup of coffee, that's for sure. It was all so confusing, you know? I didn't know what I was supposed to be feeling. Was I putting out some kind of signal I didn't know about? Why would Doug Goble buy me coffee after all these years if it didn't have something to do with touching penises?

"Let me give you a lift," he said.

There it was. The proposition. Or maybe it wasn't. Fuck, I didn't know. All I knew was that a lift would save me two bucks in bus fare, but it wasn't worth sucking Goble's dick, or even touching it. I figured if he tried anything, I'd punch him in the throat and jump out of the car.

On our way out the door, we passed Marlin, banging out a ham-fisted rendition of "Tom Sawyer." Doug stopped to watch him for an instant before dropping a fiver in his guitar case.

"Hey, I got a request," he said. "How about 'The Sounds of Silence'? Go ahead and learn that one."

Marlin looked a little pissed off until he glanced down and discovered it was a fiver.

"Peace, bro," he said.

"Get a job," said Goble.

With that, Goble led me briskly across the parking lot to a black Lexus convertible.

"Nice car," I said.

"Yeah, it's okay."

At the stoplight on 305, Doug pulled out a tube and started applying cream around his eyes. I thought it was sunscreen at first, but then I recognized the extra-long yellow nozzle.

"Dude, hold up!" I said. "That's not sunscreen!"

"Yeah, I know. It's for hemorrhoids. It contracts the blood vessels—gets rid of my wrinkles."

"You don't have any wrinkles."

"That's what you think."

He pulled out his phone and glanced at the screen again. "I've got an open house at five thirty," he said. "Kinda late, I know, but I wanna wow them with the sunset view. It'll distract them from the fugly kitchen."

"Look at you," I said. "Driving a Lexus and shit. I can't walk a hundred yards without seeing your face. What I don't get is, how did you make any of this shit happen? You came from the res, just like me. Your mom, she didn't have any money, just like mine."

"Money's not the only resource, bud. There's sweat."

"Then I should be rich."

"You gotta sweat smart, though. You can't just grunt your way to something better. Landscaping, you any good at it? You a pro?"

"Hell yeah, I'm good. I'm fast as hell, and my edges are gold. I can make your yard look like a million bucks. But my real specialty is topiary."

"What, like bird watching?"

"Plant sculpting."

"Hmph. How much do you make landscaping?"

"Actually, I'm between jobs."

"How much *did* you make?"

"Twenty bucks an hour," I lied.

"How much does your boss make?"

"I don't know."

"Well, there's your problem right there."

"Is it?"

"You're good, you said so yourself. But you don't even know what you're worth. How are you supposed to advocate for yourself when you don't know what's at stake?"

"How should I know?"

"You've gotta know exactly where you stand; otherwise, how

can you possibly make your position seem better? You've got to leverage yourself. How else can you create the perception that you're actually in control when you don't even know what it is you're trying to control?"

"I give up."

"You wanna get out of the ghetto, Mike, you gotta follow the money."

"What money?"

"There's always money. You just gotta look closer."

"Like under the couch cushions?"

"No, Mike, that's not what I mean at all."

"You mean like I gotta think big?"

"Anybody can think big. Prison is full of big thinkers. Think smart, Mike."

"You mean like smoke and mirrors?"

"No, Mike. I don't even know what that means. Look, I'm not sure why I'm telling you any of this. These are the keys to my success. This is about the will to power. This shit is gold. I don't even offer this stuff in my seminars. I guess I find you nonthreatening somehow. And maybe I feel a little sorry for you—which is unusual for me. But the way out of poverty is to infiltrate communities. Communities within communities. Communities under communities. Communities that exist invisibly inside other communities. Communities outside your community that might possibly profit from your community. *¿Comprendes?*"

"How do you infiltrate invisible communities?"

"You go to three church services every Sunday, plus a Thursday mass at St. Cecilia. You go to fund-raisers and dodge out right before the bidding. You go to city council meetings—even in cities you don't live in. You go to Little League games—yeah, a little weird, since you don't have kids, but you've got a four-by-eight-foot billboard in center field, plus one in the lot adjacent to Rotary Park, and a realty sign in front of the duplex two doors down, so it seems pretty natural, you being at Little League games, know what I mean? You're a sponsor. The point is, you be there. That's how you earn trust. Just by being there. Attendance is gold."

"But . . ."

"No buts. You just always gotta be in the right place. You're the writer, what's the word I'm looking for? *Ubiquitous.* You gotta be ubiquitous. Where do I turn?" he said when we hit Division.

"I'll just jump out here."

"No way, pal. I'm taking you door to door. For old times' sake."

There he was with the old times again but no mention of penises. How could he act so familiar and not talk about it, like it wasn't sitting there between us like a goddamn elephant?

"Well," I said as he pulled up to the house. "Here we are: Rancho Dumpo."

"Ah, it ain't so bad," he said. "You gotta see the potential. They call me the House Whisperer down at RE/MAX. What you ought to do is strike that old canopy and make a few trips to the dump. Get rid of the jalopy. Put a skirt around the bottom of the unit, so it looks more like a foundation. Plant some hedges, front and side, to break up the rectangularity of the place and give it a little buttress. Couple of planters under the window. Half-dozen paving stones and a little paint would add some serious curb appeal, too, and cheap. You own the place?"

"No."

"Never mind, then. As you were."

As I climbed out of the car, Freddy appeared on the porch in his underwear to admire the Lexus, scratching the springy hairs of his chest and hocking a loogie. Goble didn't even flinch—the guy was unflappable. He gave Freddy a familiar little wave and Freddy waved back, visibly confused to see me in a Lexus convertible with a guy wearing a dress shirt.

"By the way," said Goble, producing a business card. "Give me a call on Monday. I might have a job for you."

Before and After

Monday morning, I called Goble. He was currently managing six new properties on the island, all in need of regular maintenance. And get this: he'd pay me twenty bucks an hour—cha-ching! He instructed me to meet him out at the first property in an hour, which was on Wardwell, just off 305. I crammed the mower in the trunk of the Tercel, along with the edger, the weed whacker, and the rake, then got Freddy and Nate to give me a push for a compression start.

When I arrived at the first property, Goble wasn't there yet, so I parked on a hill and began unloading my gear. The house was your typical McMansion. Gray and boxy, with some corny flourishes intended to look classy: a pergola, some pillars, a roundabout driveway. It sat on a big lot, mostly wooded. What lawn it afforded needed some work, especially around the edges.

Just as I was getting ready to fire up the mower, Goble pulled up in his Lexus, top down, auto-tuned pop music blaring.

"Dude, you can't park there!" he shouted. "You're blocking my sign!"

So much for parking on the hill. I put the Tercel in neutral and started rolling her down toward the corner. That's how I wound up with two wheels in the ditch.

Despite his annoyance, Goble was pretty cool about the whole thing. He called a tow truck and gave me his AAA card. My debt to Goble was mounting by the minute.

"I really appreciate it, man," I told him as the tow truck pulled away.

"Just do a good job," he said. "I gotta move this place."

He walked me around the property, soliciting my opinion on a few matters. Should he stage some lawn furniture on the flagstone patio? What did I think about painting the front door red? Should we clear out some of those junk trees around the perimeter?

"Mike, I need your professional opinion here. Where do we start?"

"I don't know."

"Really? That's the best you've got?"

"You've seen my house. How the hell would I know?"

"You're a professional landscaper. I asked you, and you said yourself you were good. You've got to act the part."

"Okay," I said. "The lawn needs some work. The edges are rough, and you've got a dandelion problem. The reason it's bald under that walnut tree isn't because of the shade, it's the high acid content of the soil. I'm betting some fescue would take root there. Four bucks at Bay Hay and Feed. Done and doner. And yeah, if you lose a few of those alders, you might lighten up the place. That Japanese maple would do better with more light. I'd also square up that laurel and deadhead those rhodies."

"Now that's more like it, Mike. You sound like a gamer."

"I could also carve you a sculpture out of that boxwood there. Maybe like bald eagle with a rabbit in his talons."

"Quit while you're ahead, Mike."

"What about a fish?"

"No, Mike."

"In his talons, I mean."

Goble didn't even reply this time, just glanced at his cell.

"See how far you can get by two thirty, then meet me at the Baker Hill property."

"Ten-four."

"You've got the address?"

"Got it."

"And no sculptures," he said. "Not ever."

"Got it."

Man, it was great working without supervision. No Lacy looking over my shoulder. No Truman peering out the window. No old lady in a wheelchair busting my balls. And let me tell you, in just a few short hours, old Mike Muñoz reinvented that yard. I took out the alder saplings that were strangling the maple and started a discreet dump pile back in the cedar bog, out of sight. I forgot my weeder, so I used the flathead screwdriver from my glove box and must have dug out a hundred dandelions before I mowed the lawn. I cut a new edge along the perimeter. I weed-whacked along the foundation and deadheaded the rhodies. I'd have to come back next week for the laurel, but the place looked way better. I wished Goble were there to see it. I really should've taken before-and-after pictures.

Driving to the second property, I felt like a lion. A few blisters from the weeding, but that was nothing compared to the satisfaction of a job well done.

When I arrived at the Baker Hill place, I parked on the incline a few doors down. Goble was already waiting, leaning up against the Lexus, texting. He always looked fresh, Goble. His hair was never mussed—even though he drove a convertible. No wrinkles, not on his clothes or on his person. Just enough cologne. No wonder he was well liked at all those churches—the guy was squeaky clean, at least on the surface.

"How'd it go at Wardwell?" he said, without looking up from his cell.

"Good. Really good."

In one swift movement, he finished texting and pocketed the phone.

"Let's see the pictures."

"I didn't take any."

"No before and after?"

"I didn't think of it until after."

"So you got an after?"

"No."

He suppressed a sigh and patted my back.

"Mike, you've got to think proactively if you ever wanna get ahead. You can't just roam the earth dragging your lawn mower and hoping some old lady hires you. You've got have an angle at all times. You take pictures, you build a portfolio. You start calling yourself a landscape architect."

"But I'm not an architect."

Goble shook his head grimly. "Look, just take pictures next time around."

The Baker Hill property was another McMansion. Somewhere in its outsized boxiness there lurked a hint of Victorian. And Edwardian. And Tudor. The lawn was in decent shape. The cedars around the edge were a little shaggy and the rhodies needed deadheading. The kidney-shaped flower bed in the center of the lawn could use some cleaning up, and I told Goble as much.

"Okay, then," he said, unpocketing his cell again. "Hop to it. I'll swing by Wardwell and take a look. Oh, and Mike, next time park even farther down the street. At least until you get a decent car."

"Got it."

I snapped a few pictures of the problem areas before I set to work. The first order of business was bringing up the canopy on those cedars and opening up the yard. They were old trees, with big buttressed trunks and oddly bowed limbs, some of them as low as knee level. I took up the canopy uniformly to six feet, cleaning out the scrub plants and vine maple and raking up the windfall along with my trimmings. I started a dump pile down the hill, out of sight from the house. All the clearing and the canopy work gave the place a park-like feel around the perimeter. As I unloaded my mower, my phone rang. It was Goble in his convertible. I could hear his pop music and the wind rocketing past the phone receiver.

"Wardwell looks dynamite," he said. "Like a different property. One of my clients drove by an hour ago and called me to ask if I'd had the place painted or something. You weren't lying—you're good. You're a landscaping genius. When you wrap up there, meet me at the Harbor Pub in Winslow, say around five thirty. I wanna buy you a beer."

You heard the man: I was a genius. Imagine how good those words sounded to my ears—almost as good as that free beer. I had a little extra spring in my step as I mowed the lawn. I whistled as I cut the edge, hummed Roger Miller as I pruned, gutted, and raked out the big flower bed. My creative juices were flowing. I even jotted down a few notes for the Great American Landscaping Novel while catching my breath.

The first thing I did when I got to the pub was let Goble buy me that beer.

"Damn, it looks like a park," he said, perusing the pictures on my phone. "Creating all that space under the cedars was a genius move."

Twice a genius!

"Did you redo the edge on that big bed?"

"Yeah."

"Nice. Really makes the lawn pop."

That's when Goble reached into his back pocket, took his wallet out, and handed me a crisp hundred-dollar bill.

"You're gonna pay me daily?"

"That's a tip. Put it toward buying a new car."

"So I'm gonna get paid, too?"

"Yes, Mike. That's how a tip works."

Truman had never tipped me, that's for sure. Or the old lady. Or Lacy, for that matter. Even as I thanked Goble, I was a little incredulous.

"Why are you doing all this for me?"

"I needed a landscaper."

"No, really."

"Really, I'm just building my network, Mike. Like the man said, a man's net worth is only as good as his network."

He was right, of course. Just look at my network: a bass player, a tire technician, and likely a convicted felon in Chaz. No wonder I was penniless.

"Remember how I told you about infiltrating communities? About being there?"

"Yeah. Attendance is gold."

"Actually, it's only part of the equation, but I didn't want to overwhelm you at the time. The way you build an ironclad network is by doing favors for people. Especially if it helps you. Case in point, hiring you: I get a bunch of landscaping done, *and* you owe me a favor."

Oh God, here it was. And what could I say? The guy was paying me twenty bucks an hour. He got my car towed out of a ditch. He bought me coffee and now beer. Plus he gave me a hundred bucks. I'm no dummy. Now I had to touch his dick.

"I get it," I said.

"Do you?"

"This is where I gotta do you a favor."

"No, that's the catch. I never call in my favors. Not unless I absolutely have to."

My shoulders slackened immediately.

"But here's the other catch," Goble said, leaning in closer. "Say, I wanna do somebody else a favor, but I can't really perform that particular favor. Like, say my girlfriend needs a new muffler."

"You have a girlfriend?"

"No. But say she needs a new muffler. Better yet, say she needs a mental-health professional or a veterinary surgeon. Well, obviously I'm not gonna operate on her dog's colon. But I know a guy. Are you following me here?"

"Yeah," I lied.

"And this guy, this veterinary surgeon, I've done him a favor, too, see, a couple of favors? I helped him refi, I structured his escrow conveniently, moved some numbers around, and I didn't charge him for any of it. No closing costs. So he owes me one."

He took a long draw on his beer and held up his finger to let me know he wasn't finished yet.

"But here's the next catch: I'm not really asking for a favor, not for myself, so it doesn't really count as a favor. I mean, you and I know it does, but it doesn't, not in the guy's mind. It's not *my* colon. It's just me doing this girl and her dog a favor, like I once did him a favor on the closing costs. I'm the guy that does favors for everybody. You still following me?"

"Yeah, I think."

As close as I could figure, this meant that one day Goble was gonna call me and ask me to do a guy a favor—and I'd still owe *him* one. This was not shaping up well for me.

"So," he says. "Now I'm one favor ahead in the ledger: I got my girlfriend's dog's colon operated on practically pro bono (except for the anesthesia—they gotta account for that stuff), the guy still owes me a favor (which I'll never call in, because I only call in favors for other people), and I come out smelling like roses. Hell, if the dog could do anything for me, I'd be up two favors in the ledger. But what's a dog gonna do, lick peanut butter off my dick?"

He took another pull of his beer and patted his lips dry with a napkin. "Sounds sort of sinister in a way," he said. "But the best part of the whole arrangement? Yep, everybody wins."

"What about the guy doing all the free colon operations. How does he win?"

"He already won. With the refi and the escrow. Plus I helped him find his dream house. And I listed his sister's place."

"Will he ever win again? Does he ever get any credit for the colon operations?"

"Oh, I'll do him another favor down the line. He won't even have to ask. I'll just wait until it's convenient for me to do it, and it probably won't be a direct favor. It'll probably be a favor somebody offers me as payback for one of my favors, but then I'll just offer the favor to him. Like a pair of tickets to *Jersey Boys* or something."

"But wait. Doesn't that mean that your indirect favors are worth direct favors, but their indirect favors aren't worth anything?"

"Not bad, Mike. You're catching on."

"What if they ask you for a direct favor? Do you do it?"

"If it's convenient, sure."

"What if it's inconvenient?"

"Depends how much you can do for me. Can you help me stash some major assets offshore, or are you just mowing some lawns for me? No offense. I mean, I'm paying you, right?"

"You're paying me well," I said.

He sighed. "Not really, Mike. I'm paying you a few bucks over minimum wage."

"So give me a raise."

"Not gonna happen. I only pay what the market can bear—and that's maximum. My last guy was Mexican. I was paying him ten."

"So why pay me twenty?"

"I know, right? I guess because I like you."

"No, really, why?"

"Because you do superlative work?"

"C'mon, Goble. Why?"

"Well, you do good work, you really do. But the fact is, prospective home buyers—the ones I sell to—they don't want to see Mexicans in their prospective neighborhood. You get one Mexican in there, and pretty soon you've got a crew of Mexicans in there. You may as well park a taco truck in the driveway."

"Oh, so that's how it is."

"That's them, understand, the clients," Goble said. "Not me. Don't confuse me with my clients. I'm fine with Mexicans. I just ate at Casa Rojas the other day. And yeah, I know you're Mexican. But not Mexican Mexican. Not that it makes a difference—to me, anyway. Besides, you don't look too Mexican, that's the important thing. As long as you don't grow one of those peach-fuzz mustaches, or start wearing cowboy boots on Saturday night, or listening to salsa really loud, you'll be okay."

I needed Goble to stop talking before I punched him in the throat and fucked up the best opportunity anyone had ever offered me.

"Anyway," he said. "You did nice work out there today, Mike. Really nice work. Welcome to Team Goble."

He raised his beer and I raised mine, at once hopeful and a little heavy of heart, like maybe I just sold part of my soul.

"Goble or go home," he said, and we clinked glasses.

I was still a little conflicted about my new job when I got back to the shed. More precisely, I was conflicted about my new employer. In a way, he was like Chaz: shrewd, self-assured. He knew how to think big. Like Chaz, Goble always had a plan, an angle, an objective. But Goble was different. Whereas Chaz was chasing his dreams and schemes to achieve personal freedom—the freedom to sleep, the freedom to drink at 9:00 a.m., the freedom to be your

own boss, the freedom not to work hard, etcetera—Goble seemed
like he was after something more. You got the feeling Goble didn't
even enjoy his freedom. He filled his free time with more work.
He worried about his weight and complexion. He ironed his jeans.
Quite simply, he strove in a way Chaz didn't strive. Like Chaz, he
extended goodwill, but only if he thought it could help him win.
That was the thing: Goble had to win. Old Chaz knew when he
was beaten. Once they put you in cuffs and chained the door, you
had to shrug your shoulders and start making lemonade. But not
Goble. You got the feeling he would never submit. Whereas Chaz
was bullishly optimistic, even careless in his pursuit of upward mobility, Goble was calculated. And I guess that's what unnerved me.

The Monkey

That hundred bucks from Goble hadn't been in my pocket more than an hour before I texted Remy:

You want to hang out this weekend? Dinner? Beers?

An hour later she replied:

Pizza?

Perfect.

That Friday after work, I drove the Tercel, which nearly quit on me at the junction, and met Remy at Campana's out on Viking Way, where my mom had worked when I was a kid. Still the same decor, the same hot breadsticks, the same stale mints at the cash register. Remy's eye wart didn't seem as prominent in the low light of the bar. She was wearing less makeup, too. Tonight she looked more like the girl I fell for all those months ago at Mitzel's—minus the frumpy work uniform.

"Oh my gosh, what happened to your teeth?" she asked when she noticed.

"Had to get a couple pulled. It's only temporary," I lied.

"Who's your dentist?" she asked. "I need to find a new one. Mirkovich is my guy. He's got fingers like bratwursts, though."

"I don't remember my guy's name," I lied. "He's in Silverdale."

We ordered a pitcher of Silver City pale and a pizza with anchovies, which seemed like a good omen, since nobody ever agreed to anchovies, let alone enthusiastically. We talked pretty easily over breadsticks about movies and Remy's job search and my recent good fortune. The more I got to know her, the more self-assured she seemed, unafraid to speak her mind or say something irreverent. And she was generous with her encouragement.

"You really should write it," she said of my doomed novel. "Just go for it, Mike. Don't overthink it. It'll be great."

"I dunno. Who wants to read a novel about a landscaper, anyway?"

She set one of her hands atop mine and looked me straight in the eye.

"You do," she said.

Chalk it up to nerves, but when we got on the subject of landscaping, I began to wax poetic and maybe carry on a little too long, though Remy seemed impressed through much of it. I pontificated on the attributes of native ground covers, decried the evil of invasive species, held forth on the expediency of the mulching mower, summarized the myriad advantages of the shade garden in the northwestern climate zone.

"Wow," she said. "I wish I were that passionate about my job."

After the leftover pizza was boxed to go, we stayed for another pitcher, during which Remy confessed her dissatisfaction with waitressing, a dissatisfaction I was, of course, well acquainted with.

"What could you do instead?"

"More."

"More of what?"

"Just more. I don't know, that's the problem. Maybe I should go back to school and become a teacher."

"Do you wanna teach?"

"Not really. But at least it has meaning. I feel like I have these qualities, and this energy and this desire, but I can't find the wall to throw any of it at."

"I know the feeling."

I squared the check with my hundred-dollar bill from Goble, leaving an inordinately large tip that was not lost on Remy.

"Your mother taught you well."

And there we were in a parking lot again, leaning against Remy's car, waiting for a cue to proceed.

Remy finally made the move, and we were soon kissing. She tasted of lip balm and anchovies, and her tongue was much more active this time, slithering around in my mouth like a live goldfish. I didn't really know what to do with my hands, until Remy placed them around her waist. We were conjoined for a good five minutes, her hands patrolling my denim-clad butt cheeks without ever straying toward my crotch.

Finally, she pulled away, breathless.

"You wanna come to my place?" she said.

And there it was: the monkey, the burdensome, shameful, flea-bitten pest that had been clinging mercilessly to my back since the dawn of puberty, the one howling ceaselessly in my ears through adolescence and into adulthood, the one Nick continually teased and fed peanuts to, that monkey had just been served to me on a golden platter. How much nagging insecurity and self-doubt, how many flinty, overcooked, indigestible rib eyes and flat sodas had I endured to get to this point? No way was I going blow this.

"Uh, I've actually got a big day tomorrow at work."

"On Saturday?"

"Yeah, I know. The guy I work for is a real dynamo. You've probably seen his realty signs all over town—'Team Goble. Goble or Go Home'? Anyway, he's got all these new properties that he wants me to—"

"I get it," she said.

"You do?"

"Yeah, I do. It's actually kind of sweet."

"It is?"

"Most guys want to move too fast. I think it's nice that you don't want to rush."

"You do?"

"Like I said, your mother taught you well."

She gave me a little peck on the lips and touched my cheek. "You know, we don't have to have sex."

"We don't?"

She smiled mischievously, squeezing my butt and pulling herself into me. "Not right away."

Clubbin' It

The next morning, Goble knocked impatiently on my shed door. Before the door had fully opened, he ducked inside and started sizing the place up, which didn't take him long.

"Mike, you really need some new digs."

"I'm working on it."

"C'mon, let's grab some breakfast. I've got a proposition for you."

He took me to the Agate Pass Café, the new place next to the Tide's Inn. We call it the I Got Cash Café. But since Goble was buying, I had an omelet with salmon and capers in it. I wasn't crazy about the capers, to tell you the truth. Goble had two egg whites and a slice of sprouted-wheat toast.

"Look, Mike," he said, sipping his coffee and patting his lips dry. "I've got a very exclusive job for you. Can you borrow a truck?"

I immediately thought of Dale's truck, then Rocindo's truck.

"Something that looks decent?" Goble added.

I tried unsuccessfully to think of someone else's truck.

"Fine," he said. "I'll borrow one. Hell, maybe I should just buy one. It'd be handy. Look, this is the country club we're talking about. It doesn't get more exclusive. This place has zero turnover. If they do sell, they usually use Sotheby's or one of their own. I had to do several favors to land this listing. And I mean direct favors. Three percent of 6.6 mil—do the math. I'll do it for you: it's a lot. So don't fuck this up, Mike. And I don't mean the yard. I know you're good. But you gotta *look* like a pro for this one. This is one of the most exclusive communities in Washington we're about to infiltrate. They don't want to see For Sale signs in their neighborhood, and they don't wanna see Mexicans, either—Mexican Mexicans, I mean. You're okay, we already went over that. What they really want to see is a whole lot of old white people eating leg of lamb and swinging croquet mallets. But times are tough, even for some of these people."

"Screw those people."

"Shhh," he said. "See, this is what I'm worried about with you. Team Goble has to look like a classy outfit. You've got to suck it up a little and quit with all this grumbling. I'm not asking you to go to Princeton and start wearing a bow tie, but clean up a bit, comb your hair. Go out and buy a pair of coveralls—white, if you can find them. Yeah, white, that's genius. Rich people like stuff that's hard to maintain. I'm going to get you a truck temporarily. But eventually, you're going to have to buy your own. You can't drive around with a lawn mower in the trunk of your Datsun and expect to make a living wage."

"It's a Toyota. So pay me more, and I'll get my own truck. I'll get some white coveralls. I'll get a haircut. I'll get new tools."

He considered me closely for a while—my dark hair, my olive skin, my dark eyes, my missing teeth. "If you don't fuck it up, I'll pay you twenty-five."

"That's too much," I said.

"Make it twenty-four, then."

"Twenty-three," I countered.

"Deal."

"So, what about the other properties?" I said.

"You'll still handle the old ones. But those are still twenty, understand. Not twenty-three."

"Got it."

"Except for Wardwell."

"Wardwell's twenty-three?"

"Wardwell sold."

"Wow, congratulations," I said.

"Twelve grand above asking. You deserve some of the credit, Mike. They really liked the yard."

He reached for his wallet and pulled out a twenty. "Here, put it toward the coveralls."

Monday morning, bright and early, old Mike Muñoz, inveterate profligate and poster boy for the unwashed peasantry, donned his squeaky-clean white coveralls and climbed into a brand-new forest-green Ford F-350, in the bed of which he'd already neatly packed his gear. There was a magnetic sign on each door: TEAM GOBLE. GOBLE OR GO HOME.

I'd never been more alert, more awake to life's possibilities, or more enthusiastic about a day's work, than when I climbed into the cab of that truck. The interior of that beautiful machine smelled like a fresh start. This was the vehicle I would pilot to a brand-new Mike Muñoz. A Mike Muñoz who made nearly twice the money he had previously. I was about to make twenty-three big ones an hour. I was a goddamn king. I doubt my old man ever made half that much.

Before Goble enlightened me, I didn't even know the country club existed. It was located at the very southern tip of the island, where a natural bottleneck separated the community like a peninsula. There's only one old road in and out of the place, and it's private. And yes, there's a security gate. The same families have been living out there or keeping residences there for four or five generations, according to Goble. I recognized some of the names, but I'm not going to use them. It's called discretion, and I'm told I must have it.

So, at twenty-two, old Mike Muñoz finally got his first close-up look at how the other half lived—and by half, I mean .001 percent. This place made most of Bainbridge look like Hansville. It made Truman's place look like a McMansion. The neighborhood was outrageously idyllic, with gently meandering lanes, lined by colonnades of ancient oaks and maples, some of them seven or eight feet in diameter. In the middle of everything lay parklike grounds, punctuated sparsely with old cedars. The grass was old and cropped close like a tennis court, a little piebald in places, but green and neatly uniform.

Predominately old, some of the houses showed signs of tasteful updates. Ivy-clad palaces, hemmed in by boxwood and wrought-iron gates. Not one of them under six thousand square feet, all of them with guest quarters, and each lot had at least two hundred feet of waterfront. The whole development was tidy. Not a scrap of litter. Everything had its place, especially the help. No wonder some of these people would do anything to preserve their way of life. It was spectacular. No Dale, screeching away on his fucking band saw. No blue tarps on the roofs. No broken-down Festivas or busted swamp coolers in the front yards. No dirty-faced kids spoiling their finery. Nobody stealing their lawn mower or bashing in their mailbox. Nobody with brown eyes or calloused hands. No nail salon, no minimart. No blacks, no Mexicans, no Asians, no shanty Irish, no Indians, no kid with a scorpion tattoo on his neck or underfed pit bull or pregnant girlfriend. No Marlin, no Freddy, no Mike, no Nate, no Mom, no Nick. The place was paradise by omission.

Fuck these people, I started thinking. No, no, stop that, I told myself. Team Goble. Follow the money. Be at once ubiquitous and invisible, like a servant. Do your best work, cash your paycheck. Shed your legacy of squalor and dysfunction. Elevate yourself, Mike Muñoz!

Nobody had their addresses displayed, but I recognized my destination by the smaller-than-normal Goble sign out front—tasteful by Goble standards. Forest green. Classy white script. No Goble jack-o'-lantern leer, no slogan, but a sign nonetheless. BY APPOINTMENT ONLY, DOUGLAS GOBLE. The sign was a victory for him, even though nobody besides the residents of the country club would see it, since it was by appointment only and casual browsers couldn't get past the gate.

"Exactly," he had explained at the Agate Pass Café, forking the last of his egg white. "I want them to know I'm coming. I want them to fear me."

The house possessed none of the hokey pretense of the McMansions. Its beauty was effortless. Maybe eight thousand square feet, situated on a high bluff, the structure so well established that it might have been part of the landscape. Here, from these venerable brick walls 150 years ago, the English ivy began its invasion of the western forests, though it looked anything but insidious clinging to the eaves. The sash windows were all ancient, single paned, and perfectly preserved, the roses heirloom, the fruit trees ancient. It was a revelation to me, this place. I'd always associated money with newness. Because, well, new stuff worked. Not like the old crap lying around Dale's yard. Not like the moldering automobiles we parked in our driveways. New meant fresh. It meant things got replaced. It meant reliable. But here, everything was old and yet still working. It was a different kind of reliability. The message seemed clear: This is the way we want to keep things. Have a look around, Mike Muñoz, but don't get too comfortable. You don't belong here.

As I walked the grounds, I saw very little work for myself. Though the boxwood was plentiful, it was already scrupulously maintained. The sprawling lawn was like the rest of the grass in the area, cropped close with a natural edge. The orchard was sporting a year's overgrowth, but it was too early in the season to prune. What was I supposed to do, how was I supposed to busy myself?

Finally, for lack of anything else to do, I retired to the truck for my spanking-new broom and began sweeping the brick walkways. After a while, I was visited by the distinct sensation that someone was watching me, like I was back at Truman's all over again. Once, glancing at the fortress next door, an equally formidable Victorian edifice, I saw an upstairs curtain waver, then a shadowy figure peeking out from behind said curtain. I pictured Miss Havisham or some other waxworks skeleton lurking up there, subsisting on a diet of dust and spiders. It gave me the creeps. So I swept my way farther in the direction of the greenhouse, but the whole time I felt like I had a target on my back. Finally, I swept my way around the far corner of the house, where I was free from observation.

With nothing to occupy myself, I returned to the truck for my rake, figuring I could clean up the rose beds. As soon as I was out front of the house, the eyes were on me again. I could've sworn I'd seen some movement behind the hydrangea next door, maybe fifty yards away. Otherwise, the whole country club was eerily still. The place seemed deserted. No kids shrieking, no dogs barking, no bottle rockets whizzing overhead. No idling diesel delivery trucks. What seemed idyllic a half hour ago felt suddenly haunted.

Shrugging off my uneasiness, I set to work on the rose beds, raking out the debris. I was at it about five minutes, marveling at the fact that for every two and half minutes I worked, I was making a buck, when a voice startled me from my reverie.

"'They would fall as light / As feathers, smelling sweet; and it would be / Like sleeping and like waking, all at once!'"

I turned to find a silver-haired fox about sixty, in wire-rimmed glasses, pink chinos, and a baby-blue polo shirt. His hair was perfect: thick as hell, powder white. Good-looking guy, too, and statuesque. Imagine a third-term senator, with a slight drinker's tan.

"Those autumn damasks came all the way from Europe," he said. "My mother remembers when they put them in the ground. Jud Piggot," he said, extending a hand. "You must be Doug's new lawn boy."

"Yeah. I guess."

He smiled, but I didn't smile back, because I didn't want him to see my teeth.

He looked me up and down like a side of lamb. I couldn't help but straighten up a little in my white coveralls, aware of my scuffed boots.

"What do you think of this old place?" he said.

"It's beautiful."

"Think somebody will buy it?"

"If they can afford it, yeah."

He chuckled like I'd made an inside joke. "Say, when you're all done here, suppose you could come over and take a look at my Cartiers? Fear I've got a touch of black spot."

"Uh, sure. I guess that'd be cool."

"Great. Come around to the side door when you're ready."

He gave a little nod and walked away. The guy had a breezy walk and an altogether breezy manner. Hands in pockets, shoulders loose.

Roses were not my specialty, but I knew my way around them a little bit. Not that I was any expert in black spot, but I had a few ideas about roses based on years of observation. In my experience, most rich people liked to tend their own roses.

Viewed from the outside, Piggot's place was meticulous: a neat wall of laurel, pruned to a vertical face. But inside the perimeter, the place was wild. Out-of-control hydrangeas. Blighted juniper. Rogue lavender. My old nemesis, morning glory, had claimed one of the outbuildings.

I was greeted at the side door by a pair of fat little pugs, snuffling like emphysemics. Persistent little fuckers. One of them started lifting his leg on the cuff of my coveralls, so I gave him a little nudge with my boot. That's when Piggot emerged from the side door.

"Willoughby!" he scolded. "Stop this instant."

The little pug kept at it, nuzzling my ankle.

"Willoughby!"

Piggot's second command unheeded, the other pug scurried for the hedges just as Piggot strode up and gave Willoughby a swift kick in the ass. The little guy squeaked like a rubber toy, but within seconds, he was back at it, panting and wheezing like he was in heat, his tongue darting rapidly in and out of his ridiculous sad-eyed face. You had to admire his spirit.

Finally, Piggot scooped him up and banished him inside.

"Territorial," he explained.

Piggot led me around the old house to the small rose garden, which was the only feature on the grounds, aside from the laurel blockade, that had undergone any recent attempt at cultivation. Still, it was pretty sad. There were four or five varieties, all suffering one malady or another.

"What's the prognosis?" said Piggot.

"That big spruce on the bluff isn't helping your cause."

"I don't follow."

"See how it's starting to lean to the south as it slides down the bluff? It's blocking your sunlight."

"Ah," said Piggot.

"But that's only part of the problem. I don't think you're getting good drainage. This is low ground. Either you've got to do something about that spruce, which is holding up your hillside from the looks of it, or you've got to move the roses somewhere else. That's probably the better option."

"The Cartiers?"

"All of them."

"Will they survive?"

"Maybe. But left here, they're only gonna get worse."

"Listen, Mike. I've got a proposition for you." Piggot was standing a little too close for comfort now. "How would you like to be my official groundskeeper?"

I looked around the place. Certainly, it could use me.

"Well, um, I guess I'd have to ask Doug. I'm supposed to be working next door. I mean, that's what I'm getting paid for."

"Whatever Doug Goble is paying you, add fifteen percent."

I started doing the math. Apparently, Piggot mistook my numeric fumblings for deliberation.

"Make it twenty-five percent," he hastened to add.

Let's see, twenty-three divided by four, plus twenty-three . . .

"Fine, thirty percent," said Piggot, who apparently shared my knack for negotiation. "You don't have to make up your mind right now," he said. "Come out to the party this Friday at the clubhouse, we'll talk more about it. There will be young people there. What do you say?"

Twenty-nine ninety an hour! That was (let's see, thirty, give or take, times forty, give or take, times fifty-two) over sixty grand a year! Holy smokes! What I could do with sixty grand a year! I'd rent my own house. I'd buy unlimited data. Health insurance. Dental.

"Bring your girlfriend," said Piggot.

"I don't have one."

Piggot gave me a wink. "Ah," he said. "Well, come stag, then. Maybe I can introduce you to someone."

A Generous Offer

left the country club feeling guilty. Here I was being offered my
second substantial pay raise in a week, without hardly lifting a
finger, and all I could think was that I'd be screwing over Goble
if I took the job. Okay, Goble is kind of a douche bag—agreed. But
he'd taken me into his confidence, taught me how to improve myself, given me sound professional advice, and bought me a bunch
of beers. Not to mention the great money he was paying me—and
the tips. Plus there was no denying that Goble and I had history,
unresolved though it might have been. How could I turn my back
on him?

All week long, as I worked the other accounts, I was anxious
about the decision. I just didn't have it in me to talk to Goble about
it. If I was going to jump ship on Team Goble, I was going do it in
the most cowardly fashion possible: take the money and cringe.
Hide behind Piggot's laurel hedge every time Goble came to check

on his sign. I told myself Goble would do the same thing, at least the take-the-money part. Heck, he'd relish the opportunity to watch somebody fade to nothing in his rearview mirror. So what was wrong with me? Why was I still a slave to some loyal impulse that never seemed to benefit me? Why did I lack the impetus to get ahead? Christ, it's like I wanted to be broke my whole life. I had to do this, I told myself. I had to suppress my pride, I had to ignore my instincts, I had to look out for number one. I had to play the Goble card and suck up to these wealthy fucks, get them to accept me, admire me even, so that I could move on up the ladder, so that if I ever managed to get a girlfriend or a wife, and we decided to squirt out a few kids, they wouldn't be eating stale saltines in a library somewhere while we slaved away at our evening jobs. You'd think that would be motivation enough for old Mike Muñoz to take a job that could change his life, but, oh no, I continued to wrestle with the proposition.

In addition to the job dilemma, and all its traitorous implications, I was nervous about the party itself. What was I supposed to wear? What was I supposed to say to a bunch of wealthy people with whom I had nothing in common? My conception of a party was dirty jokes around a bonfire, flannel shirts, and Jägerbombs. Canned beer and pretzels. But this was going to be something different, and I wasn't sure what. It should've been exciting, right? If only I could blend in, the way Goble managed to blend in, who knew what opportunities might become available to me. I just had to look and act the part.

Friday afternoon, I spent nearly an hour in front of the mirror trying to look the part. I tried on beige cotton Dockers and the same tie I wore job hunting, but I only looked like a manager at

Starbucks. I tried black slacks and a white dress shirt, but I looked like a busboy. Dockers and white shirt, no tie, I looked like a guy trying to sell you a time-share. Dockers, dark shirt, tie, I looked like a strip-club doorman. Whatever combination I tried, I wound up looking not wealthy. Eventually, my efforts soured me. Fuck this party, I wasn't going. I was gonna stick with Team Goble and quit trying to be something I wasn't.

Fortunately, Freddy talked me down from the ledge.

"That tie is your problem, boy. Look like you goin' to a trade show in Tukwila. Freddy got just the tie for you."

Freddy had a tie, all right. It was midnight blue, about six inches wide, and had a hand-painted naked lady with torpedo tits, playing a harp.

"I can't wear this, Freddy."

"That's art, boy. Hand painted. Wealthy folks love art."

"Thanks, anyway," I said.

I went with the busboy look. If nothing else, I'd blend in with the help.

I thought about inviting Remy, I really did. Maybe she would have been impressed. But what worried me was that seeing me around all those breezy, carefree wealthy people would only make her see me even more for what I was: unbreezy, uncarefree, un-wealthy. The fact that I was driving the Team Goble truck to this clandestine affair and that Goble himself was conspicuously not invited only made me feel guiltier for considering Piggot's proposi-tion. On top of that, I took the magnetic Team Goble signs off both doors, and you can just imagine how Doug would have felt about that. The whole drive there, I was nervous and miserable. Look at me, moonlighting on the guy who gave me the best job of my life.

The guy who towed my car out of the ditch. And it's not like he didn't appreciate me. He called me a genius—twice.

By the time I cleared security and arrived at the country club, I was resenting the place all over again. I parked about a half block down from the clubhouse and made my way toward the festivities with a heavy heart. Drawing nearer, swing music and laughter could be heard wafting on the warm evening air. It was all so goddamn idyllic. And still, I felt like a shitheel. Suddenly I wished I'd gone ahead and invited Remy. Maybe I would have felt more confident with her at my side, maybe coming to this party would have felt like the right decision.

There were a hundred or so people socializing in the clubhouse, an airy and effortlessly elegant structure, with a high ceiling, its bare rafters strung with white Christmas lights. Four or five couples danced before the grandstand, where six old fogies blew brass and woodwinds, while one dude with a shock of white hair was beating the drums and looking like he might have a heart attack.

Piggot stood poised by the bar, looking his breezy self, dressed in peach-colored slacks and a white dress shirt. Standing nearby, a formidable old woman with a proud bearing, wearing a half ton of makeup, patted her sculpted hair.

"Mary, I want you to meet Mike, my new yard man." *Wink wink.*

"Pleased," she said, holding out her palsied hand like she was Queen Victoria.

I wasn't sure if I was supposed to kiss it or what, so I shook it limply, not wanting to crush it.

"Is this the writer?" she inquired.

I looked at Piggot for an explanation.

"Doug enlightened me regarding your literary ambitions," he said.

"You talked to Goble?"

"Indeed, and he told me about your novel."

"Uh, oh yeah." I should have never told Goble I was writing a novel.

"Sounds ambitious," he said.

"My nephew Richard wrote some poetry in college," Mary informed us haughtily. "But nothing published, of course. Have you published?"

"Not yet."

"Oh," she said, averting her eyes and waving curtly at someone across the room.

"Grab yourself a drink, young man," said Piggot.

I moved about ten feet to the bar, delighted to discover the booze was free—cha-ching! Not that I was planning on getting drunk. Not with the company truck. Plus I needed to make a good impression on these people. They didn't have Jäger, so I ordered a beer and a shot of whiskey. They didn't have Old Crow or Wild Turkey or even Jack Daniel's, so I ordered some shit called Bushmills. I tried to tip the bartender, but he told me they weren't allowed to accept tips.

"Why not?"

"Don't get me started," he mumbled.

As I was tossing back my shot, an old sheepdog in a worn tuxedo muscled up next to me at the bar and ordered a scotch. His bow tie was hanging loose. He sported some ruddy cheeks and the shaggiest eyebrows I've ever seen. Tufts of gray hair sprouted from his ears.

"You must be the writer," he said.

"Uh, yeah, I guess."

"Anything published?"

"Not yet."

"Ah, I see," he said, arching a shaggy brow. "You know, my son Richard wrote a little poetry in college. Nothing published, of course. Eventually, he outgrew it."

"I guess there's hope for me," I said.

He considered me briefly, like one might consider a doorless bathroom stall.

"Perhaps," he said, taking his scotch without so much as a nod at the bartender. Then, just like that, the old sheepdog walked off toward the bandstand.

And here I thought wealthy people had good manners.

"That's the guy who hired me," the bartender said, his voice lowered. "Loaded as they come—old logging money or something. He's a real grab-ass. You know all these people are related, right?"

"I didn't know."

"They inbreed so their money stays in the family. Check it out. They all kinda look alike—weak chins, thin lips, wide hips."

To be honest, I hadn't seen the resemblance up until that point, beyond the fact that they were all conspicuously white.

"Don't bother sucking up to them. That's not what they want from you."

"Oh?"

"Me, they want to suck up. But not you."

"What do they want from me?"

"They want you to be yourself. The more yourself you can be, the better. You're an exotic."

"Me? Exotic?"

"Yeah. Catholics, artists, Jews. They get a real kick out of them."

Piggot approached the bar, dragging a young lady with a weak chin and thin lips.

"Mike, I want you to meet Kaitlin. Kaitlin studied English literature at Tufts. I thought you two might find something to talk about."

"Hey," I said.

"Pleased, I'm sure," she said, but only after Piggot gave her a nudge.

No sooner did Piggot plant her at my side than he wandered off again. We stood there uncomfortably for a moment, me and the girl from Tufts, while the bartender withdrew to polish glasses.

"Uncle Jud says you're a writer."

"Yeah, I guess that's kind of the consensus around here."

"Have you published?"

"Not yet. First, I've just got to finish my novel."

"Hmm," she said. You could tell she wasn't convinced. "What is the subject?"

"Landscaping."

"Ah. You should talk to my cousin."

"Is he a landscaper?"

"No. He used to write poetry. He wasn't published, either."

I didn't really know where to go with the conversation, so we stood in silence for a minute longer.

"Well, nice meeting you," she said at last. "Good luck on your publication."

She left me standing there, holding my beer. I drifted off toward the rear of the clubhouse, Piggot patting my back on the way past.

"Enjoying yourself, young man?"

"Yessir."

"Good, good," he said, turning his back on me again.

God, I wanted to get out of there. I didn't like being exotic. I weaved my way through the party toward the back patio to get some fresh air. There, I found a wrought-iron chair in the shadows and nursed my beer along, with half a mind to flee the country club altogether. These people were reptiles. The more I thought about taking the job, the more I appreciated Team Goble. At least Goble believed in some kind of racial equity, some kind of upward mobility. These people wanted to live in stasis, swilling gin and congratulating themselves for doing nothing.

It took me a couple minutes to realize I wasn't alone in the shadows.

"You must be the writer."

I turned to find a skinny guy in a rumpled seersucker jacket and bow tie, slumped in a chair behind me. He had a weak chin and thin lips—unmistakably one of them.

"Richard Freeman," he slurred. "Call me Richie."

"Mike," I said.

"You know, I fancied myself a poet once. Back at Yale. Too many years ago to count. Of course, I never published anything."

"I heard."

"Of course you did. They're supportive in their way. Financially, I mean."

"Do you still write?"

"Gads, no."

"Why not?"

"What's the use? I was never any good. Everything I wrote was derivative. Nothing unique to write about, no noble instincts to draw upon. Never did anything of any real benefit to the world, or even myself. Started on third base and still couldn't score. I suppose I must seem like a tragic—*hic*—figure to you."

"Not really."

"Well, I am. You're looking at an unmitigated failure. I've foiled expectation at every turn. I've done nothing to distinguish myself, nothing on the strength of my own character. I'm a walking disappointment—to myself, to my family, to the world at large."

"Take it easy, dude. Seems like you're doing okay to me."

"Yes, but you're not a failure."

"I'm not?"

"You're here, aren't you?"

"So are you."

"Yes, but on different terms."

"I don't see how being here makes me a success. Couple of free drinks, a few pats on the back. It's not like I've published anything."

"Yes, but already you're exceeding anybody's expectation of you, am I right?"

He was right, of course. The bar was set pretty low for old Mike Muñoz.

"I see you two have met," came Piggot's voice. "Now it's a bona fide literary roundtable."

"*Hic*," said Richie.

"Sorry to interrupt," said Piggot.

"Are you?" said Richie.

Piggot ignored him and sat down beside me. "So, have you thought about my proposition?"

"Yessir. I've thought a lot about it."

"And?"

"And I'm just not sure."

"It's thirty percent more money."

"It's a generous offer, sir. And I like the yard—er, the grounds, I mean. There's a lot of work to be done. We could save those roses. We could maybe even save that bluff with a little help. It's just that . . ."

"Yes?"

"I just don't think I can do it, sir. As much as I appreciate the opportunity. I'm pretty happy where I am right now. I wouldn't want to—"

"Take the—*hic*—money," said Richie.

Piggot patted me on the shoulder and smiled knowingly. "C'mon, let's get you a drink."

The Art of Favoring

'll admit to feeling pretty proud of myself for doing the right thing, I mean by passing up Piggot's job offer. With the dilemma resolved, I didn't see the harm in telling Goble. In fact, I saw a distinct advantage in demonstrating my loyalty to Team Goble. Maybe he'd bump me up to $23.50.

So Monday, before reporting to the Baker Hill property, I met Goble at Starbucks and told him about the offer and that I'd turned it down.

"You what? Why the hell would you do that?"

"I would have never been in the position for the opportunity if it weren't for you."

"And?"

"Well, I didn't want to screw you over."

He ran his hands over his face. "Mike, do me a favor?"

"Direct or indirect?"

"What I mean is, do yourself a favor."

"Don't think I haven't tried."

"No, really, Mike. I'm not joking here. Look out for *número uno,* *¿comprendes?* Just this once. I know you've got people, your re-tarded brother and that black dude and whoever. But that job will pay way more. That would be helpful, no?"

"He's not actually retarded."

"I meant retarded in a good way. Look, I appreciate your loyalty. But you better take this job, or I'm going to fire you. I don't want to pay you twenty-three bucks an hour."

"Uh, okay."

"Good," he said. "It's settled, we're in. Now, I need you to keep your ears open and your eyes open. Mouth shut. Don't talk—that won't help anybody. Just listen when they talk among themselves. If anybody starts talking about selling, I want to know. And by anybody, I especially mean Piggot."

"Okay," I said.

He searched deep in my brown eyes again and apparently saw no light there.

"Look, I wanna turn that neighborhood over. I wanna bring the country club up to date, so to speak. And I'm not talking about closeted gay ex-professors or reprobate judges. The clubbers love that stuff—that's as close as they get to interesting. I'm talking about X people, self-made types: athletes, entertainers, rich people of color. I've got a potential black buyer, and that could really stir things up. A Seahawk. One felony arrest, couple of misdemeanors, but otherwise a good family man. I wanna get this guy and his family in there."

"That's cool. So I just . . . ?"

"You do recon. How do you think you got the job offer? I need some eyes and ears out there."

"Wait, you got me the job offer?"

"Get me a listing, and I'll give you the truck, Mike—outright."

"How can I get you a listing?"

"Just be yourself—except don't talk."

"Okay. But who would I be ta—"

"Don't talk."

"Got it. I'm just ask—"

"Stop talking."

"Right, I understand. But what—"

"No, really. Stop talking."

"You mean now?"

"Yes." He rubbed his temples. "Sorry, I think I'm dehydrated. Your voice grates on me sometimes. No offense."

"Here, drink some water."

"I'm trying to lose weight."

"But you're skinny."

"Says you."

"No, really, dude, you're skinny."

"Please stop talking for a minute."

He continued to knead his forehead and temples, jaw clenched. I tried not to talk, but I couldn't help myself. I was still putting things together.

"So, wait. When you told me I should take the job because I should look out for myself, you really meant I should take the job so I could look out for you? Like literally?"

He grimaced through his headache. "Yeah, well, both. Look, you can talk some. Just stick to gardening and the writer shtick, they like that. Piggot especially. Just don't make it sound like you're writing some kind of manifesto. Tell them you're writing about horses."

"What about the truck?"

"You continue to make the payments until you get me a listing."

"Will it be mine?"

"No. You'll just be making the payments."

"To the dealership?"

"To me. I'll need five hundred up front for a deposit."

"But I'm not really sure if I can swing five hu—"

"Trust me," he said. "You need the truck. How else are you gonna haul all your equipment back and forth? You think they're gonna let you into the country club in that Datsun?"

There was no getting around it. "Okay, fine," I said.

"I'll also need the first payment of three hundred."

"Doug, that's eight hundred bucks. I haven't got it."

"Fine, I'll take it out of your last paycheck. But whatever you do, don't take the signs off the doors ever again."

"You know about that?"

"I know a lot of things."

"But I won't be Team Goble anymore."

"Sure you will."

"How? You're not paying me. You're just renting me a truck."

"I got you the job, right?"

"Well, yeah."

"That's four favors you owe me."

What Are You Trying to Prove?

Turns out, the five-hundred-dollar deposit just about cleaned me out. But I figured with all the money Piggot would be paying me, I'd be able to build my savings back up in no time. Twenty-nine ninety an hour! What was a three-hundred-dollar-a-month truck payment next to sixty grand a year? Think of the things I'd be able to do with that kind of money! I could move out and still help my mom with the rent. I could take everybody on vacation next summer. We could rent a cabin on the beach somewhere. I could buy my mom a decent car. As much of a dickhead as Goble was, I was grateful to the guy for getting me this gig. And to think I almost passed it up.

Sunday night, I texted Remy:

Hope you're good. We still need to have that beer!

A few hours later, she texted me back:

Long time no hear.

Been stupid busy. New job. How about that beer?

Pretty busy with a new job myself. But maybe soon.

On Monday morning, I suited up in my white coveralls and drove out to the country club, my intent being to tell Piggot that I'd changed my mind about the job. Recognizing the truck, they let me through at the gate. I parked in front of Piggot's and rang the bell. I waited about thirty seconds, listening to the dogs wheeze and skitter around in the foyer. I was about to start poking around the side yard, when the door opened a crack and one of the pugs wiggled out and started customarily snuffling all around the cuff of my coveralls.

"Willoughby! Down!"

The pug ignored Piggot's command. Just as the little fucker was mounting my ankle, Piggot gave him a kick, and this time he scurried off under the hedges.

"What brings you back here, Mike?"

"Well, sir, after further consideration, I've decided to take you up on your job offer."

"Oh, that," said Piggot. "Unfortunately, I'm afraid I can't extend that offer at this point in the game."

My heart sank. He must've have found somebody else. This is what happens when opportunity knocks and you hide in the bathroom.

"What I can offer you is fifteen dollars an hour."

"But sir, that's—"

"Yes, twenty-five percent less than what you were making for Mr. Goble, I realize that. He called me yesterday with the recommendation."

"But you said—"

"Circumstances have changed, young man. You already had a

job when I was courting you, did you not? Having discussed the matter with Mr. Goble, I'm given to understand that he can no longer afford your employ and that you're currently in need of a position. He suggested fifteen dollars would suffice."

"So, wait, you talked to Doug?"

"As I said, he called to recommend you."

"And he told you to pay me less?"

"He made a recommendation."

"That fucker," I said.

You see how it is, people? The money grubbers of the world will collude and conspire, and they'll stop at nothing to keep you down. They'll trade your sorry ass like a commodity, then laugh about it over cigars. So get ready for that ride downriver.

"Do we have a deal?" said Piggot, extending a hand.

"This is bullshit," I said, hating my white coveralls.

"Be that as it may, in light of all this, I'd say fifteen dollars an hour is a nice offer. So, what do you say?"

"Sixteen-fifty," I said.

"Fourteen," countered Piggot.

I could see where this negotiation was leading. Part of me wanted to turn and walk away.

"Okay, fine," I said, shaking his hand.

Within the hour, I was clearing a spot on the bluff for the roses. But believe me, I wasn't happy about it. Piggot donned a pair of navy-blue duck boots, as though he planned on working side by side with me. But he didn't lift a finger. He only watched, always standing a little too close for my liking.

"I taught English for eight years at the university level," he informed me. "Bet you didn't know that."

"No, I didn't."

"As a matter of fact, I'm still on the board of directors at a certain prestigious university press."

"Congratulations," I said. "Could you please move?"

To my surprise, Piggot didn't object to my tone, or didn't notice. I couldn't help it, I was irritated. Yes, fourteen bucks an hour was more than I was making with Lacy back when, but I felt cheated. It was considerably less than I was making yesterday. Fourteen bucks an hour left no room for my big plans. No beach cabins, no new cars for my mom. I'd be damned if I was going to suck up to Piggot for fourteen bucks an hour.

"I could be quite helpful, you know," said Piggot from my back pocket.

"Then how about grabbing a wheelbarrow?"

"In your bid for publication, I mean. I have influence. God knows, you don't want to end up like Richard."

"Filthy rich and drunk? Sounds okay to me."

Piggot smiled at that one. I think he liked me at fourteen bucks an hour.

"How about using your influence to pay me what you offered me in the first place?"

That one got a full-fledged chuckle out of him.

I couldn't see what he was driving at with all this influence stuff, anyway. I really didn't want to hear it. Anyway, how could he help me publish? I didn't have anything to publish. The Great American Landscaping Novel was a Great American Joke. I had exactly eleven pages of overwrought, steaming dung. It was worse than the MFA crap I'd checked out at the library—at least they could write sentences.

I had no business transplanting those roses in September, but they were struggling and who knew what they'd look like come winter. I probably should have watered them for about a week first, and if I were making $29.90 per hour, like I should've been, I would have insisted on it. I would've pruned them back a week before I moved them, too. But I was only making half that, so fuck protocol. I dug each bush out to a depth of a foot and a half and moved them over to the bluff, four at a time in the wheelbarrow. I should have amended the soil, but that, too, seemed like a lot of effort for fourteen bucks an hour. At this point, I didn't care if they lived or died.

Piggot followed me breezily back and forth from the bluff, hands in pocket, twice stepping on my heel. Now and then reciting a line of poetry. Every time I stooped to plant one of the Cartiers, he stood right over me, blocking the sunlight. It wasn't until he started beating around the bush about the place next door that I recalled Goble's directive to gather recon—the real reason I landed this job, the one Goble forced me to take, negotiating the terms without my consent. I wasn't exactly in a hurry to do any favors for Goble, since the guy sold me out to the tune of a 50 percent wage cut, but I have to admit I liked the idea of a black guy moving in next door. That stuffy old neighborhood needed a shaking up. An All-Pro defensive back with a criminal record might be just the ticket. I hope the guy drove a ghastly green Humvee limo emblazoned with a silver Seahawk and a vanity plate that said CAN'T TOUCH THIS or U MAD BRO. I hope he parked it right out front where everybody had to look at it.

"I understand your friend Mr. Goble will be showing the Swanstrom estate next Thursday."

I remembered Goble's other directive: don't talk. But fourteen bucks an hour didn't seem like much incentive for silence.

"He's not really my friend," I said. "And yeah, he's gonna show it."

"What do you know about this football player?"

"I know he had six interceptions last year."

"That's good?"

"Yeah, that's good."

"I understand he's had some character issues."

"Yeah, he punched a cop. But that was years ago, back when he was at Stanford."

"Stanford. Hmph," he said disparagingly.

"And who knows," I said. "The cop probably deserved it if he was anything like the cops I know."

Even as we were discussing it, through the laurel hedge I saw Goble roll up in his convertible and pull in next door, where he immediately hopped out of his car and started fussing with his sign.

"I don't like it," said Piggot. "This is a well-established neighborhood. These families go back generations."

"Don't all families go back generations?"

"Not like these families."

"So, what's wrong?" I said, hefting a rosebush out of the wheelbarrow. "You don't want a black neighbor?"

"It has nothing to do with being black. I haven't got a thing against people of color. This is about a time-honored standard. This is about legacy. You can't just move into this community because you've got a little money. It's not about money."

"You ever think of moving?"

"Why should I move? My family has been here for over a hundred years. We settled this island."

"Before you, it belonged to the Suquamish tribe. They used it as a hunting ground."

"Not anymore," said Piggot.

I kept expecting Goble to make an appearance, but he stayed next door, looking over the place, picking up stray leaves, dusting ledges, admiring his sign, and snapping pictures from different vantages. At one point, Piggot tiptoed over and peered through the laurel to see what Goble was up to.

"Frankly," he said upon his return, "I don't see what makes your friend think this football player will even want to live here. Especially not in that drafty old house."

"Maybe not," I said, mounding soil around one of the Cartiers.

"I can't imagine he'd be comfortable with the arrangement. He'd feel like an outsider—he'd have to. Why would he want to move here? I thought they all lived on the Eastside."

"Black people?"

"The players."

"Maybe he likes the view."

"Hmph," said Piggot. "Of course he does. But you'd think he'd want something a little more garish, wouldn't he?"

Something I've observed about rich people: when they pay you, they assume they're buying your confidence, even when they're getting you at a discount. They expect you to agree with them.

"Beats me," I said.

Piggot straightened himself up and, for the first time all day, reached for the shovel.

"We'll just see about this," he said.

The next hour was the only time I'd seen Piggot attempt anything resembling work. And he wasn't very good at it, severing
roots with the blade of his shovel, toppling the wheelbarrow, and
generally getting in the way. He managed to get his hands dirty, all
right, but otherwise he was more of an obstacle than he was a help.
By the time I broke for lunch, Piggot had worn my patience to the
ragged edge. I needed to get away from him for a while, so I walked
out to the truck, where Goble was sitting in the cab waiting for me.

"So?"

"So, what?"

"You got anything for me yet?"

"No," I said, wishing I had a lunch. "And by the way, I'm only
making fourteen an hour."

"Yeah, sorry about that. I recommended fifteen. So, you've got
nothing for me?"

"He doesn't know shit about football, how's that?"

"Is he scared?"

"How should I know?"

"Did he say anything about the sign?"

"No."

"Are they circling the wagons?"

"Fuck, I don't know. I just want a sandwich."

"Mike, listen to me: if we can spread fear, we can bust this
neighborhood wide open. We could clear huge dollars."

"That's you, man, that's not me. I just want a sandwich. Personally, I'd like to bomb this neighborhood."

"Shhh. Jesus, Mike, don't blow this."

Maybe I was just hungry, maybe my blood sugar was low. Certainly, I was disgruntled. Two hours in the company of Piggot, at

fourteen per hour, had simply exhausted my goodwill. Something in me snapped—my tolerance, I guess. Suddenly I didn't give a shit about the world in which I'd found myself hopelessly enmeshed, through no fault of my own. I didn't care about the money or the truck or what happened to anybody involved. I just wanted to go back to Suquamish and read a book and eat a sandwich.

"I'm out of here," I said, firing up the truck.

"What, you're taking lunch?" said Goble, checking his watch.

"That, too."

"Good, we can talk strategy. Leave the truck, so they have to look at my signage. We'll take my car."

"Get out," I said.

"I'll drop you back after lunch."

"Out."

"What's got into you, Mike?"

"I'm not coming back, Doug. My work is done here."

He checked his watch again. "But it's only noon."

"I'm quitting."

"You can't quit, Mike."

"Watch me."

"But you still owe me."

"Out of the truck, Doug."

"You can't take this truck. It belongs to me."

"Then give me my five hundred bucks."

"That was a deposit. To protect myself from a situation exactly like this one, Mike."

I started pulling out of the driveway.

"Stop the truck, Mike, I mean it."

I stopped with a lurch. In the rearview mirror, I caught a

glimpse of Piggot prairie-dogging behind the Japanese holly. Fucking weirdo.

Goble leveled a meaningful gaze at me. "You're not taking this truck."

"Give me my five hundred bucks."

"The truck belongs to me, Mike. You'd be stealing it."

"Fine," I said, swinging my door open and stepping out of the cab.

"What are you doing?"

"I'm not taking the truck."

"Well, who's going to drive it back to town?"

"Fuck if I know. But if I don't see my five hundred bucks by the end of the week, I'm gonna tell anyone who will listen about how you put a dick in your mouth."

"Jesus, what the hell are you talking about? Get back in the truck."

I made a little cock-sucking gesture and turned so Piggot could see it from behind the holly.

"Get back in the truck! You're making a scene."

"It was your idea, Doug. Remember? Out behind the parsonage."

"Jesus, Mike, you're seriously losing it here."

"Let's talk about favors, Goble. Let's talk about me putting your dick in my—"

"Stop!" he hollered, reaching for his wallet. He started rifling through bills. "I've only got one eighty here."

I grabbed for the cash.

"I'll get you the rest next month," he said.

I narrowed my eyes menacingly and shook my head.

"Ugh, fine," he conceded.

I followed Goble directly to the cash machine and collected my three hundred twenty bucks. It killed him to part with it, believe me. Then I followed him to his condo and parked the truck, lingering in the cab in wistful silence for a moment. What was I giving up here? Sure, it was only fourteen bucks an hour, but it was bound to go up if Piggot wanted to keep me. And losing the truck, that hurt. After months of limited transportation, months of schlepping around Kitsap County on the shame train, I hated giving up that truck. But I had to. It was an imperative. I couldn't be around Goble or Piggot anymore. Goble wore too many faces, and Piggot probably collected Nazi paraphernalia. I'm telling you, Tino and his cousins never looked so good.

When I finally got out of the truck, Goble was waiting for me, and I handed over the keys.

"Mike, what are you trying to prove here?"

"I just wanna mow lawns and prune shit, dude. I don't want to be your secret agent. I don't like that place. And I don't like Piggot standing so close to me all the time. The guy's got no boundaries. Next thing you know, he'll be expecting me to walk his dogs and go to the dump for him. You want me, hire me back. I'll do your properties."

"Can't do it, Mike. It's coming on fall. Most of the gardening stuff takes care of itself. I'll hire a Mexican with a leaf blower for ten bucks an hour. Unless you wanna do it for ten bucks an hour . . . ?"

"Fuck you."

"I didn't mean it as an insult. It's just the reality, Mike."

The smug little fucker. The sad thing is, it actually hurt my feelings. I really thought I had value in Goble's eyes.

"It was your idea behind the parsonage," I said.

"What are you talking about?"

"You know exactly what I'm talking about."

"No, Mike, I have no idea what you're talking about."

"I'm talking about youth group."

Goble checked his watch, then pulled out his cell and checked that, too.

"Youth group? You mean with the Bible songs and the crackers? What the hell? You're fucking crazy, Mike. Good luck," he said, without looking up. "Nice job on the Wardwell place."

"Why won't you admit we sucked each other's dicks?"

He looked up from his phone. "Excuse me?"

"You heard me. Why won't you just acknowledge it?"

"Mike, you're talking nonsense. Did you forget to take your meds or something? Look, I gotta run. I'm doing an open house at one thirty."

"Wow," I said. "You are really in denial."

"I don't think so, Mike. But you may want see a psychiatrist."

The fucking nerve of the guy! I wanted to punch him in the throat! How could he look me in the eye and just flat-out deny something we both knew was true?

"You hatched the plan, Goble, and you know it. You lured me behind the parsonage. We talked about girls. We shared a Hershey's bar. Then you showed me your dick."

"Whoa. What the hell are you talking about?"

"The next thing I know, it's in my mouth."

"Are you high?"

"I can't believe you, Goble! Dude, you're insane. We sucked each other's dicks, and you're pretending it didn't happen."

"Have a nice life, Mike," he said, repocketing his phone.

And just like that, he turned and started walking toward his condo.

"You're the one who needs a psychiatrist!" I yelled, practically foaming at the mouth. "You're fucking crazy!"

He didn't even look back, the cold-blooded little prick. That's when I realized what I should have realized years ago: that there were people in this world who either had no conscience or just severe memory deficits, tailored to their convenience. I could see the advantage of either one immediately. Yet both ideas were abhorrent to me. Either you didn't care, or you chose not to care. The way I see it, you've got to be accountable, or you're nothing. Without personal accountability, you can talk yourself into anything. You can leave rubble in your wake and never look back. That could mean wars. Genocides. Ecological disasters. And what for? What was the advantage?

Fuck those guys, and their money and their power.

It was starting to sprinkle, and a wave of futility washed over me.

"Hey, wait!" I yelled after him, the logistics of my situation suddenly dawning on me. "What about my gear? You gotta drive me to my house!"

"Yeah, sorry," he said. "Gotta freshen up for my open house. Good luck."

The rain was picking up force, starting to blow in slantwise.

"This is bullshit!" I hollered. "You sucked my dick, you crazy fuck!"

Goble just kept walking. A little old lady on the second floor opened her window and peered out to see what all the shouting was about.

"Your neighbor Doug Goble likes to suck dick!" I yelled up to her. "And he doesn't want anyone to know about it!"

Doug stopped his forward progress just long enough to give the old lady a little wave and a bemused shrug before she shut the window and abruptly lowered the blinds.

A Good Place to Start

Over the next week, I tried to be as invisible as possible on the home front. I started avoiding the house, mostly for the sake of everybody else, so I wasn't using hot water or electricity, or eating other people's food out of the refrigerator, or even taking up space. I must have lost five pounds that first week. When I wasn't out fruitlessly submitting résumés—Safeway, Central Market, even Walmart—I found a warm place to sit and read, the only place where nobody gave me the stink eye about loitering.

One day at checkout, I got in Andrew's line, even though it was longer than the other one. As usual, his thick, curly hair was all over the place. Bald guys must hate him. He was wearing one of his cardigan sweaters, a bile-colored affair, and a T-shirt that said COEXIST. The instant he opened his mouth I was confronted with a gleaming mouthful of braces—the big clunky kind that looked like you might get radio reception on them, the kind that always seemed to be digging into tender flesh. Normally a guy would look like a mouth breather or a dweeb with that much metal in his mouth. But Andrew didn't appear to be self-conscious about it.

"Michael!" He sounded genuinely happy to see me. "I see you're reading *Timbuktu*. I love that book."

"Yeah, you recommended it."

"I did, didn't I?"

We talked for a minute about books, me looking back over my shoulder every ten seconds to make sure I wasn't holding up the line.

"So, what do you do for work, anyway?"

"Look for it, mostly," I said.

"What are you doing at three?"

"Nothing."

"You wanna occupy Walmart?"

"What, you mean like buy stuff?"

"No, I mean picket."

"Picket what?"

"Pfff. Where to begin? No paid rest, no meal breaks. Inhuman wages. Sexual discrimination, urban encroachment, union busting. Don't even get me started on sweatshops."

I didn't have the guts to tell him about the job application I'd submitted to Walmart not two hours earlier. But what was there to lose? Let's face it, I probably wouldn't get the job, anyway. And deep down, desperate as I was, I didn't really want to work at Walmart.

"Sure, I'm in."

"Great," he said. "Come back at three."

I didn't have anywhere to be, so I just waited at the library, scanning the fiction section aimlessly. At three o'clock, when Andrew's shift ended, he led me briskly and purposefully from the library and across the parking lot.

"Hop in," he said.

His red Subaru was old but scrupulously maintained. Not a speck of dust on the dash. No dog hair on the seats. No errant coffee cups or empty Burger King bags. In the backseat, a bunch of hand-drawn picket signs were stacked neatly alongside a pair of walkie-talkies, some yellow rope, a case of bottled water, and a Kinkos bag full of fliers.

"Ever occupied before?" he said as we swung onto the highway.

"No."

"Well, this is a good place to start."

I'd heard the talk about Walmart and its shady business practices. I'm not oblivious. I remember all the hemming and hawing when they moved into town, back when I was in high school. How they were gonna put everybody out of business with their aggressively low pricing. And, well, they did, pretty much. Coast to Coast Hardware, Schuck's Auto Supply, Payless—they all went belly up within two years. But the truth is, I shop at Walmart quite a bit. It's got a way of stretching your money—and when you don't have much to work with, inexpensive is a very attractive quality. Two bucks for a block of cheese? Get out of here! Ramen at six for a dollar? That's what I'm saying. And that's why everybody I know shops at Walmart.

But to hear Andrew tell it, Walmart was the evil overload, victimizing poor people by selling them cheap stuff. And I have to admit, he was pretty persuasive.

"The problem, as I see it," he said, "is that a lot of people, and not just poor people, equate value with savings—like the two are synonymous. That value is measured in savings is a tenet of consumerism. It's shoved down our throats. People forget what real value is. Money is not the only measure of value. What about quality of life? What about community? These things are more fundamental to our happiness than saving a buck."

One eye on the road, he proceeded to explain how the value we equate with savings is only an illusion.

"Take a can of spray paint," he said. "Say there was a hardware store next door—not that one could actually survive next door to Walmart, but just for the sake of argument. We'll call it Richard's Hardware."

"Dick's," I said.

"Okay, Dick's. Let's say Dick's and Walmart were selling the same can of spray paint."

"What color?"

"Does it matter?"

"I guess not. But still, it helps me imagine the scenario."

"Okay, black. The same can of black spray paint. Dick's Hardware is selling it for three bucks."

"Two ninety-nine," I said. "They always get you with the nines."

"Let's just call it three, for the sake of argument," he said, the slightest hint of impatience creeping into his tone. "Three bucks is reasonable. The markup is fair—not a rip-off at all."

"Yeah, but you could probably get it for one ninety-nine at Walmart," I said.

"I'm getting to that," he said briskly. "The point is, the value doesn't end there, with the savings. Let's follow the exchange further. What happens to that extra buck? Well, for starters, Dick sponsors a Little League team. He's also in the Kiwanis. Turns out, he votes for school levies. He has three kids that go to school with your kids. He lives right down the street from you, as a matter of fact. Once, he found your freaked-out beagle in a thunderstorm and brought it back to you. Dick shops local, he buys Girl Scout cookies, and he pays his employees a fair wage."

"He sounds awesome."

"He is awesome. But even if he's not, the point is that the extra buck goes right back into the community. It keeps your sidewalks clean and your boulevards narrow. Do you want to live in a world of wide boulevards, no sidewalks, and nothing but box stores on all sides? A world where nobody walks? A world where one percent of the population accounts for eighty-five percent of the wealth?"

"Hell no."

"Well, that's why we're doing this."

Andrew made it sound like we were about to save the world. Like we were being the change we wanted. I didn't need any more excuses to stick it to the man, believe me. Here was an opportunity to stand up and make a difference. And all I had to do was occupy space. I could do that.

Occupying Space

When we arrived at Walmart, there were seven or eight young guys, mostly with beards, and one middle-aged lady in sweatpants, loitering out front. A scruffy bunch, all told, signs dangling limply at their sides. One guy was texting. Another guy was holding a boom box. The lady in sweats was smoking a cigarette and talking on her cell phone. Surely a lone blast of pepper spray would end this flagging occupation and send this group of protesters scurrying like roaches. Immediately I could see that what this protest needed was a Goble-type personality to buoy them. Somebody to go around yelling, "Get those signs up!" Somebody with a vision. Somebody who could motivate and galvanize and all that. A politician, I guess. And so I took it upon myself, the best way I knew how.

"Shouldn't they be holding those signs up a little?" I whispered. "You know, so people can read them?"

"Excellent point. Let's get those signs up, brothers and sisters!" Andrew announced.

Up came the signs: POVERTY WAGES! STOP THE WAR ON WORK-ERS! One kid named Moses looked really stoned. He was wearing a beanie and held a sign that said STANDING FOR OUR JOBS!

"So, does he mean 'Standing *Up* for Our Jobs'?" I asked.

"I'm not sure," Andrew said. "I guess."

"Do any of these people work here?"

"No."

"They used to work here?"

"Not that I know of."

"None of them?"

"The people who work here can't afford to protest, Mike. They're too busy occupying their checkout stands or bagging your off-brand Doritos. They don't even get breaks or lunches. We're here as their advocates."

He made it sound noble, standing around in a Walmart parking lot. At least I was finally doing something besides complaining about the system. I was actively striving to effect change. I was advocating. I was standing up and saying, "I'm not gonna take it anymore!" Or, more precisely, "*He's* not gonna take it anymore!" In my small way, I was helping bring down the man or, at the very least, obstructing his progress.

And yeah, it felt pretty good.

One thing I learned in the Walmart parking lot was, hold a picket sign and nobody wants to go anywhere near you. They're afraid you're going to try and recruit them or make them sign a petition, when all they want is some cheap laundry detergent and a two-liter bottle of Mountain Dew.

I whispered other suggestions to Andrew: Maybe we should spread out a little. Maybe the lady in sweats should quit smoking. Tell Moses to spell-check his signs next time. Maybe we need a chant. I was proving to be quite the field marshal. And Andrew saw to it that each and every one of my suggestions was implemented, except for the chant. We never thought of a good one.

If I was a little reticent to fully embrace my new revolutionary persona, it's only because Poulsbo is so small. Even when you figure in Kingston and Suquamish and Indianola, and all the unincorporated areas, you're not dealing with that many people. I routinely recognize faces at stoplights. Or standing in line at the DMV. Or strolling the aisles at Walmart. I suspected it was only a matter of time before I started running into people I knew: Nate's physical therapist, my middle-school gym teacher, maybe even Remy.

And sure enough, around four thirty, as I was standing there holding my #1 IN EMPLOYEES NEEDING MEDICAID AND FOOD STAMPS sign, absorbing dirty looks from the morbidly obese and bitterly diabetic, not to mention a few hot soccer moms, I heard the unmistakable cadence of white-boy rap and its attending thump, and I spotted a familiar purple blur with spinning LED rims, cruising briskly past Home Depot toward Walmart.

I suppose I could've dodged Nick, though I'm pretty sure he spotted me. I'll be honest, it took some wind out of my revolutionary sails. How was I supposed to convince people to change their ways when I was inextricably bound to my own? How was I supposed to change the world when my best friend acted like such a dick most of the time?

Nick was wearing his twelfth-man jersey, and a Les Schwab cap, his goatee neatly trimmed. His eyes looked a little bloodshot, and he was already trailing a fog of Jäger, so he must have got off work early.

"What the hell are you doing here?" he said.

"What does it look like I'm doing?"

"It looks like you're just standing there."

"Exactly. That's what occupying is, Nick. You stand."

"Occupying, huh? Gotcha. Looks like a bunch of Girl Scouts standing out front— but without the fucking cookies. Try occupying a job for a while, dude. I ran into Freddy at the Masi. He said you still haven't found a job."

"It's only been a week."

"I can't believe you're still living with your mom, bro."

"Shhh," I said.

"So, who's this," Nick said, acknowledging Andrew with a nod. "Your new boyfriend?"

I cast my eyes down. "Nick, Andrew. Andrew, Nick," I mumbled.

Andrew stepped forward winningly and extended a hand, smiling so that his mouthful of braces were shining in all their glory for Nick.

Nick winced and shot me a look when Andrew released his grip.

"Go Hawks," said Andrew.

"Yeah, whatever you say."

Nick opened and closed his hand a few times like he was trying to regain some feeling in it.

"So, they payin' you to protest? Payin' your rent in slogans now, is that it?"

Why did he have to be that way? Why all the bravado, the constant razzing, the persistent alpha-male hectoring?

"Hey, so what's with the auto-picks on fantasy last week? You fucking benched Matty Ice, bro. Guy threw for like four hundred fifty yards. You've got to get on the ball, man. Whitehead is killing everybody already."

"I've been busy."

"I can see that."

"We gotta hang out, man. You're like off the radar lately. You want to watch the game Sunday?"

"Maybe."

"Maybe, he says," said Nick. "Pretty weak. Whatever you do, don't bench Matty Ice again. And why the hell did you pick up Eddie Lacy?"

"Just a hunch."

"His ankle is toast. Anyway, I've gotta buy some shit. Have fun with your little protest," he said, pleased with himself as he sauntered off toward the entrance.

"Who was that?" said Andrew.

"Some jerk I went to high school with."

"Nice guy," he said.

"Yeah, he's a prince."

Nick was right, unfortunately: our protest was a flop. Nobody wanted an informational flier summarizing the insidious business practices of Walmart, except for one guy in rubber boots and a bicycle helmet covered with bumper stickers. Seemed like maybe he'd started wearing the helmet a little too late, if you know what I mean. And while it's true that a few people paused long enough to read my sign, none of them seemed to comprehend it. The guy with the bike helmet bought Andrew and me a jumbo dog with sauerkraut, which was thoughtful and also sort of surprising, since he looked like he was homeless. I didn't eat mine. I'd like to say that I didn't eat it on principle, but the truth is, I couldn't stop thinking about *The Jungle.* Even though Andrew usually didn't eat red meat or support Walmart, I couldn't blame him for inhaling his, being that he came straight from work and hadn't eaten since lunch. So I wasn't about to deprive him his nourishment by saying anything about the working conditions in meatpacking plants.

Before long, our numbers began to dwindle. Moses had to pick up his girlfriend from work. The lady in the sweats had to split at five fifteen, but not before she ducked into Walmart for a carton of smokes. Around five thirty, I spotted Tino and two sleepy-eyed companions I didn't recognize in the northeast corner of the lot, spilling out of Tino's beater van.

"You work here now, *ese*?"

"I'm protesting."

"Yeah, but do you work here? You get any kind of discount?"

"I don't work here. I told you, I'm protesting."

"They fire you?"

"No. I've never worked here."

"So why you protesting, then?"

"Because," I said. "Walmart is exploitative."

"Okay, *ese.* I believe you. Hey, you still live with your mom?"

"Shhh."

He said something in Spanish to his sleepy-eyed companions. They all laughed. Once again, Andrew came to my rescue, braces gleaming in the weak sunlight. "We've got signs, brothers. Join the resistance."

"No, thanks, *mano.* I got enough trouble." Tino turned his attention back to me. "Hey, Miguel, you still got your mower?"

"I got a new one." If I could ever get it back from Goble.

Tino nodded, looking impressed. "I keep my eye out for you."

He set a hand on my shoulder and gave me a pat before the three of them proceeded on their way into Walmart.

"Give me a call, Miguel," he shouted over his shoulder. "We grab a beer!"

It wouldn't be a proper protest unless the cops showed up eventually. Well, cop, in our case. I guess I really shouldn't have been surprised that the cop happened to be Jar Jar Binks, the racial profiler, who tried to shoot my tire.

"You," he said. "What are you doing here?"

"I'm occupying."

"Yeah, a parking lot, I can see that. You and your friends need to disperse."

Lowering his sign, Andrew stepped up, a little sauerkraut still stuck between his braces.

"We're not doing anything illegal, officer. We're exercising our right to assemble. As a matter of fact, you ought to be protecting that right."

"Well, I don't know about that," said the cop. "But we've had two complaints about the music. And you're blocking the entrance—which is a fire hazard, last I checked. If I can't get you kids to clear out, hey, no sweat off my back. I'll just leave it to the hose jockeys. It'll be fun breaking up their barbecue."

"Or you could just shoot somebody," I observed.

He narrowed his eyes. "Don't tempt me."

"We're doing absolutely nothing unlawful here, officer," said Andrew.

"Yeah, you already said that."

"The right to peaceably assemble is an inalienable—"

"Save it, Cesar Chavez. Just quit blocking the entrance. If you want to save the world from great prices, move it over by the shopping carts."

Needless to say, Andrew wasn't happy about the move, but we didn't really have much choice. It took some more wind out of our sails, that's for sure. Three more folks took the opportunity to drop out, and the few who remained started playing hacky sack. By six, the resistance folded once and for all.

"You hungry?" said Andrew.

"Starving."

We never did use the walkie-talkies.

Lists and Reminders

At Central Market, Andrew bought a couple of wild salmon fillets (sixteen bucks!), a bag of organic salad greens (six bucks!) and a six-pack of something called Hopjack (ten ninety-nine!). I figured the library must pay pretty darn well if Andrew could afford to shop like that. Or maybe he was a Trustafarian, but I doubted it. I mean, he was from Belfair, how could he be rich? He was gracious about not accepting my six bucks.

We drove to Andrew's apartment, which was way up on the hill above Rite Aid and Albertsons. It used to be a green belt up there, but developers gave the hill a buzz cut about ten years ago and started putting warts on its forehead. *Developer* is a bit of a misnomer, if you ask me. Rite Aid and Albertsons used to be wetlands. All that's left now is a sad little swathe strewn with swamp grass and scraggly trees. It's great for catching discarded Big Gulps and stray plastic bags, but I can't say I've seen a lot of waterfowl there.

I'd be lying if I said I wasn't jealous of Andrew's apartment, which was at least six times the size of my shed. It was beautiful chaos: books stacked everywhere, boxes of old records. A receiver, turntable, and speakers. A writing desk, a brown sofa, an old wooden coffee table riddled with tea candles, rolling papers, and dental floss. A great big overgrown herb garden in the windowsill of the kitchen. There was a saxophone, some picket signs, a dented globe, and no TV. Everywhere you looked there were lists tacked to the wall.

Places to go: Solomon Islands, Dublin, Aruba, Patagonia.

Bucket list: Space travel. Adopt children. *Finnegans Wake.*

Values: Gratitude. Curiosity. Empathy.

What I liked about Andrew was that he was earnest and easy-going at the same time. He obviously had ambitions, among them civic-mindedness and straight teeth. But he wasn't about to beat you over the head with his semivegetarianism or anything. Heck, he'd even eat a hot dog in a pinch.

He opened us a couple of those expensive beers, and I sat at the dining-room table and watched him prepare the salmon on one of those wood planks they're always gushing about at Red Lobster. There were even more lists plastered in the kitchen—on cabinets, on the refrigerator, over the sink.

Qualities: Kindness. Thoughtfulness. Forgiveness.

Ambitions: Strong heart. Clear mind. Pure body.

Dos: Listen. Learn. Love.

Don'ts: Judge. Project. Hold grudges.

"Oh, the lists?" he said, registering my curiosity. "My constant attempt to be mindful. I tried yoga, but it gave me gas."

"So what are you trying so hard to achieve?" I asked.

"I'm just trying to figure out how to be happy without being the best at anything, you know? What about you?"

"I kind of want to be a writer, I guess. Or make some kind of splash with my topiary."

"An artist! Why didn't you tell me that? That's amazing. How could you not tell me that?"

"I'm just a wannabe."

"Well, isn't that where everybody starts? C'mon, no limits, no excuses. Get after it, Michael! Fake it till you make it. You can be anything you want."

"Pfff. I doubt that."

"It's true—anything."

"I couldn't be an astronaut."

"Sure you could."

"I'd have to be a pilot first."

"So?"

"I'm field independent."

"What's that?"

"It's a brain thing. I have trouble separating details with the surrounding context or whatever. It means I could be flying upside down and I wouldn't even know it. They don't let people like me be pilots."

"C'mon, Michael, rules are made to be changed."

After dinner, Andrew and I took our beers and sat on the veranda overlooking the Rite Aid parking lot. What with the glow of the lights, and the traffic on 305, and a whiff of Taco Bell in the gentle breeze, it was sort of pretty. Even the Taco Bell smell was okay. I'm not saying I was famished or anything, but I should've eaten that jumbo hot dog back at the protest, instead of taking the moral high road. Those exorbitantly priced organic greens didn't stretch too far, if you know what I mean. Not that I didn't appreciate Andrew's effort.

"What made you decide to get braces, anyway?" I asked.

"The usual: I wanted to feel better about myself. I thought straight teeth might boost my confidence."

Instinctively, I ran my tongue over my recently vacated teeth.

"The plan was to get the invisible kind, but I only had four grand. And that's only because my uncle died and left me the money. I probably should have paid off my student loans."

"No, they look good," I said. "I mean, they will. You know, afterward."

The truth is, I hardly noticed Andrew's braces anymore. I could already see his future smile, and it was a winner. As far as I was concerned, all his lists and reminders were working, too. He was someone to aspire to: kind, thoughtful, and forgiving. He had a strong heart and a clear mind. I had no doubt that he'd see Patagonia and Aruba and that he'd read *Finnegans Wake* eventually. Shit, he'd probably find a way to do a little space travel, the big goof. The guy had a plan. Not an angle, like Chaz, not a self-serving dictate, like Goble, but an actual plan for a better life, a better world. He wasn't about to sit there with crooked teeth and take the scraps the world offered him. He did things. He attended lectures. He bought local. He joined a Toastmasters group. He was going to mindfully plot his course, and I respected the hell out of that.

As the evening wore on, Andrew shifted the focus to me, asking me questions as though he was hungry for the answers. What books had changed my life? What were my five favorite movies? He asked me about Suquamish, and I didn't really have much to wow him with—no great bookstores or Ethiopian restaurants, no killer nightspots. Just the Tide's Inn and the minimart and the abandoned grocery store. But Andrew was interested all the same. We didn't talk about football or chicks on TV we'd like to bang. No complaining about gays and Mexicans. There was here and now, and the future, wherein anything was possible, at least that's how it felt.

Andrew actually listened to me when I talked—not like a lot of people, who only seemed to be waiting for their own turn to talk. He asked me about Nate and my mom and Freddy. He said that he wanted to meet them all, that he wanted to come to our house and cook for us. He wanted to know all about the Great American Landscaping Novel. He wanted to be my first reader. He wanted to see my merman and my mushrooms and my pipe-smoking gnome.

After a while, I began to feel like I was talking too much about myself.

"Not at all," he insisted. "I want to know more. What about your dad? You never talk about him."

So I began to regale him with what little there was to tell about Victor Muñoz and the shadow that he didn't much cast. I told Andrew about the time my dad took me to Disneyland and told me they moved. Most people get a kick out of that story. I mean, it's pretty funny, even though the experience broke my heart. Even if it largely defined my expectations for the life that lay ahead of me, even if the yearning and disappointment, the sense of possibility that died that day, still reverberated somewhere down deep inside of me. I recalled clutching that chain-link fence in the spitting rain and looking out over the sea of pitted concrete and the half-barren shipyard beyond, the putrid stench of clams assaulting me, the seagulls jeering at me from above. And the whole time I told the story to Andrew, he seemed to vacillate between horror and indignation. He didn't laugh once. In fact, for an instant, I thought he might cry.

"It really wasn't a big deal," I insisted. "I mean, at least he made an effort, right?"

"Hmph," Andrew said, looking vaguely out over the lights of the strip mall. "My father hasn't spoken to me in four years. I'm dead to him. He won't even acknowledge my existence. People ask him about me, and he shrugs or waves me off. My mom talks about me, and he changes the subject."

"That's fucked up," I said.

"But it's my mom who really kills me. Every single time I talk to her, she wonders aloud where she went wrong with me, you know? Like I'm a mistake. And it doesn't matter who I am, or how decent I am, or how hard I try, or what I believe, or what I accomplish—there will always be something fundamentally wrong with me in her eyes. A parent's love is supposed to be unconditional. But if my mom had a choice, she'd have me be somebody else entirely."

I couldn't help but wonder if my mother felt the same way about Nate and me.

"Dude, you're amazing how you are," I said.

"Stop," said Andrew.

When I looked at him, he sort of grimaced like he was about

to get sick, but then I saw that his eyes were brimming over with tears, so I set my hand on his knee and gave it a little pat and tried to think of something lighthearted to say.

"I'm sorry," was all I could think of.

And that's when Andrew did a very unexpected thing, something that made me a little uncomfortable: he clasped my hand in his own, and he squeezed it.

Making a Stand

Though I possessed zero street cred as a protester, having never been arrested, detained, gassed, or beaten, Andrew didn't hold it against me. He assured me that I'd get my opportunity sooner or later. As for him, he'd been arrested twice. Once at the Bangor nuclear submarine base for attempting to serve coffee to state patrol officers and once for chaining himself to the wrong tree. The fact that it was the wrong tree was immaterial.

"These are the sacrifices we make," he explained.

Maybe today was my day to get arrested, I kept telling myself. Or gassed. Or beaten. But secretly, I hoped it wouldn't be.

We were scheduled to occupy the southwest corner of a strip mall in Silverdale, protesting a pet store that allegedly purchased their puppies from a notorious puppy mill in Kansas. The previous week, Andrew had sent out press releases announcing the protest. He'd been recruiting aggressively. Moses was bringing his little sister. The lady in sweatpants was bringing her son.

"Gandhi said that 'the greatness of a nation and its moral progress can be judged by how it treats its animals,'" Andrew told me in the Subaru as we were passing Skippers. "Somebody has to advocate for these animals, Michael. They can't advocate for themselves."

When we arrived at the pet store ahead of schedule, nobody was waiting for us. For the next fifteen minutes, Andrew checked his phone obsessively. I guess he figured there'd be at least one TV crew since he sent out all those press releases.

"Where the hell is everybody?" he wanted to know. "Where's the commitment? Doesn't anybody care?"

"They'll be here," I assured him.

I knew I was lying, but I think it softened the blow when nobody else showed up. Not even Moses. Not even Sweatpants and her son. So the puppy mill protest wasn't exactly the March on Washington. Nevertheless, we did occupy space, and nobody could take that away from us. And we carried ourselves with dignity and the requisite amount of moral outrage, hoisting our picket signs high, marching purposefully to and fro in front of the entrance like a pair of armed sentries. Not that there was any traffic to contend with—not like Walmart. Nobody was going to the vacuum repair or Radio Shack. Mostly people were going to T.J. Maxx and Starbucks, and one or two people to the hair salon.

Around noon, we got our first potential convert when an earnest, dirty-faced girl of eight or nine in a grease-stained sweatshirt stopped short of the entrance to read our signs.

"Where's your mommy and daddy?" I asked.

"My daddy is in Pensacola with that whore Loretta," she said. "And my mommy is at T.J Maxx."

"Does she know where you are?"

"She lets me wait at the pet store."

"What's your name, sweetie?" said Andrew.

"Waverly," she said.

"Well, Waverly, you don't want to wait at this particular pet store, because they get their puppies from a puppy mill."

"What's a puppy mill?" Waverly asked.

"A puppy mill is a terrible place," said Andrew. "It's a place where little puppies die of neglect and starvation."

"Oh," she said, visibly unnerved.

In my opinion, Waverly didn't need any more convincing. I think she was ready to boycott the place, I really do. But Andrew was too impassioned to notice. And I couldn't really blame him. Finally, somebody was listening! This is how you made change happen!

"Some puppy mills," he explained, "are littered with piles of dead, partially eaten dogs, stuffed in corners and hanging from rafters. And in some puppy mills, starving adult dogs eat their newborn puppies."

Around now, Waverly's face muscles started twitching visibly, and her chin began to quaver. I nudged Andrew, but he was in the zone.

"One miller stuffed five Rottweiler puppies into a birdcage and left them to starve. Except that they kept growing, anyway. And eventually they were too large to be extracted from the cage, and they had to be euthanized through the bars."

I think it was about at this point that Waverly began to hyperventilate. But Andrew was on fire.

"When the females are no longer fertile, they're left to starve, and their bodies are fed to—"

I would describe it as a screech, the sound Waverly made. Or maybe part screech, part squeal. Have you ever stepped on a puppy's tail? Like that, but sustained—really sustained. It was goddamn unsettling. Only when shoppers started converging on us from all directions did Andrew realize he'd miscalculated.

"What have you done to that child?" demanded the lady from the travel agency, having charged out the door.

"Hey now!" said a fat guy in front of the vacuum repair.

"Yo!" cried a nearby tweaker in a filthy Ravens cap.

People were now rushing out of T.J. Maxx and the hair salon to see what all the fuss was about. Still screeching like a banshee, fists clenched, Waverly clutched her arms tightly to her chest. Setting our picket signs aside, we did our best to deal with the situation. Lots of shushing and considerable shoulder patting. But Waverly couldn't be reached. She was a human teakettle.

It took five minutes to finally calm her down and disarm the gathering mob. It took another ten minutes to locate the mother, who was summoned from T.J Maxx, a sallow-faced woman with skin like mangy camel hide and two missing teeth. Honestly, she seemed to be the least concerned party involved, until she recognized the opportunity to make herself the center of attention, whereupon she yelled at Andrew and me, calling us "freaks" and "molesters." She said we were no better than fucking Clint and that dirty whore Loretta, down in Florida. But apparently her outrage wasn't very convincing. Even the sketcher cut us some slack.

"That skeez should *not* be a mom, yo," he said, scratching his stubbly face. "Hey, you got two bucks?"

So maybe the protest wasn't a huge success. Andrew meant well, I know he did. Maybe he didn't exercise his best judgment in a delicate situation. But in my opinion, he took the setback harder than he should have. After we left the pet store, we walked down Silverdale Way, dragging our picket signs to a grubby little *pho* place in a different strip mall. The restaurant was maybe two hundred square feet and might have benefited from dimmer light. I didn't want to assume Andrew was buying, so I just ordered a spring roll, because I only had four bucks and three of them were in quarters. Andrew ordered me the works, anyway, and insisted on paying. He was classy that way.

The instant the waitress left, he turned mopey, and I guess I couldn't blame him.

"Who am I kidding, Michael? I'm a phony. All my lists are bullshit. All my talk, all my posturing, all my big ideals. No wonder my father's ashamed of me and my mother's embarrassed of me."

"Dude, that's not true. You're an inspiration."

"Michael, I traumatized that little girl. I ate a hot dog at the Walmart protest! I'm a complete hypocrite! Look at me: I wear leather shoes. I bank at Wells Fargo. I've never even had a dog. Who am I to decry puppy mills?"

"You're somebody trying to make a difference."

"I'm nobody trying to make a difference."

"You're a librarian. A librarian is a public treasure, a respected community resource. A goddamn saint in my book!"

"No, Michael, I'm a substitute library assistant. I don't have a degree. I got that job off the bulletin board. I shelve books. On Thursdays they let me put the flag up and take it down if I'm working. I'm basically a lackey."

"Well, at least you're trying."

"Am I? Oh, Michael, it's vanity, that's all. Like these stupid braces. I just want to look good, so I can feel better about myself and convince other people I'm somehow better than what I am or, even worse, better than what they are. I'm shallow, Michael, you may as well know it before we go any further. In fact, there are a lot of things you should know before we go further."

"Where are we going?"

He looked at me searchingly, almost like he was asking me a question, then waved it off, smiling sadly.

"Oh, never mind," he said. "Anyway, you're sweet to say those things."

"They're true," I said.

"Thanks," he said, and I thought that sounded a little sad, too.

Following Up

Two days after the puppy mill protest, I ran into Goble outside Central Market. I was hoofing it from the bus stop on 305 when he whizzed past me on the frontage road at about forty miles per hour with the convertible top down, crappy pop music blaring. As always, his hair was impervious to the wind, and he was wearing one of those puffy ski jackets that somehow make people look skinny in spite of the fact that they're puffy.

I watched, only slightly incredulous, as Goble blatantly cut off an old lady in an Oldsmobile and shoehorned in on her parking spot before closing his automatic convertible top. Hopping out of the car, he activated his car alarm over his shoulder with a stylish flick of the wrist. The audacious fucker waved at the old lady, flashing a saccharine smile.

Immediately, I realized that I wasn't mad at Goble anymore. I'm not sure the guy could help himself. He wasn't all terrible;

almost nobody is, deep down, once you strip away all the terror and trauma and neurosis and bad conditioning. The thing with a guy like Goble was that he scratched and clawed to get where he was. Being a creep was an imperative to his way of thinking. Anything less was weak. Like me, Goble started on the ass end of an uneven playing field. But unlike me, he had a nose for the goal line. While I was perfectly happy to settle for a midrange field goal or even a punt, Goble drove ninety yards uphill into the jaws of his adversary (the world at large), scratching and clawing the whole way to the end zone. And here's the thing: people who scratch and claw tend to be shortsighted.

Apparently, Goble was harboring no ill will toward me for outing him as a cocksucker to his neighbor, either. For whatever reason, he'd never admit what happened between us, and I just had to accept that. What did it really matter?

"How goes it, *hombre? ¿Cómo estás, amigo? Mucho tiempo sin verte.*"

"I have no idea what you're saying. How'd it work out with your Seahawk, anyway?" I said. "Did he buy the place?"

Goble winced. "Yeah, well, turns out the team's not gonna exercise his option. I guess I didn't get the memo. Come to find out, they all live on the Eastside, anyway. Every last one of them."

"Piggot must be relieved."

"For now. But that old highballer is going down, sooner or later. I've got a close eye on his place. I think he took a pretty big hit in '08. What about you? How's unemployment working out?"

"Couple irons in the fire," I said.

"Like what?"

"You know, just . . . irons."

One of the irons was a bag boy application at Central Market, which I submitted last Thursday, upon which I was presently "following up." But Goble didn't need to know that. I figured the less Goble knew about me, the better our standing.

"Ah," he said. "Well, as fate would have it, I have an opportunity for you, actually."

"Nah, I'm good."

"Full access to the truck," he said.

"Thanks, anyway."

"I'd take care of the payments." *Wink wink.* "We could even talk about sweat equity if the arrangement works out."

With nothing but bus fare in my pocket and dwindling possibilities ahead of me, I have to say, the offer was awfully tempting. Not that I thought for a second he'd ever actually deliver on the equity arrangement. But working for Goble definitely had its advantages.

"C'mon," he said. "What do you say? Goble or go home."

Yes, it was irresponsible of me to decline the opportunity. I see that. If nothing else, I should have said yes for everyone else's sake—Mom, Nate, Freddy. But looking at Goble, with his bronzed skin and his orthodontically straightened pearly whites, standing next to his stupid luxury convertible, clutching his cell phone in the same hand that once clutched my penis, I just didn't want any part of it, you know? I guess I was finally learning not to settle for less, even when it looked like more.

"Yeah, sorry," I said. "I guess I'm gonna just 'go home' this time."

I guess that expectation may have been a little naive, but my declining didn't even faze him like I'd hoped it would.

"Well, suit yourself," he said, firing off a text. "Hey, you know any good Mexicans?"

"What do you mean good?" I said.

"Cheap."

"Nah, sorry."

Maybe good things do happen when you don't settle for less. Because the very same day Goble offered me a job, Nick called to offer me a job at Les Schwab. I didn't mean to be rude, but I was almost out of cell minutes and I wanted to save them for prospective employers, and Andrew. And honestly, the very idea of working alongside Nick all day was too excruciating to even ponder. How many fag jokes would I have to endure? How many wrongheaded, misinformed opinions would I have to hear? I was trying really hard to tolerate the guy, in spite of his huge warts. Sometimes you have that responsibility, or at least that's how I've always felt. But at this point, being in close proximity to Nick for any substantial length of time would render that good intention patently impossible, and I saw that now.

"Thanks, anyway," I said. "Not interested."

"Dude, what do you mean you're not interested? I pitched you hard to Whitehead. I told him you were a natural."

"I appreciate that, Nick. I'm just looking to go in another direction."

"You mean homelessness? You gotta get your own place, bro. Your mom and Freddy want you out of there. Besides, I can't go back to Whitehead and say my friend's not interested. I had to beg the fucker, and he loved every second of it. You gotta do this interview—and do not fuck it up, Michael. If you fuck this up, I'll kill you. I put my ass on the line for you."

"I don't want the job, Nick."

Two or three seconds of stunned silence followed before Nick finally responded. "You're fucking stupid, you know that?"

"That may be the case. I'll admit, there's plenty of evidence to support it. But the thing is, I don't want to work on tires, I just don't. I don't want to wear that uniform. Or smell popcorn and rubber all day. Or read four-year-old *Auto Traders* on my break. Or have to run out into the parking lot to greet everyone. Don't get me wrong, I like that you guys do that, I think it's really professional. I just don't want to do it. And I'm tired of doing things I don't want to do. I've gotta start doing things I don't hate."

Again, incredulous silence, followed by the slightest of gasps. "What the hell happened to you, dude? You sound like you're from Bainbridge."

It stung, but it was true. Why should it sting? That's the part that still bugs me. Was I a traitor for empowering myself, for indulging a sense of self-worth? For finally holding out for something better than pumping air into tires and wearing a uniform five days a week? Or digging up roses for some racist old wealthy dude like Piggot? Or selling my soul to Team Goble just so I could drive a new truck? I'd way rather bag groceries, at least until I could get back to landscaping. Yes, I was leaching off my support system at the moment. But it's not like I was leaving a big footprint. And six months ago, wasn't I a veritable rock? Hadn't I always been there for my family? Remember that big breakfast at the casino? All those Indian tacos at Chief Seattle Days? Was I presumptuous to believe that somehow, some way, I could get off the hamster wheel on my own terms? Even if my mom and her boyfriend wanted me out of the shed? Isn't that just the sort of

delusional psychology and unqualified confidence it takes to suc-
ceed in this world? And don't you need it in greater measure when
you're a tenth-generation peasant with a Mexican last name, raised
by a single mom on an Indian reservation?

The answer is yes.

Bumps

I was sitting with Andrew at the Starbucks in Poulsbo on his lunch hour, discussing various subjects, including, but not limited to, union busting, campaign reform, gun control, locally sourced beef, Pez dispensers, and Liza Minnelli's big eyes. This is how our conversations usually ran: one minute we were railing on the Republican establishment and lamenting greenhouse gases, and the next minute we were discussing '90s TV shows or tropical fruit. They were like no conversations I'd ever had before, and they energized me.

As I was bidding Andrew farewell outside of Starbucks, I spotted a familiar car in the Albertsons parking lot. I'll give you a hint: it was a BMW. The driver was not so familiar, at least not right away. This guy was feral: unkempt beard, baggy clothing, flip-flops in the rain. If there would have been even a sliver of the patented optimism in his bearing, or maybe a vodka mini in his hand, I might have recognized Chaz sooner. I'll be honest, and I'm not proud of this, but the first thing I thought of was the last paycheck he owed me.

"Chaz!" I called out.

He looked around a little dazedly.

"Chaz!" I cried again.

This time, I got his attention. I can't blame him for looking a little startled, the way I charged across that parking lot, just as sure as if he was dangling a fourteen-hundred-dollar check with my name on it. He was visibly relieved when I didn't tackle him. The instant he stopped flinching, he started demonstrating a little of the old exuberance.

"Muñoz!" he said. "How goes it? Have you been thinking big? Keeping your nose to the grindstone?"

"Giving it the old college try," I said.

"Wow, you're going to college now?"

"No."

"Ah, right, figure of speech. You working?"

"Not so much."

So as not to leave you in suspense, the instant I got a whiff of my old mentor (think vinegar and damp wool), it was readily apparent that I would not be seeing that final, fourteen-hundred-dollar paycheck anytime soon. I decided to just let it rest. I guess I believed that if Chaz had the money, he would've given it to me. I also suspected he would have given me the same pass. You really can't ask for more than that, unless you want to be some kind of bloodsucker.

"How about you?" I said.

"Well, you know, a few bumps in the road," he said. "A few

twists and turns. Maybe a cliff or two. Nothing major. Where you headed?"

"Bus stop," I said, flashing my transfer.

"C'mon," said Chaz. "I'll give you a ride. Like old times."

The BMW was chaotic on the inside—shit strewn everywhere.

"So, where you living these days?" I inquired. Though from the bedroll, the pillow, the spit kit, the squashed loaf of bread, the fast-food bags, and the general disarray of the car's interior, I'd say the answer was pretty obvious.

"Around," he said.

A few bumps in the road? The guy was living in his car! You had to admire his grit and determination. Chaz had the American can-do spirit in spades. He simply refused to be defeated. Not even in defeat was he defeated. Yep, it seemed old Chaz still had a lesson or two to teach Mike Muñoz.

Chaz activated the blow-and-go without my assistance.

"Been in the program now for two months," he explained. "Feeling great. I haven't seen things so clearly in years—personally, spiritually, financially. As a matter of fact, my sponsor Lamar and I are working on capitalizing something at the moment. Could be a real cash cow. Little start-up called Fried Chicken."

"Like a restaurant?"

"No, e-commerce."

"So, like online chicken?"

"Nothing to do with poultry. We just like the name. Import and distribution—mostly import. You know how to build a website?"

"No."

"You know anybody who does?"

"Sorry, man. But if you ever need a pair of tires."

Chaz began tapping triplets on the steering wheel, biting his lip in a pensive manner, eyes fixed straight ahead on the roadway.

"What about money? Got any?"

"Eight bucks."

He stopped tapping the wheel. "Ah, well, had to ask. One way or another, we'll get her done, don't you worry. I've got a few leads. Gonna talk to my parole officer. And Lamar's got a rich aunt who's pushing ninety-five. Who knows, anything could happen with her. But just so you know, once I get this thing up and running, I've got a place for you on the ground floor."

You laugh, but I believed him, and I still believe him. You wait and see, Chaz will pull through in the end. Good intentions often fail us, but not always. Chaz will stay in the game long enough, keep stepping into the fray and punching with enough grit and determination that he's bound to make something happen eventually. It's the American way.

When we arrived at the house, Chaz pulled into the driveway and shut off the engine.

"So, um, you wanna come in, and like, I don't know, have a sandwich or a cup of coffee or something?"

"Can I use your shower?" he said.

"Yeah, that'd be cool, I think."

Freddy and Nate were at the kitchen table playing Candy Land. It must have been a tense game, because neither one of them looked up from the board when we walked in, socks and sleeves hanging willy-nilly out of Chaz's overstuffed duffel bag.

"Double green," said Freddy. "That's what I'm talkin' about, big dog! Old Freddy just caught a free ride over Gumdrop Pass. Booyah! Peanut Acres, here I come."

"Hey, this is Chaz," I announced. "He needs to use the shower."

Freddy looked up. "This mean you got your money?"

"No. But Chaz is starting a new business, and he's gonna get me in on the ground floor."

"It's called Fried Chicken," Chaz said.

"Mm. Like the sound of that," said Freddy.

"Nothing to do with chicken, actually."

"Well now, I'm sorry to hear it."

"Import and export," Chaz explained.

But Freddy ignored him, immediately turning his attention back to the game. "Your turn, dog."

I know it seems like Freddy was being a dick, but he was only looking out for my best interests. And in the end, he let his true colors show. It was Freddy's idea to let Chaz sleep in our driveway, just until he got Fried Chicken up and running. Say what you want about Freddy. He may be a little unorthodox, and maybe he's not the most ambitious guy in the world, and yeah, maybe he'd do well to keep his nuts in his pants and quit smoking so much Blueberry Kush, but he's a good man.

Legit

Ready for this? Further evidence that good things happen if you can somehow manage to hold out for what you want: three days after Chaz started using our driveway as the headquarters for Fried Chicken, I got a call from Tino.

"*¿Qué onda, Miguel?*"

"Are you ever gonna stop calling me that?"

Tino laughed. "C'mon, *ese*, it's a joke, man."

"So, what up?"

"I got an offer for you, *ese*. You wanna have lunch?"

We met at Los Cazadores, a grubby little taqueria on the ass end of Viking Way. Tino ordered a tamale plate, so I figured "when in Rome" and ordered the same thing. Though I'm okay with most Mexican food, I'd always avoided tamales. I don't know what all the fuss is about. It tasted like a wet loaf of corn bread to me. And I'm not really into the whole shucking-my-food thing.

I asked Tino how his family was doing, and he told me how little Izzy had potty-trained herself and how Emilio was the star of his soccer team, and Arturo was quite the young ladies' man. I could see him trying to muster his pride, but really, he seemed as sad as hell the whole time he talked about them, like he'd lost them already.

"Every stinking day I think about them. Every week, they getting bigger, they growing further away from me. I feel like *pinche* Santa Claus, like some myth, you know? He lives up north, he sends gifts to the children. But don't nobody ever see him. I tell you what, Miguel. Don't have kids, don't do it. They tear your *pinche* heart out. What about your family?"

I told him how Nate had lost a bunch of weight and how my mom was about the same as ever, except maybe a little happier. I asked him how things were at the trailer with Rocindo and Ramiro, and he said he was moving out, splitting a one-bedroom apartment with his cousin Sergio and his friend Ernesto in Silverdale, near the mall. I told him that sounded great, and that I was still living with my mom, but he didn't make fun of me this time.

"Shit, Miguel, at least she don't fart like Ernesto."

Right around the time I was choking down the last of my tamale, we finally got around to business.

"So, what are we're talking about here?" I said.

Tino looked me right in the eye and held my gaze.

"Look," he said. "For three years, we doing all the work. Lacy, he's no good, you know it. He used to be but no more. Most of the accounts, they don't like him anymore. He pads the hours. He charges for product we don't use. They not always happy. And the shit, it all roll downhill, you know?"

"So what are you saying?"

"On Sundays, I already been working my own accounts, old ones that dropped Lacy. Larsen, Buchholz, and sometimes Fetters. They not much, but they pay."

"And?"

"And I wanna find more, *ese*. I want you to be my partner. T&M Landscaping—you know, for Tino and Miguel."

"Mike," I said. "Mike. And why would you want me to be your partner? I don't even have a truck."

"Because you the best, Holmes. Nobody mow like you. Your edges are *muy bueno*. Your pruning, it's *fantástico*—like the best I've seen. You an artist, *ese*."

"What about a truck?"

"I'll get to that, amigo."

"You got any money for start-up?"

"A little bit."

As much as I wanted to believe I was some kind of lawn-mowing savant, I knew from experience there had to be more to this. Nobody ever complimented me without asking me for something.

"No, really, why me? Why not Rocindo or Ernesto or Che?"

Tino looked down at the bar top, softly drumming his fingers on it once before letting out a sigh.

"Because you're not Rocindo or Ernesto or Che. Because you're Mike, man, you're white—whiter than me, anyway. The clients, they lowball me every time, *ese*. They think they can pay less for a Mexican. That's just how it is. If you wanna get in touch with your inner Mexican, cut your salary in half."

"No, thanks. Already been there."

"Miguel, you could be like the face of the business. I give you fifty percent. And I be calling you Mike all the time. We can even put Mike first, if you want. You know, like M&T Landscaping."

I don't know why, but all I could think of was Goble and his shopping carts and how I never wanted to be the guy that leveraged himself at the cost of everything else. I didn't want my life to be a negotiation, where the sole point was to come out on top of the other guy.

"I'll take forty-five," I said. "And T&M sounds better."

Tino took a bite of tamale and chewed it deliberately as he searched my face.

"Nah, *ese*. I give you fifty. But you right, T&M sounds better."

"Forty-five," I said.

He stabbed his tamale a few times and mopped up some hot sauce with it, shaking his head side to side.

"But I came to you, Miguel."

"Exactly."

"I dunno, *ese*. Why you wanna take less? It don't make no sense."

"It's how I negotiate," I insisted. "Besides, you've already got accounts, you already laid some of the groundwork."

"Yeah, *ese*, but you white. They pay you more. It gonna even out quick."

"I'll take forty-five," I said. "And that's my final offer."

Tino did his best to act like he wasn't altogether comfortable with the terms, but he couldn't belie a sly little grin.

"Deal," he said, extending a hand.

We made it official. Then I raised my Mexican soda, some flavor I'd never heard of called *tamarindo*, which, as far as I could tell, was a mix between orange soda and ditch water.

"To T&M Landscaping," I said.

"We gonna kill it, *ese*."

We clinked bottles, and suddenly my mind was racing with possibilities.

"You know, we should poach Knowlton," I said. "Lacy never did move that pergola like he said he would."

"Hell yes. And the old lady, we should take her, too."

"Nah," I said. "I'm done cleaning her garage and jockeying her cars around. Only the mellow ones for T&M."

"If you say so, *ese*. Also, I got my eye on some new accounts, on this side of the bridge. Not so much competition over here. And Silverdale is *caliente* right now. They building like crazy—big yards!"

"I like it."

"And my cousin Rodrigo, he got a Ford truck that look pretty good. He sell it to us for two thousand."

"We can get some of those magnetic signs to put on the doors," I said, thinking of Goble.

"Yeah, *ese*. 'T&M Landscaping.' We gonna be legit."

I played it cool, but the truth is, I was over the moon. This was better than a winning scratch ticket, better than an all-you-can-eat-buffet, better than the $29.90 an hour I almost made working for Piggot, even better than getting in on the ground floor of Fried Chicken, whatever the hell that was. See, the thing is, I was telling the truth when I said I love to get my mow on. I love to prune and rake and edge. I'm good. Maybe not a genius, but I'm conscientious and efficient, and I'm getting better all the time.

To you, it probably looks like old Mike Muñoz is right back where he started, in work boots and a green sweatshirt, mowing your lawn. But see, here's the thing you're failing to understand:

I'm mowing your lawn on my terms now. I'm making my own rules and punching my own clock. I'm blazing my own trail, yo! No cheapskate boss exploiting my ass. Nobody making me shovel turds when I don't feel like it. That's your Great American Landscaping Novel, right there. I even came up with a slogan for T&M Landscaping: "Saving the World, One Lawn at a Time."

The minute I left the taqueria on foot, I used all but the very last of my cell minutes to phone Andrew on his lunch break and tell him the great news. He insisted we celebrate that night, and not at Tequila's, either, but somewhere classy, like the Loft.

"Dinner and drinks on me," he said. "Pick you up at five fifteen."

Making It Official

lways punctual, Andrew knocked on my shed door at 5:12
p.m., wearing a pea-green cardigan over his PETA T-shirt
and a pair of Levi's so new that they still had that fuzzy
sheen. Completing the look were Birkenstocks with white socks.
Quintessentially northwestern. Having recently undergone some
misguided attempt at subjugation, his hair remained suppressed
for the moment, though it was beginning to show signs of immi-
nent revolt in the back.

"Well, if it isn't Mr. Small Business Owner," he said, clapping
me on the shoulder.

"Yeah, well," I said.

"C'mon, Michael! This is huge," he said, shepherding me around
to the front of the house. "How can you be so matter of fact? This
is amazing! Who knows, maybe some of your accounts will want
topiary."

"I doubt it."

"You can't think that way. You've got talent, Michael—I wish I had your talent. Your merman is sublime. And it's fun. I'm telling you, you've gotta put yourself out there."

In the enclosed space of the car, I could smell Andrew. He smelled like a library, like books and dust and photocopies and hand sanitizer. I was so grateful for him just then. It was so obvious that his excitement for me was genuine. He actually believed in me, apparently more than I believed in myself.

"Okay, so tell me the details," he said.

I gave him the rundown, and he asked me some savvy business questions about T&M Landscaping along the way, stuff about bonding and licensing, insurance and payroll taxes, and the like. At just about every juncture, I told him I was pretty sure Tino was handling that end. I told him about the magnetic signs.

"Smart," he said. "And cheap."

I told him about the slogan.

"Brilliant," he said.

When we were seated in a window booth at the Loft, looking out over the marina, Andrew beseeched me to order anything on the menu and then some, but I didn't want to break the bank. The guy was a sub library assistant, after all. He bought me coffee and lunch almost daily. How many times had he hauled me all over town? I felt like I was taking advantage of him. The least I could do was go easy on him at the Loft. But Andrew wouldn't hear of it.

"We're celebrating, and you're ordering a Caesar salad and water? C'mon! I've got my credit card."

So I decided on the fish and chips at $13.95—still the cheapest thing not on the children's menu. But Andrew made me order the

Caesar salad, too, and insisted that we share some hummus and a cheese plate. He kept bringing up T&M and the exciting possibilities, and the importance of getting bonded and insured, since his uncle's tree service in Belfair had failed to do either before felling a hundred-foot cedar on some rich guy's garage. His uncle ended up living in his truck for six months after that.

"All I'm saying is, people who can afford to be are litigious. My other uncle was a contractor, and one time he did this big remodel for some lumber-baron guy, and not only did the guy refuse to pay him after he finished the whole ninety-five-thousand-dollar job, he also sued my uncle for finishing two weeks behind schedule, and all because the guy's wife kept changing her mind about the floors. Not only did Uncle Pete have to eat the ninety-five grand, he had to pay the guy thirty grand in damages. Put him completely out of business for a while. Ah, but what am I saying? We're supposed to be celebrating, and here all I can talk about is calamity! Eat, drink!"

I was about to spear another mozzarella ball when a woman at the bar caught my eye. I'll give you a hint: it wasn't Hillary Clinton. It was someone with a little skin tag on her arm that looked like a toasted Rice Krispie. She must have felt me staring, because she looked right back at me and smiled, giving me a wave. I'd hardly thought of Remy in weeks.

Andrew craned his neck. "Um, Michael, in case you didn't notice, that girl is flirting with you big-time."

"Nah," I said. "She just knows me."

"No, Michael, she's hitting on you. It's obvious. She's been looking over for the past five minutes. Go on, go talk to her."

"Nah."

"What are you waiting for? Seriously, you have to go."

"You think?"

"Yes, I know. Just go," he said with a regretful sigh, as though my departure was something he'd already prepared himself for.

Even as he said it, I caught Remy glancing my way. And here's the thing: I wasn't scared and I wasn't intimidated. If anything, I felt guilty. On a different night, in different company, I probably would've felt the way I usually felt: that I ought to be interested in Remy, that I ought to be compelled, that if I had any guts, I'd be over there chatting her up. Because maybe she really was the one.

"Go on," Andrew said. "Don't blow it."

"I don't feel like it."

"Michael," he said gravely.

I stood up and obediently made my way to the bar, glancing back at Andrew, who encouraged me along further with a little hurry-up gesture.

"Hey," said Remy. "Long time."

"Hey. What's up?" I said.

"Just got off work. Thank God."

"Here?"

"Yeah. Sandy cut me loose—too slow. Nobody's sitting here," she said, indicating the empty stool next to her.

"Oh," I said, then nodded toward Andrew.

"Ah. Well, how have you been? Haven't heard from you. How's your brother?"

"He's good. He's lost twenty pounds so far."

"Wow. Good for him. You look good," she said.

"Thanks," I said, still insecure about my missing teeth. "You, too."

She caught me glancing back at Andrew again.

"Who's your friend?"

"That's Andrew."

"Ah," she said. She waved at Andrew, who manufactured a smile and waved back.

I should have invited Remy to join us—I think that's what she was waiting for. But I couldn't do that to Andrew. It would've been awkward.

"How's your writing?" she said.

"Meh," I said. "It pretty much sucks."

"Geez, that's a glowing endorsement."

"Yeah, well. It's true. I've been rethinking the whole writer thing. In terms of my art, I'm more into my topiary these days. How about you? What've you been up to?"

"Working, mostly." She glanced at the stool, wondering if I would ever sit down. "Buy you a drink?" she said.

"I've got one," I said, nodding toward Andrew, sitting solo with two beers.

"Oh, right," she said.

How can I explain it? It had nothing to do with Remy. Remy was fine. Remy was great. Probably not "the one" but certainly the closest thing I'd encountered so far. She was nice and funny and down to earth. The thing is, I guess I didn't feel like trying anymore. I felt like being myself. Rather than having to perform, I just wanted to celebrate with Andrew, he of the clunky braces and the organic lettuce and the freakishly clean automobile. Andrew, who changed my thinking about Walmart, who opened my eyes to the inhumanity of puppy mills. Andrew, who chose to believe in me, despite all the evidence against me. I looked back at him, alone at the table, a little forlorn, smiling sadly to make the best of it.

"Well," I said.

"You'd better get back to your friend," said Remy.

"Great seeing you."

"You, too," she said, and I thought she sounded a little disappointed.

"Text me," I said.

I realize it makes zero sense, but more than anything, I felt relieved to be walking away from Remy.

"Struck out, huh?" said Andrew, upon my return.

"Pretty much."

"Well, at least you tried."

"Let's do some shots," I said.

Andrew submitted to a Jägerbomb, quickly followed by another. After the second, I saw Remy set her half-empty drink down and walk out of the restaurant, not in the highest spirits. My guilt bloomed anew, and I was a little confused that I could have such an effect on anybody. Andrew must have misinterpreted my concern.

"Forget about her," he said.

And just like that, I did. There would be plenty of time to feel guilty later. Andrew and I proceeded to eat like lions, and talked in our familiar way of books and oral hygiene, and ancient aliens, politics and recycling, and rotisserie chicken.

After Andrew squared the tab—eighty-six bucks with tip—we ambled aimlessly down Front Street bumping shoulders, then cut back across the public lot toward the water and down the boardwalk to American Legion Park. You could feel the very last vestiges of summer in the not-so-cold air, but mostly you could feel fall.

We got weightless on the swings for a while, until my fish and chips started turning somersaults and I thought it best to sit.

We parked our butts on a picnic table in the dusk and shot the shit.

"When did you know you were an artist?" he said. "C'mon, don't think about it too hard."

So I told Andrew the story of my mermaid and how vividly her form insinuated itself on the holly, and how that one stupid limb refuse to submit, and how eventually I had no choice but to embrace it, and how the hard-on was there all along, and all I did was liberate it.

"Truth," he said.

And we both laughed, and when we finally stopped, I noticed his upper lip had snagged on his braces and was bleeding. Without even thinking about it, I leaned forward to dab off the blood with my thumb, and he leaned into me, a little unsurely, until I felt his breath on my face and his clean-shaven chin against mine, and that's when I pressed my lips into his lips, blood and all.

After a moment, he pulled away.

"Are you sure?"

It was a fair question, and I'm grateful that he asked. And the truth is, no, I wasn't sure, not exactly. I was conflicted about a great number of things at that moment, but the act of kissing him was pretty low on the list.

"Yes," I said. "Yes."

And I pressed myself back into him without reservation.

And yeah, I guess that officially makes me a fag. Or maybe it doesn't. I'm not big into labels at this point. All I know is that my life seemed to make a little more sense being with Andrew.

I won't bore you with the particulars: how I staunched his bleeding lip with the pressure of my tongue, or how I cut my own lip on his braces, and how he stopped my bleeding lip, or the rest of that intimate stuff about our breath growing heavy and our hearts beating furiously and our man parts straining against our stout denim trousers. I'm not writing erotica here. I won't give you any literary pretense, either. You don't need to know about the aching ferocity of my tumescence or the cataract of guilt frothing weightlessly over the yawning precipice of my personal dawn, like that fucking even means anything. Yes, there was guilt, and there was ferocity. But all you need to know is that kissing Andrew made perfect sense at that moment. And I intended on kissing him as long as he'd let me, no matter how faggy that was.

"Why weren't we doing this all along?" I said when we finally stopped for air.

"I wasn't sure you wanted to," he whispered.

Hours later, still flush from the action, still quickened and hyperalert from taking the leap, I sat in the kitchen of Andrew's apartment and watched him make breakfast at two in the morning. Sitting there in my T-shirt and underwear, I tried to convince myself that I ought to be more anxious about the repercussions of what had just transpired, that I ought to just stop and reconsider my actions and save myself from . . . well, myself. Where was the ambiguity, the guilt, or the doubt in my decision? Why wasn't I terrified? Part of the answer is that the stakes simply didn't seem that high, which says a lot about my pitiful life up until that point. And I guess the rest of the answer is Andrew. Being with him on every level felt natural.

He scrambled free-range eggs wearing boxer shorts and an

apron, and we drank Equal Exchange coffee and talked just as easily as ever about melting glaciers and privatized education, but mostly we talked about the future of T&M Landscaping and my renewed passion for topiary, and the prospect of a more abundant life, one that didn't involve me living in a shed behind my mom's house.

"Let's make you a list," he said.

And so we made me a list. Things to do:

> Get bonded.
> Get licensed.
> Move out.

And we made me another list. Places to go:

> New Zealand
> Disneyland
> Dentist

And we made more lists: books to read, skills to learn, tools to develop. And it seemed like the more lists we made, the bigger my life felt by extension and the more possibilities that seemed to be out there for old Mike Muñoz, if he was only willing to think beyond the confines of his experience, if he could only summon the courage and the wherewithal to break the patterns that defined him, raze the walls that imprisoned him. If only he could believe in himself. And I was beginning to.

The Day After

When I awoke at dawn, Andrew was still fast asleep with his head on my shoulder, wheezing through chapped lips. Without moving a muscle, I stared at the ceiling and began to panic, harassed by doubt, hounded by guilt, tormented by my unknown future. My old life seemed irretrievable. What was I supposed to do now? Who would I be disappointing? Who would I be walking away from? Where was I going? Would I be with other men, or was this something specific to Andrew? What were the moral implications of changing my identity, of making my loved ones uncomfortable, of forcing them to accept me?

In the darkness of Andrew's bedroom, I tortured myself with such considerations, inching away from him so that the bare skin of our shoulders was no longer touching. I was on the verge of extricating myself completely from the mattress when Andrew woke up. And no sooner did he stretch, yawning his alfalfa breath directly into my face, than my anxiety quickly dissipated.

"That was amazing," he said.

We lingered in bed without talking for a few minutes. Lying there beside him, I felt at home. But I knew that back in Suquamish, things were about to get complicated. I'd never been much good at asking for things, and now I had to ask the people I loved to reimagine me as somebody else.

I didn't go home that day. Long after Andrew left for work, I stayed in his apartment, lying in bed, flipping through books, and looking out the window. It wasn't only that I was avoiding the world at large; it was also that I felt so comfortable at Andrew's place. I could be whatever I wanted in that apartment. Everywhere I looked, something was daring me to be a more expansive and adventurous person. Whether it was Andrew's lists, or his goading me to pursue every challenge and seize every opportunity, or the picket signs and stray protest fliers exalting me to make the world a better place, the expectation in that apartment was that Mike Muñoz be a bigger and better person.

I picked up one of Andrew's numerous empty notebooks and started dashing off a series of playful sketches: Bigfoot eating a triple-decker ice-cream cone; a big-headed alien wearing a cowboy hat, riding a unicorn. Two swans humping. I must have made a dozen sketches, and not one of them was trying to save the world. But any one of them would've made the world a slightly better place, at least in my opinion.

What if I started using mesh and wire? How much could I elevate my game? Think of what I could do with ivies, like all that Duck Foot in front of Bainbridge city hall. Imagine a sea serpent with arms, wearing a jean vest, shredding a solo on a Flying V guitar. He could be sticking his tongue out like Gene Simmons. I'd tilt the headstock up at 180 degrees, so he was obviously in the middle of a solo. And think of all that red sedum along the foundation, and imagine a roiling sea of blood. Oh, man, how cool would that be?

Or what about all that privet in front of the tribal center? I could do a bear on all fours, an eagle, a raven. I could sculpt a fishing party in a dugout canoe. And how about all that holly on the new traffic island on the south end of the Poulsbo junction? Imagine a Pegasus, muscular and proud as hell, a friendly ogre, a pair of gigantic cobras, and a group of enchanting rabbits. Damn, I was good. Andrew was right, I had to put myself out there.

Restless to create, I located a pair of scissors in Andrew's desk and a couple of empty coat hangers from the closet, and retired to the kitchen, where I set about patiently to work reshaping his herb garden so that when Andrew arrived home from the library four hours later, he would discover on his windowsill Cupid shooting an arrow straight at the ass of a sumo wrestler, who was reaching out to touch a panda bear in a pirate hat, who was sitting next to an elf, who was swinging a golf club.

The Beginning

I decided Freddy would be a relatively easy place to start. Freddy, who was rarely quick to judge. Freddy, who seemed willing to accept just about anything. When I finally came home from Andrew's that second morning, I found Freddy in the kitchen, standing at the stove in his underwear, frying an egg.

"Look who's back," he said. "You want an egg, boss?"

"Nah, I'm good."

I stood there silently a few seconds too long, watching Freddy until he glanced sidelong at me.

"What? You need to borrow money or somethin'?"

"Freddy, what if I told you I was gay?"

He pursed his lips thoughtfully, considering the information for a few seconds as his fried egg shimmied in the pan. "Are you tellin' me you are?"

"Yeah."

"Hmph," he said. "Didn't see that one comin'."

Removing the skillet from the burner, he clapped me on the shoulder. "Look at the bright side: at least you ain't black."

I found Mom in the bathroom, a glacier-blue wad of paper towel in her clutches as she scrubbed toothpaste off the mirror.

"Michael," she said. "I've been worried sick. Where have you been? Why haven't you been answering your phone?"

"Yeah, sorry, I've been at Andrew's."

"Ah," she said. "The mysterious Andrew."

It's true, she'd never met Andrew. I'd never invited him to hang out at my house or tried to encourage any familiarity between my family and him. I'd sheltered them from Andrew, just as I'd sheltered Andrew from my home life.

Again, I just stood in place, letting the silence linger a little too long, until Mom turned and looked at me curiously.

"What is it?" she said.

"I've got some news," I told her. "I'm going into business with Tino."

"That's wonderful," she said. "Good for you, sweetie."

"I'm going to be my own boss."

"Lucky you."

"Yeah," I said. I let the silence settle in again until the only sound was the squeaking of her towel on the mirror.

"Mom, maybe you oughta sit down," I said at last.

She paused in her scrubbing. "Michael, what's wrong?"

"Well, uh, it turns out that, well . . ."

"That what?"

"Mom, I'm gay."

Visibly relieved, she resumed scrubbing the mirror. "Oh, thank God. I thought you had a tumor."

How could she be so matter of fact? Look at Andrew's mom,

all but estranged. His dad, who refused to even acknowledge him. How could my mom just go on scrubbing the bathroom mirror?

"Aren't you going to say anything?" I said.

"What would you like me to say, Michael?"

"I don't know. You're not surprised or anything?"

"Are you?"

"Kind of, yeah, I guess."

"You never knew?"

"You did?"

She narrowed her eyes and gave me a knowing look. "Well, I am your mother."

"But how could you possibly know?"

"I can't say exactly. Just a feeling."

"A feeling? C'mon, how did you know?"

"Just a feeling, that's all I can really call it. Ever since you were a boy. Before you ever dated anyone."

"I didn't date anyone."

"There was that, too."

"I guess that makes me feel pretty stupid," I said.

"Why should you feel stupid? If we're lucky, Michael, we grow into ourselves." Without looking, she threw the wad of paper towel toward the wastebasket and banked it in.

"That makes you lucky," she said.

Dickless

Finally, there was Nick. I'd saved the toughest for last. I wasn't sure there was room in my life for both Nick and Andrew. The combination seemed irresolvable. They'd met only once for about thirty seconds at Walmart—thirty of the most uncomfortable seconds of my life. The idea of the three of us hanging out was pretty hard to imagine. Andrew was only a casual football fan. He didn't know a cornerback from a safety, let alone a three-technique from an edge rusher or a cover 3 zone from a man defense. He deplored the Seahawks' colors. He thought the cheerleaders were tacky. Andrew liked Russell Wilson's wife because he thought she was courageous. He thought Bobby Wagner was sexy. He thought Kiko Alonso was a beautiful name, though he couldn't remember whom he played for or what position he played.

A future with both of them in it seemed unlikely. I'm ashamed to admit how easily I accepted this. It was with something of a heavy heart that I met Nick for a pitcher at Tequila's.

"Dude," he said. "You benched Julio Jones last week? You think a sprained knee is gonna stop that guy? He's a fucking monster! His catch radius is like a square mile! Carolina's corner is what, five ten? Seriously, what were you thinking? Michael, you're in fifth place! Dickless is using auto-pick every week, and he's thirty points ahead of you."

"Who's Dickless?"

"Whitehead! His fucking auto-picks beat you head to head in week four. And it wasn't even close. Might have helped if you hadn't picked the Packers defense with Peppers and Matthews out. I swear, you must be high, Michael. This isn't March Madness! You can't just fill in your bracket and get lucky. You gotta manage your roster. You gotta pay attention. It's a commitment—it's a fucking discipline, Michael. How do you think I won three years ago—and two years before that? Honestly, dude, it's a fucking miracle you got second place last year."

"I'm gay," I announced.

"News flash," he said.

"No, really." I said. "Like actively."

"Yeah, I believe it. No wonder you picked the Packers."

I looked at him meaningfully. "Nick, I'm, like, actually gay."

To his credit, he didn't looked repulsed, just confused, like his nose was bleeding and he didn't know why.

"It's really no big deal," I insisted.

"It's a pretty big deal, considering," he said.

"Considering what?"

"That I'm your best friend for like how many years? And suddenly you're gay. And I'm just hearing about it now?"

"I'm just figuring things out now, Nick. It doesn't change anything between us."

Nick put a hand up in a yield gesture and grimaced as though he were experiencing gastric reflux.

"Ugh. Okay. Fuck," he said. "Can we just play some darts and not talk about this?"

And so we retreated awkwardly back to the machines, already the distance between us widening. We hardly spoke the whole time we played cricket. I welcomed the focus. I was money right out of the gate: trip twenty, triple nineteen. Near miss on eighteen. I closed eighteen and seventeen next time around as Nick watched on dazedly. The poor guy was reeling. He couldn't hit a twenty to save his life. Under practically any other circumstance, I would have relished destroying Nick. But that night, I took little pleasure in winning.

After the game, he drained his glass and consulted his phone.

"I gotta bolt," he said. "Good darts."

He didn't clap me on the back or shake my hand or punch me affectionately on the shoulder on his way out.

Watching him go, I told myself I really didn't care if I ever saw him again. Already, Nick was starting to feel like someone from my past. Maybe loyalty was conditional, after all. Maybe my burgeoning sense of self, my developing identity as a socially engaged, newly gay, working-class half-Mexican topiary artist demanded such wholesale sacrifices as leaving my old friends in the dust.

The Mixed Parts

And what about Remy? Didn't I owe her an apology? At least an explanation? Had I not willfully led her on all that time, buying all those crummy meals at Mitzel's and having my water refilled every five minutes? Asking her out on dates, confessing my literary ambitions to her, texting her and not texting her, kissing her in two parking lots, and all the while sending her mixed messages, without ever understanding why myself? Suddenly it seemed cruel and fickle of me.

Remy was still working when I arrived at the Loft. Rather than sit in her section, I took a place at the bar and ordered a Sprite. When Remy registered me there, she did a quick double take, though it was impossible to read her expression. Already, this was starting to feel like a mistake.

Twice she passed me on her way to the kitchen and said nothing. On her third pass, she stopped at the bar for a drink order, flirting conspicuously with the bartender. When she caught me looking at her, she immediately cast her eyes down and started organizing tickets.

I sat at the bar through one more Sprite, wishing I'd brought a book, so I could at least pretend to be reading it. When Remy's shift finally ended, she stationed herself at the exact opposite end of the bar and tallied her receipts, never looking up to catch my eye. When she was done with her reckoning, she swept up her tips and her tickets and ducked into the office, reemerging moments later with her coat and her purse. Clearly, she had no intention of talking to me.

I caught her at the door on her way out.

"Hey," I said.

I thought for a moment she was just going to walk around me, but she decided to indulge me momentarily.

"I want to apologize," I said.

"For?"

"Sending you mixed signals, I guess. Not texting you back."

"That seems pretty straightforward. Where does the mixed part come in?"

"The thing is, I was figuring some stuff out."

"Okay."

"I wasn't really sure what I wanted, you know? I thought one thing was going on when really it was something else. What I'm trying to say is, it's not you, it's me."

Remy rolled her eyes and buttoned up her coat and fished her car keys out of her purse.

"Look, Mike, you're giving yourself way too much credit," she said.

"What I mean is—Remy, I'm—"

"No, really," she said.

And then she stepped past me, keys jingling, and walked out the door.

Baby Steps

W hen I had all but decisively closed the book on my friendship with Nick, he called me early one Sunday morning in November.

"Dude, you actually did it! You beat Whitehead! I'm in second place now! Cha-ching!"

"That's cool," I said.

"How did you know Rawls would break out against Detroit? And benching Brady was genius! Dude, you may not finish in last."

"That's quite a distinction," I said.

"Anyway, not why I'm calling. Remember this summer when I had a line on those tickets for the Arizona game?"

"Yeah."

"The ones on the fifty yard line, from the big-shot contractor who I sold those all-season Toyos to?"

"Yeah?"

"Well, I didn't get them."

"Bummer."

"You wanna watch the game at the casino?"

"Yeah, sure."

I had no idea that I'd feel so heartened by such an invitation. I didn't want to lose Nick. He was family.

"Is it cool if Andrew comes?"

There was a brief silence in which I could feel Nick wanting to sigh. "Whatever, sure. As long as he doesn't talk during the game."

If you're still wondering why I love Andrew, consider that he insisted on dropping me off at the casino, and begged off watching the game with Nick and me, sparing me the inevitable discomfort.

"If you guys need a ride home, call me," he said. "Especially if you're drinking."

When he dropped me off out front, I almost leaned over and gave him a peck on the cheek, but I chickened out.

Nick was waiting for me in a high-backed booth at the back of the bar, with a clear shot of the big screen.

"Dude, I got twenty-six points out of Antonio Brown this morning," he said before I'd even sat down.

The Hawks jumped off to an early lead, and by midway through the second quarter it was clear they had the game under control. The Cards were shit without Palmer. Too bad the guy was made of glass.

At halftime, Nick ordered us both Jägerbombs, and we were about to hoist them when Nick turned serious.

"Look, bro. I got to thinking about it. And as much as it grosses me out, you sucking dick and the rest of it, I gotta admit you're pretty fucking brave. It takes guts to be a fag—I couldn't do it."

"Is this some kind of an apology?"

"Look," said Nick. "I don't wanna sell tires the rest of my life, either. But it takes more balls than I've got to pass up a job when you're flat broke, and your mom and her boyfriend want to kick you out, and you have no idea what your future looks like."

"I know, it was a dumb move not taking the job."

"No. It was risky, but it wasn't dumb. That's what I'm trying to say. Sucking dick is dumb—dicks are dirty, dude. Really dirty. Mine sure is."

"Well, maybe you ought to wash it."

"Ugh. Can we not talk about my dick?"

"You brought it up."

"All I'm trying to say," said Nick, "is that whatever it is you're holding out for, I hope you get it. You deserve it, Michael, you actually do. Working for yourself, writing your dumb novel, making your stupid sculptures, all of it. And good luck with the sucking dicks. I don't wanna hear about it, though."

"Good."

"And please," he said. "Promise me you won't get a sex change, Michael."

"I'm gay, Nick, not transgender."

"Same diff," he said.

Baby steps, I keep reminding myself, baby steps.

The Good Life

Remember back when I used to carry on about how if I ran the show, I'd run things this way, and if I were the boss, I'd only service a certain kind of client? I'll be honest, I wasn't daydreaming, I was only grumbling. I never truly believed in the possibility, not for a minute. That would've required thinking big, and I didn't know how to do that back then.

But this is now. Meet Russ Walcott, 9120 Lemolo Drive. Russ is single, as far as I can tell, midforties, by my guess. He's got an acre-plus on the hillside, overlooking the bay, and it's teeming with holly—a huge clutch of the stuff every fifteen feet, and you can see it all from the road, which is another perk, because Russ is going to let me put a tasteful little T&M Landscaping sign with a phone number out front when I'm all finished.

Russ gets me. Russ is a fan of my work, and by work, I mean topiary. Not that he doesn't appreciate my sublime lawn mowing or my superlative edging, but Russ especially loves my creations. See, Russ is also an artist, which explains why he dresses like it's 1993, but still doesn't explain how he has any money at all, especially to hire a landscaper, let alone a guy to sculpt his bushes into knights and gladiators, but hey, none of my business. I don't care if he sells coke, frankly. He always pays on time, and he never makes me clean his garage.

Today I'm putting some final touches on the centerpiece. It's unseasonably warm. Folks are honking as they drive by on Lemolo, slowing to admire my work. It's been this way all week. Wait until they see the finished product.

Every now and again, Tino waves to me from the little orchard, where he's raking up the fallout from this weekend's blow, his headphones blaring salsa. When he stoops to gather his load, I can see the crack of his ass, and somehow it makes me love him a little bit more.

I pause to oil my new Felcos, then take a step back to consider my next move. It's all about work flow with a big piece like this, all about eating that elephant one bite at a time. If I want to get the flow and the movement right, everything has to develop organically. Should I do a final pass on the second sea horse? Is his dorsal fin too big? What about his snout? And what about the first knight, is it me, or is his helmet slightly oversized? Is the snorkel ambiguous? Should I make the shield smaller? How much of that limb can I utilize for the lance before I'll need to extend it?

These are the problems I now face. Don't let anyone tell you it's not tough being an artist.

Maybe the biggest lesson I've learned, in art and in life, is that when the questions become too numerous and the considerations begin to feel a little overwhelming, you just have to look away for a minute and regather your vision for the thing, try to see it the way it originally came to you. Ask yourself, how did I arrive here? What was I trying to accomplish?

I take a step back, gazing up the hill toward the house, where I discover that Russ is watching me through the big picture window. Not like Truman used to watch me, though. Or like Piggot. No, Russ is grinning like a senator at a whorehouse, and he's giving me a double thumbs-up.

God love the guy, even if he is gacked out of his mind.

My Knight in Shining Armor

I suppose you could make a good case that Andrew was my knight in shining armor, or shining braces, anyway. After all, not only did he help deliver me to my sexual identity, it was Andrew who drove me down to Verizon and staked me to thirty bucks' worth of wireless minutes to help T&M Landscaping hit the ground running. It was Andrew who did all the research about business licensing and bonding and insurance, Andrew who helped Tino and me navigate the necessary evils of bureaucracy.

And you could make a very convincing argument that Tino was my savior for delivering me to my dream job (collections, cash flow, billing, payroll, and quarterly taxes aside). Tino, for coming to me with the greatest opportunity of my professional life so far: the chance to be my own boss.

And don't forget Freddy. Old Freddy would also prove instrumental, as the world's most unlikely investor. The morning after I gave him the news, he sat me down in the kitchen.

"Dog, I want to help bankroll this venture. I believe in you. Besides, the sooner we can get that guest cottage back, the better."

"Thanks, Freddy. But we're gonna need like four grand, at least."

Freddy cleared his throat. "Well, it just so happens that Freddy's got some savings tucked away."

"Wait," I said. "How do you have savings?"

"Ain't always been a doorman, Michael. Used to be a licensed electrician. Made good money for eighteen years."

"So, um, if you had money all along, why did you move into the shed?"

"All part of the plan, my man. Wasn't shelter old Freddy was after. You think I couldn't do better than no shed?"

So it was Freddy who lent Tino and me the money for the truck and the trailer and the riding mower. And my debts don't end there. Chaz gave me something, too, even if I'll never end up collecting my fourteen hundred bucks. Chaz taught me the imperative of thinking big, even when you couldn't afford to—*especially* when you couldn't afford to.

And even Doug Goble imparted some wisdom to me, if only in a cautionary way, about the trappings of ambition and the vacuum of the tireless pursuit. The fact is, everywhere I look, somebody has been giving me something. If I do an honest accounting, I owe just about all of my good fortune to someone else. And yeah, I realize my fortune isn't measured in millions. But it's my fortune, and I'm grateful for it. And I'm grateful for a lot of other stuff, too. My health, my family, tallboys. I'm grateful for the first goddamn caveman who ever gazed up at the stars and paused to wonder. I'm grateful for that ringing silence, that stillness in the Suquamish night when Freddy finally lays aside his bass and Dale calls it a day on his band saw and the last M80 has exploded, and I can finally lay my head down to sleep. And furthermore, it's my opinion that those who claim their accomplishments all to themselves, those who are the heroes of their own stories, are liars.

No man is an island, even if Bainbridge Is.

Gravy

Well, old Mike Muñoz could probably go on forever entertaining, enlightening, and edifying you. I could tell you how to vote and what books to read, how to spend your money, and all the rest of it. But it's up to you to make your own lists. What the fuck do I know? I've got a fledgling business to operate. I've got bushes to carve into dragons and giraffes and dangling monkeys with big swinging balls. But since I may never actually write the Great American Landscaping Novel, the least I can do is circle back and begin wrapping up this story the way they do in most novels, before I hit you with the big finish.

So, here I am on Thanksgiving, eating a turkey leg. Except this time I'm not on the crapper, I'm seated at the head of the table, and Andrew is right beside me. My mom and Nate are directly across from me. And Freddy is here, too. And yes, my old friend Nick, warts and all, is seated right beside a clean-shaven Chaz, who is really close to getting back on his feet. Fried Chicken is just about to launch, whatever the hell it is.

Here is Mike Muñoz, in the bosom of his ragged tribe. Maybe we're not the Du Ponts or the De Beers or the Rockefellers or the Rothschilds, but at least we're not perpetuating world domination, at least we're not fracking, or drilling the Arctic, or hiding our money offshore, or bankrupting schools, or foreclosing on anyone for our own profit. Hell no, we're just trying to make an honest living. And our numbers are growing. Tino and his roommates are swinging by later with a case of Tecate. Goble might even drop by for a little dessert, but I'm not holding my breath.

Just as I'm about to tear into my drumstick, Andrew taps his wineglass and clears his throat, and everybody lowers a fork out of respect.

"Friends," Andrew says, the candlelight hitting his braces just so. "It's true, we all rage. We all hate. We all fail. But . . ." And here, he raises a finger, pausing for dramatic effect, something he learned at his Toastmasters group. "That rage and contempt, that disappointment, that's what makes us yearn so hard. Those deficits, they make us reach, they stretch us. They make us fight back when it matters."

"Life shits on you, and you turn it into fertilizer," I say.

"Exactly," Andrew says. "And then there is this: Community. A village. A shining example of—"

"Yo, Mr. Jaws," interjects Nick. "When you're done with your little elocution over there, could you pass the fucking gravy?"

Did Nick just say *elocution*? You see, anything can thrive if you give it a chance.

So, whoever you are, whatever your last name is, wherever you came from, whichever way you swing, whatever is standing in your way, just remember: you're bigger than that. Like the man said: you contain multitudes.

Today Is the Day

'm not going to tell you that the Days Inn in North Anaheim is some kind of paradise. As far as I know, the swimming pool in Paradise actually has water in it. And I'm pretty sure there isn't a nail salon and a Qdoba across the street, but don't quote me on that. I'm not going to tell you that the eighteen-hour drive to get here was anything less than hellish, what with the five of us crammed into a midsized rental and Nate suffering an acute gastric disturbance the entire way. I'm not going to lie and tell you that the weather in Anaheim—sixty-four degrees with a chance of showers—isn't a little disappointing, or that the traffic doesn't suck, or that the endless parking lot is not a clusterfuck from hell. I'm not going to tell you that the line to gain entrance is not soul crushing or that the admission is not overpriced.

"You bring the camera?" says Freddy.

"Got it," says Andrew.

"What about the sunscreen?"

"It's in Mom's purse," I say.

"What about the—"

"Freddy, relax."

I'm not going to tell you that Freddy's shorts provide sufficient cover for his nuts. Let's just say I wouldn't want to ride the Tea Cups with him.

What I am going to tell you is this: that standing here, fifty feet from the turnstile, my heart is in my throat, because already I can hear the children's laughter. I can see the castle spire stretching skyward in the distance, and just beyond the gates of the Happiest Place on Earth, an outpouring of floral promise, red and white, and blue and yellow, in the thick of a great green expanse of new-mown grass.

Today is the day. I finally made it.

ACKNOWLEDGMENTS

Big thanks to my early readers for their generosity and input: Jim Thomsen, Brock Dubbles, Willy Vlautin, Drew Perry, and Mara West. I'm forever indebted to Cassidy King for employing me all those years as a landscaper and being a great boss and a kind person. And Arnie Sarma, my old landscaping mentor, may you rest in peace, brother. Hardly a day goes by when I don't think of you and your old Vanagon, and your cheap cigars, your stale raisin bread, your Braunschweiger liver sausage, your bourbon and coffees, your astrophysics lectures, and your landscape mastery.

I'd be nowhere without my beloved editor and honorary pops, Chuck Adams, always so instrumental and patient in helping me find my way and, in the case of this book, letting me draw from his personal experience to get there. One of the great blessings of my life as an artist has been working with the amazing team of publishers at Algonquin Books: Elisabeth Scharlatt, Craig Popelars, Ina Stern, Michael McKenzie, Brooke Csuka, Brunson Hoole, Jude Grant, Carol Schneider—you are all rock stars.

And while we're on the subject of professional associates that rock: thanks to Jon Cassir at CAA for finding new audiences for my stories. As always, thanks to my stalwart agent and longtime champion, Mollie Glick, for her amazing guidance and stewardship, both editorially and professionally, and for her loyalty and friendship.

Lastly, thanks to my amazing wife, Lauren, for her endless patience, understanding, and support. Did I mention patience? Without her yin to my yang, I'd be even more of a hot mess than I already am.

LAWN BOY

The Great American Landscaping Novel
An essay by Jonathan Evison

Questions for Discussion

The Great American Landscaping Novel

An essay by Jonathan Evison

B efore I became a bestselling writer, I was perpetually broke. For me being broke was not only an enduring condition, it was my legacy. For generations the beleaguered Evison tribe had been all kinds of broke: hopelessly, urgently, even willfully. I can honestly say that young Johnny Evison never expected to be anything but broke. That I decided to become a writer in third grade ought to be proof enough.

The fact is, I'd always sort of resented money. When you grow up broke, you don't learn much about money except that there's usually not enough of it. Nobody teaches you how to attract money, or leverage it, or even save it. And capitalism is not exactly teeming with possibilities for those individuals who lack capital. Basically, you're just left with the ism.

In 1976, four years after my sister died in a freak accident and our family life began its not-so-gradual unraveling, my old man managed himself a work transfer from Sunnyvale, California, to Keyport, Washington, moving us eight hundred miles north to the relatively affluent community of Bainbridge Island, whereupon he promptly managed himself a transfer back to Santa Clara, effecting his escape from domestic life, and leaving my mom a broke single mother of four.

Not everybody was wealthy on Bainbridge Island, but the majority of families, as far as I could see, were getting by better than us. At thirty-nine, my mom entered the workforce for the first time in her life, as the milk lady at my elementary school. A couple years later, she landed a post as the safe deposit attendant at a bank, where she stayed for the next twenty-odd years.

I started working off the books at eleven years old, bussing tables in downtown Seattle for my older sister, a waitress, who paid me out of her tips. The next summer, I walked up and down the ferry line, selling newspapers to commuters. When I was lucky, I didn't have change. So, it's not that I was lazy or incapable of industry. I knew from the beginning that work was—and would forever remain—a necessary evil, provided I could get it.

Throughout high school I worked afternoons as a dishwasher at the Streamliner Diner. The morning dishwasher was a guy named Michael, about forty. He had laminated his master's degree and hung it above the sink. I thought it was a joke. I told him it was hilarious. He told me in no uncertain terms that it wasn't a joke, that he stared at that master's degree for six hours every day to remind himself he was more than just a dishwasher, which was a convenient stance, considering he wasn't much of a dishwasher.

After graduating high school (barely), I spent the next twenty years working dozens of jobs to support myself, none of them glamorous, all of them low paying: gas-meter-checker, auto detailer, caregiver, sorter of rotten tomatoes, telemarketer of sunglasses. If I had ever earned a master's degree, or even an associate's degree, I would have almost certainly laminated it for display at whatever my place of employment. I guarantee my co-workers would have loved it. "That's hilarious," they would have said, just like when I told them I wrote novels.

Among all those low-paying jobs, by far my favorite was landscaper, the profession I arrived at by default in my mid-thirties. By thirty-five, my tolerance for money was at an all-time low. I actually avoided the stuff, and it avoided me. Every year I got a tax refund, and it always went straight to rent or groceries. Had you asked me who was ruining the world, I would have pointed to the people with the most money.

Other than my aversion to wealthy people, I was not a disgruntled landscaper. I enjoyed working outside, provided it wasn't raining pitchforks and my back felt tolerable. The tasks were mostly satisfying: weeding flower beds, pruning hedges, raking orchards, blowing leaves, deadheading hydrangeas, spreading mulch, and mowing lawns, all tasks that lent themselves to a heady mix of concentration and abstraction, the perfect state of mental equilibrium for the author of six unpublished novels.

Mowing lawns was the most satisfying task of my trade. I liked the clean, straight lines, the visible progress the work offered, and, of course, the smell of fresh mown grass.

The only downside of landscaping was the clients—not all of them, but some of them, specifically the ones that went out of their way to let you know your place, the ones who treated you not as a professional tradesperson but as their personal lackey. The ones who asked you to clean their garage, or move furniture around, or take their garbage to the curb, without even acknowledging that you were going above and beyond your duties. Never mind that you were a virtuoso with a push mower. To them, you were merely someone they were paying, whose name they couldn't remember.

For many years I'd been stewing on a novel centrally concerned with wealth disparity and class. It's a theme I've explored to some extent in all my previous novels. But I wanted to write one that zoomed in specifically on the double standards that exist between the haves and the have-nots, a book that highlighted the myriad indignities, vagaries, and obstacles of poverty in America in the twenty-first century. I wanted to write a working class novel that did not patronize the working class, one that did not politicize them as such or ennoble their poverty, one that painted them three dimensionally, so that the characters came to life on the page.

I arrived at a single working class voice that spoke to me so clearly I couldn't ignore him, a protagonist with a worldview that brought the quagmire of wealth and class into fine focus for me. His name was Mike Muñoz, and he was a twenty-two-year-old landscaper who lived on the res and worked in the yards of wealthy Bainbridge Islanders. Mike was a bit of a misfit: brutally honest, irreverent, compassionate, conflicted, funny, full of yearning, and more vulnerable than he'd have you believe. I loved him immediately, and I love him infinitely more three years later.

Such was my unconditional love for Mike that I wanted to build a world for him in which he could reinvent himself as he wanted to be, not who the status quo set him up to be. In this world, Mike would be tested again and again, his efforts often consigned to futility, his success borne back by the ceaseless tide of cultural and financial inequity. Yet Mike would ultimately overcome, because he learned to engage the world on his own terms.

And thus *Lawn Boy* was born. With this novel, I wanted to wake up the moribund American Dream, grab it by the collar, and splash some water in its face. Or better yet, invent a new American Dream, one not beholden to the tenets of capitalism, or identity politics, or any measure but the human will to invent ourselves as we wish. Call me an idealist, but I wanted for Mike what I want for my children, what we all deserve: an opportunity to thrive.

I don't think I've ever had more fun or taken more satisfaction from the act of writing a book than I have from *Lawn Boy*. I loved living in Mike's world, and watching him own it. I loved hanging out with Freddy in his underwear, and drinking tumblers of chardonnay on ice with Mike's mom. I loved sharing their every defeat and small triumph. I laughed my ass off, and cried, too—from sadness and from gratitude. In the end, the writing of this book gave me hope and clarity in a muddled-up, crying-for-help world. It is my sincere desire that all of this translates to you, the reader. There are Mike Muñozes all around us, and in telling this story I hope I've shown him the respect he deserves.

Questions for Discussion

1. In *Lawn Boy*, author Jonathan Evison takes readers into the world of a family living on the edge, both financially and socially, and this is the environment that the novel's main character, Mike Muñoz, has grown up in. How do you think Mike's upbringing shaped his worldview as a young adult?

2. When Mike's father told his son that he was taking him to Disneyland but instead took him to a waterfront graveyard for old naval ships, it was a pivotal moment in the young boy's life. Do you think it changed the way Mike looked at the world going forward? If so, how do you think that changed view manifested itself in his life?

3. Mike's ethnicity and mixed lineage plays a big part in how his story unfolds, yet his Mexican background is something he seems to downplay, insisting he be called "Mike" and not "Miguel," and choosing not to speak Spanish with his co-workers who are of more recent Mexican descent. Why do you think he does this? Are you sympathetic to this decision? Why or why not?

4. Why do you think Mike maintains a friendship with Nick, even though Nick is constantly saying things that Mike finds offensive, and espousing points of view toward women and gays and minorities and politics that go against Mike's beliefs? Do you think less of Mike for putting up with this? What would you do in such a situation?

5. Having read *Lawn Boy*, do you have an altered opinion about the men and women who tend to lawns and clean houses? Are you able to see them more as individuals you might like personally, as opposed to a clutch of people with whom you have nothing in common? Is there any one thing in the novel that helped bring about a shift in your point of view?

6. The lives of working class characters and families are not often explored in fiction. What things did you see in Mike's experiences that were familiar to you, perhaps even a part of your own everyday life? What things were unfamiliar or new to you?

7. Have you ever been made to feel inferior because of the line of work you do, or the kind of neighborhood or home you live in? Do you feel that as a character Mike Muñoz deals realistically with these factors? Did you find yourself reacting with sympathy to his plight? How do you think you might have reacted in the same situation?

8. Humor plays a big part in *Lawn Boy*, some of it situational (the tooth extraction scene), some of it growing out of Mike's interaction with other characters (the scene at the gated country club). Did you find the humor intrusive, or do you think it enhanced Mike's story and made him more likeable?

9. In addition to humor, anger plays a substantial role in Mike's story. Were there times when you wanted Mike to rein in his anger, and times when you felt he needed to express more of his frustration? Try to pinpoint instances of each reaction.

10. Do you feel that Mike was a good brother and a good son? What do you think you would have done if you were forced to live in such a situation? And do you feel that he treated Freddy with enough respect? How would you have reacted if your mother brought someone like Freddy into your household?

11. Through Mike's almost obsessive focus on his youthful sexual encounter with Doug Goble, and his inability to focus on creating a relationship with Remy—whom he sometimes seems to think of as his "girlfriend"—it becomes apparent that when it comes to his sexuality, there is some confusion. Do you feel that the subject was handled realistically in the novel? Were you surprised when Mike finally realized the truth of his sexuality, or had you noted it as it developed in the story?

12. What future do you see for Mike and Andrew? Do you think their relationship will develop and endure? And what future do you see for Freddy and Mike's mom? Who do you think will end up caring for Nate? If you were going to write a sequel to *Lawn Boy*, how would it begin?

KEITH BROFSKY

Jonathan Evison is the author of four previous novels: *All About Lulu, West of Here, The Revised Fundamentals of Caregiving,* and *This Is Your Life, Harriet Chance!* He lives with his wife and family in Washington State.